THE BIRTHDAY PARTY

Panos Karnezis

THE BIRTHDAY PARTY

JONATHAN CAPE
LONDON

Published by Jonathan Cape 2007

2 4 6 8 10 9 7 5 3 1

First published in Great Britain in 2007 by
Jonathan Cape

Random House, 20 Vauxhall Bridge Road,
London SW1V 2SA

www.randomhouse.co.uk

Addresses for companies within The Random House Group Limited can be found at:
www.randomhouse.co.uk/offices.htm

The Random House Group Limited Reg. No. 954009

A CIP catalogue record for this book is available from the British Library

ISBN 978-0-224-07932-7

Mixed Sources
Product group from well-managed
forests and other controlled sources
www.fsc.org Cert no. TT-COC-2139
© 1996 Forest Stewardship Council

Our paper procurement policy can be found at: www.randomhouse.co.uk/paper.htm

Typeset in Minion by Palimpsest Book Production Limited,
Grangemouth, Stirlingshire
Printed and bound in Great Britain by
Mackays of Chatham plc, Chatham, Kent

to Vana

THE PREVIOUS NIGHT HE HAD GONE TO BED WITH THE windows open after the doctor had said at dinner that at his age even a minor infection could kill him. In the morning he woke up with the flutter of the curtains and the cool breeze blowing in through the french windows that faced the sea and discovered that he was still alive. He pushed the blanket aside and sat up naked in bed, contemplating the clouds with arms folded behind his head and thinking about his dream. He had managed four hours of sleep, a rare achievement for an insomniac like himself, whose nights were a torment without reprieve, but the sleep had done him no good. He had dreamed that he was a boy in Izmir and was seeing a dead man for the first time, a steward from a steamship knifed through the heart during an argument, floating face up among the filth of the harbour. In his dream Marco Timoleon was standing on the promenade, dressed in striped pyjamas, and was watching as the current pushed the sailor out into the sea where the fish waited to peck at his eyes. The curious thing was that the dead man was waving at him.

He believed in dreams and other omens with a deep faith, and although he believed in God too, he obeyed Him with less enthusiasm. He consulted astrologers, palmists and mediums on a regular basis, a secret he kept from rivals and most of his friends, thinking of his premonitions as one of the last uncharted sciences – like weather forecasts. He signed no contracts on the thirteenth of the month, banned cats from his houses with the excuse that he was allergic to them and threw salt over his shoulder to fend off the Devil. He was also afraid of being buried alive; he had read about it in Plutarch, who described the execution of vestal virgins breaking their vows of chastity in Roman times, and had come across it again in an article about Thomas à Kempis.

The interesting thing was that Marco Timoleon had never before dreamed either of death or water: until then his dreams were uncomplicated memories from his life. He had a good memory, especially for trivia. When he dreamed about women, he was able to recall the colour of their hair, their birthmarks, the smell of their perfume. When he dreamed about cars, he could remember their registration numbers. When he dreamed about a place he had visited over fifty years earlier, he could describe it down to the last detail. Furthermore: no matter how deeply he slept, he could wake himself up at will, a trick he used when he had to escape a dream that was sad or frightening. Yet the night before, he had slept through the whole thing because the sight of a dead man waving at him had neither frightened nor saddened him. It had intrigued him. Marco Timoleon tried to interpret his strange dream without success. In the end he dismissed the greater horrors suggested by his imagination, admitting that the doctor had been right: he should not have slept with the windows open.

He was much shorter than one who had only seen him in photographs would expect. His skin was not simply tanned but bruised from the sun and covered with small liver marks that resembled lichen. He was a good swimmer, and despite being old and a little overweight, his skin was tight like a corset. When he had turned seventy, he had stopped dyeing his hair, a habit he always thought a little undignified but at the same time necessary. His most distinctive feature these days was the loose flesh under his eyes that gave him the permanent expression of one about to burst into tears.

He had been born under the sign of Leo seventy-two years earlier but was still in command of his faculties and in good health, apart from a persistent cough caused by smoking and his recent sexual dysfunction. For the latter he had tried homoeopathic medicines, acupuncture and hypnosis, but neither the human nor the vegetable magic had helped. He had slowly come to terms with the end of a lifelong habit that had started at the age of fourteen in the brothels of Izmir and continued until he could claim with pride that he had sampled everything that life and imagination had to offer – among them having slept with a man, an act he could not simply attribute to the curiosity of youth because he had slept with him more than once.

It was the end of August. He had arrived on his private island, eleven nautical miles from the Mediterranean coast, a week earlier after a short voyage from Monte Carlo on his luxury yacht. Normally he could stand the rough sea, but this time he had been sick. His pride forbidding him from taking any pills, he had tried to recover by pacing the deck despite the bad weather until the captain banned him from coming up for fear he might be swallowed by the waves. He had protested but in the end had given in and passed the rest of the journey between his stateroom and the bar where he had tried to shake off the haunting shadow that had settled over his mood with alcohol.

Marco Timoleon thought about the hours ahead without enthusiasm. He had arranged every detail of the party as if

3

his daughter's birthday were indeed the true reason for the celebration. Tomorrow Sofia was turning twenty-five. He had long ago stopped celebrating his own birthday or attending those of his children and wife in order to save himself the embarrassment of having to grow old in public, but tonight he was making an exception, throwing a big party on his private island.

His villa, a three-storey house with a tiled roof, peach stucco walls and wide balconies, stood among the trees on a steep slope above a cove with shallow green waters. There were eleven bedrooms on the upper two floors, several sitting rooms and a dining room, and on the lowermost floor a vast ballroom with a black lacquered grand piano and three Venetian chandeliers. The master bedroom was on the top floor and decorated without regard for either cost or taste. Its centrepiece was a marble fireplace, and in the room were several armchairs, coffee tables and china vases filled with freshly cut roses. The walls were hung with mirrors, crimson drapes and original paintings in gilded frames. What saved the room were the four glass doors through which Marco Timoleon could watch the Mediterranean sunrise from his bed as soon as he opened his eyes. A balcony outside allowed an uninterrupted view of the sea.

His wish had been to have on his island every kind of tree mentioned in the Bible, and his gardeners had followed his instructions to the letter: there were almond and olive trees, cedars, pines, chestnut, fig and bay trees, cypresses, oaks, palms, poplars, acacias, tamarisks and willows, as well as a Tree of the Knowledge of Good and Evil. Rising above the orchards, on the top of a hill, was a small stone church with a blue dome. The church was dedicated to Saint Mark of the Cypresses, and on a plot behind it were three graves with simple marble crosses. One read: *Daniel Timoleon, 1954–1974.* In his will the ageing tycoon specified that he wanted to be buried next to it, leaving the details of his funeral to his executor.

He left his bed, walked out on to the balcony and leaned naked against the marble balustrade. The cool breeze began to resurrect his body. Watching the faint outline of the distant shore, he felt a hint of doubt about his plan. There was a knock on the door, and a young man dressed in a white uniform walked in, carrying a pack of sheets and towels that smelt of lavender. After a quick search around the room and the *en suite* bathroom, the servant found him on the balcony. He was not surprised to see him naked; it was a habit his employer had got into in recent years. The smell of lavender was enough to bring Marco Timoleon back from his contemplation, and he told his servant, in his terse tobacco voice that tolerated no delay, to run him a bath. The young man went inside to carry out his wish before making the bed and cleaning the room. When he could bear the morning wind no longer, Marco Timoleon went to the bathroom, sank into the hot water and called his servant to come and rub his back with a brush.

The preparations for the party had begun long before his arrival on the island with a close attention to detail that was intended to thwart suspicions. Invitations had been printed and posted from his Paris office to guests all over the world, a three-tiered birthday cake had been ordered from Demel in Vienna, and the twenty-one-piece orchestra of Maxim's, the Parisian restaurant, had been booked at astronomical cost.

When his servant finished rubbing his back, Marco Timoleon stood up and showered with scalding water, enduring the high temperature with a sense of self-punishment. He used to be able to wash and dress in ten minutes, a habit that had grown out of an old eagerness to accept every invitation, but success and age had long taught him how to say no. He turned off the water, dried himself with a towel embroidered with his initials and sat on the toilet seat to catch his breath. Then he over-whelmed his servant with a series of questions, fired in quick succession, about the preparations for the birthday party. He listened to the answers with suspicion, challenging every one of them with yet more questions and a stern look, finding fault where there was none, changing his mind about orders he had given only the day before. He ended his interrogation with a harsh warning: 'Don't lie to me.'

His servant nodded and reassured him once again that everything was ready for that evening. Marco Timoleon was not satisfied. He wanted to know whether the orchestra was on its way and whether the bus that would be picking them up was at the airport. He said: 'Make sure they come straight to the island. They need to practise.' His servant had already made the necessary phone calls but said he would call the airport at once.

'They don't have to go through customs,' said Marco Timoleon. 'Tell whoever's in charge they're my personal guests.'

He had an army of servants, maids and cooks, who saw to his every need with a combination of devotion and fear. He had the reputation of being very generous, giving money freely if he heard that someone was in difficulty and always at Christmas and Easter, but he could also be unkind and violent like an ancient god. The last time he had guests on the island, he had insisted that Olivia should be at his side not only to silence the rumours that their marriage was failing but also to help him charm his guests. Olivia Timoleon seemed not to have the capacity for boredom. She had an instinct for discovering the wishes of her guests, laughed at their jokes, flattered them about their appearance and gave them her full attention, fixing them with her eyes, which had once charmed Marco Timoleon too, on their first encounter.

He normally woke up at midday and immediately put on his glasses because without them he was lost in a world of ghosts and shadows. His first of many daily cups of coffee waited for him on his bedside table, and he drank it while reading the papers. He always started with the society columns, which interested him the most, and then went on to read everything, including the advertisements, the obituaries and, of course, his horoscope. Only then was he ready to leave his bed and bathe. He was an immaculate dresser. His taste had matured to the austere combination of black and white that he had made his trademark. He himself dismissed any betterment of his taste over the years, stating with good humour a different reason for his choice of clothes: 'I'm colour blind.'

He was at his desk no later than three in the afternoon. He had offices in Paris, London and New York and could be in all of them at the same time if he needed to be, a trick he had not learned from God but taught to himself with the help of telephones and telexes. Following his wishes, his offices were all furnished in exactly the same style, with oak-panelled walls and heavy, permanently drawn curtains: he had discovered that darkness gave him an advantage over his visitors. In the middle of every study was a large Louis XV writing desk with leather top and cabriole legs. Even though computers were already becoming popular, he himself did not use one and discouraged his subordinates from doing so: when it came to business decisions, he had a deep-seated mistrust of electronics.

Until he turned seventy, he worked twelve hours a day, which were not enough to go over all his business affairs. If there was a crisis, he could easily carry on for forty-eight hours without an interruption, sustained by his passion for business and his faith in alcohol. He was a heavy drinker of Scotch, and although he admitted to the fact, he also insisted that he was not an alcoholic because he drank only as much as his metabolism permitted. Whatever the case, he consumed half a bottle at work and the rest afterwards in one of the night-clubs where he usually ended his day.

He did not leave the office unless the clock had struck midnight. He owed seven black Cadillac Fleetwoods, each parked somewhere in the world with a chauffeur in attendance and the engine running. He no longer walked anywhere, no matter how close. He professed security reasons, but the truth had more to do with the spent cartilage in his knees. He shaved twice a day, once when he woke up and again in the evening, with the cutthroat razor his father had given him long before he had needed it. This morning he took his time with the blade, stopping to rinse it under the tap and dipping it in a jar filled with surgical spirit. When he came out of the bathroom, rubbing cologne on his cheeks, his servant was choosing clothes for him. The young man helped him to dress.

'Is the cake here yet?' Marco Timoleon asked.

His servant handed him the trousers he had chosen and informed him that the birthday cake was already in the refrigerator. Marco Timoleon dismissed the sweater as being too warm and chose a short-sleeved shirt from the closet. Dressed in the white linen trousers and black shirt, he stood in front of the mirror and asked about the food.

'It is coming in the launch,' his servant said.

He brought him his shoes, and Marco Timoleon put them on without socks before asking for his wedding ring, which had been gathering dust on his bedside table for several months. He put it on in a slow movement that was heavy with symbolism. When he had finished dressing, he told the servant to mop the floor in the bathroom.

'We should have flown everything in,' he repeated. 'Or at least the caviare.'

Earlier that day his seaplane had travelled to the capital to wait for his wife's arrival at the international airport. The plane was the remaining one of a pair of twin-engine Piaggio P–166s that Marco Timoleon used regularly for short trips to the capital when he was holidaying on his island, but he had not flown it since the accident that had killed Daniel, his only son and chosen heir, a year earlier.

The misfortune had torn apart a pleasant weekend Marco Timoleon had been having on the island with a casual lover, a woman half his age, which seemed to be the age of all the women he came across these days. He had noticed her at an airport café during a brief stop in a long business trip. She was dressed in a green chemise and was reading a magazine but at the same time seemed to be aware of everything that was happening around her. Marco Timoleon later insisted that *she* had seduced him.

This was typical. All his life he strove to escape not the reputation of a womaniser, which he accepted with pride, but the guilt of hurting with his behaviour those close to him. He insisted that he did not suffer from satyriasis, he was not selfish, he was not cruel, but something worse: lonely. And since it seemed to him that loneliness was not something one brought upon oneself, he was not to blame.

He had delayed his departure until he persuaded her to accept his invitation to his villa and a few days later arrived at the island ahead of her, gathered his staff and swore them to secrecy with a dusty bible he found in Saint Mark of the Cypresses. He told them that they would have to be twice as careful because his visitor was a happily married woman, that they should see to her wishes as if they were his own and then asked them to change into the starched liveries with the gold-tasselled epaulettes that they had last worn many years earlier, during the visit of his most illustrious guest: an elderly but not senile Sir Winston Churchill.

She came on a Saturday, and he met her on the jetty to help her off the launch after the short crossing from the mainland. He wore a white shirt with the sleeves rolled up and a black tie that hung loose round his neck. His hair, grey but thick as a boy's, was combed back with cream. His only request to her was that she changed immediately into his wife's clothes in order to deceive the photographers who might be spying on them from sea or air. He was not joking. Some time before a hot-air balloon painted like a cloud had flown several times over the island, day after day until Marco Timoleon's security guards had shot it down. It had fallen into the sea, and three Japanese journalists had had to be rescued from the strong current or else they would have drowned.

When the woman returned, dressed in a pair of long trousers, a silk headscarf and big sunglasses, Marco took her on a tour of the island, dazzling her with the beauty of the gardens and the variety of trees where songbirds had built their nests. She was even more surprised when he showed her the farm where the livestock were serenaded by orchestral music in order to be calm and productive.

It was a beautiful day, the sea flat as a mirror, but Marco

Timoleon was quick to notice the deception above the drone of the cicadas: a storm was on the way. He saw the slow change of colours across the horizon, the clouds above the mainland, he felt the beginning of a breeze, but nothing seemed to him like a bad omen. 'There will be a storm tomorrow,' he was pleased to forecast. 'You will enjoy it.' Then he took her hand and led her along the narrow paths to the olive grove where they lay on the floor carpeted with leaves and undressed each other without hurry, without excitement but with the easiness of two people who had undressed many times before in the presence of a stranger. Marco Timoleon had no reason to suspect that this would be the last time he would make love in his life.

Later they sat on the veranda of the villa to have coffee and sweets. When it was time for lunch, he showed his guest to a table set among the rose bushes where they could eat away from his servants' eyes. He served her himself, pouring the wine and insisting that she tasted everything his cook had prepared: saffron rice, seafood platters, various salads and seven migrating quail that never made it to Africa. While they ate, Marco Timoleon charmed his guest with imaginary stories from his life, told so many times that even he was beginning to believe them. The lunch ended with a glass of dessert wine and his favourite seduction trick: the gift of a golden bracelet inscribed with her name. In the evening they danced in the vast empty ballroom because it was cold outside, to the music of a portable record player borrowed from the servants.

On Sunday the sun had not shown and the temperature had fallen suddenly. At midday lightning had flashed, and it had started to rain. Marco Timoleon was in the hallway trying to open an old umbrella when the phone rang. His private pilot informed him that his son had taken off in one of the

11

Piaggios and was on his way to the island. Marco Timoleon tried to reach his son on the radio. After many attempts, he made contact with the plane and ordered, threatened and finally begged Daniel to turn back because a storm was brewing. Every time the reply he received was brief and resolute: 'No.'

Daniel Timoleon had loved aeroplanes ever since he was a little boy, and his dream had been to become a professional pilot, but his short-sightedness had condemned him to remain an amateur. As soon as he was old enough, he enrolled at flight school where he passed easily his examinations on navigation, flight rules, meteorology and general knowledge, completed his flight test and persuaded his father to bribe the doctors so he could pass his medical too. He received a student licence, which meant he could only fly with a qualified instructor, but it had not curbed his passion. Marco Timoleon had given in, and allowed his son to fly alone as long as he obeyed one rule: never to fly at night or in bad weather. On the day of the accident, Daniel Timoleon broke that promise.

Marco Timoleon had gone to wait for the plane on top of the hill where Saint Mark of the Cypresses was. There he stood alone under his umbrella while thunder crashed around him and the rain grew heavier. He had sent away his guest without having told her the truth, saying instead that she should go immediately because the sea would soon be turning too rough for the launch to cross the strait to the mainland. From the top of the hill, he watched the small boat brave the waves as it slowly made its way across. Then a sudden gust of wind snatched his umbrella, exposing him to the lashing rain, and he would have caught pneumonia if a servant had not brought him a blanket. But still Marco Timoleon refused to take shelter and stayed where he was, waiting for the plane to appear through the clouds.

Finally it did. The sight of the white Piaggio flying on a straight path despite the force of the wind calmed Marco Timoleon down a little. He had imagined the small seaplane thrown about by the storm, but there it was, one moment disappearing into a cloud, the next coming out again, slowly descending to land on the sea. 'God keep him alive,' he joked. 'So I can kill him myself.' He threw away the soaked blanket and took the path to the beach, but was still some way from the jetty when his joy turned into horror. As soon as the seaplane touched the water, a crosswind pushed it sideways. The Piaggio tilted to the side, and the tip of its wing hit the water not at a great speed but fast enough for the seaplane to capsize.

Daniel Timoleon was killed instantly. A melancholy boy with pale skin, who felt constantly tired because there were not enough red cells in his blood, he had grown into a detached adult with an enigmatic face and the whispering voice of a librarian. He spoke little in his father's presence, smoked constantly an expensive brand of gold-filtered cigarettes and spent most of his time either servicing the plane that would later kill him or driving his sports car. From the moment he had turned eighteen until his death two years later, he was in every magazine's list of most eligible bachelors, an unwelcome honour that only helped increase his indifference to fame. He was secretive and elusive even to his father, who often thought his son was abroad when in reality he was in his room, reading car and aviation magazines, lost in a fog of cigarette smoke that had no way of escaping through the sealed windows, and listening to the music of the Rolling Stones.

Daniel Timoleon would have been sorry for his death if only for the attention it had drawn to his person. And yet his life had always been obscured by the shadow of death, an intangible but nevertheless constant feeling that made the accident somehow seem like the fulfilment of a prophecy. This did not lessen Marco Timoleon's despair or guilt because, like Euripides, he believed that the gods visit the sins of the fathers upon the children.

Marco Timoleon stood in front of the gilded mirror to comb his hair. It was still early. Most of the guests would be arriving on private yachts that had set sail several days earlier from various Mediterranean ports, making the birthday celebration the perfect conclusion of a late summer cruise. The small marina where they would be docking was empty apart from the rubber dinghy from Marco Timoleon's yacht. Too big to berth, the yacht was anchored at the mouth of the cove. Looking through the window at its trim white shape, its Liberian flag flapping in the breeze and its yellow funnel, Marco Timoleon fought the urge to set sail rather than having to face his guests and his daughter.

His latest headache had started several weeks earlier, and it was imperative to act or it would soon be too late. Long before his son's death, he had asked a private investigator to shadow Sofia, day and night, wherever she happened to travel in the world, and report back to him. Once a week Marco Timoleon dismissed his secretary, locked the door of his office, took the phone off the hook and leafed through the latest surveillance reports. All they revealed was that his daughter was a great mystery to him. She was his first-born, brought into the world by his first wife when he was still in love with her, and since then he had had a quarter of a century to get to know Sofia but had wasted every chance. Three months before, Marco Timoleon had had a visit from his investigator. The news was so important that it could not wait: Sofia was pregnant. The private investigator had seen her visiting her doctor and the same evening had listened in on a telephone conversation she had had with the father of the baby. A tape recorder was placed in front of Marco Timoleon. He listened, drumming his fingers on his desk.

'This is unacceptable,' he had said.

Sofia had no clue about her father's plans to use her birthday celebration to persuade her to end her pregnancy. She would have been even more horrified to know that he had summoned to the island Dr Patrikios, his private doctor, and had arranged for all the necessary medical equipment to be shipped in. Then he had secretly converted one of the guest rooms into an operating theatre whose key he kept in his pocket. Marco Timoleon's private doctor had said yes to carrying out the abortion but only if his daughter agreed of her own free will.

When his servant finished mopping, Marco Timoleon asked him to prepare him a whisky and soda. He lit a cigar and started pacing the room. A stack of old books was on the floor from his collection of classics, the books that gave him the same satisfaction no matter how many times he read them. In fact, they were the only books he ever read. Their singed pages and covers, smelling of soot, had survived the Great Izmir Fire of 1922 on the shelves of his father's library: a railway engineer, tobacco merchant and amateur scholar, his father had disappeared before the war. Marco Timoleon sipped his drink and puffed on his cigar.

'Tell the doctor to come and see me,' he said.

When he was alone, he picked up a book at random that turned out to be Plato's *Republic*. He read a few of the pages where passages were marked in red ink but could not concentrate. The dead man from his dream was still in his mind, in his steward's uniform with the polished buttons, the raised collar, the big bloodstain on the chest. He may not have seen a violent death in his sleep before, but Marco Timoleon had seen one in real life, which was not ominous but gruesome: the crash of the Piaggio. There was a scratching noise on the other side of the door, and he stood up to let Soraya in. Wagging her tail, the Afghan entered and accompanied him back to his chair. Marco Timoleon sat down again and picked up his book.

He had had several dogs over the years. The fact that Miranda, his first wife, did not share his love of them was one of the lesser problems of their marriage. Dogs had always filled his solitude if not with love at least with motion. His most memorable companion had been Caesar, a large Rottweiler that his staff had given him as a wedding present, a calm pacifist who had fallen victim to his breed's reputation. His wife had demanded that he got rid of him as soon as she gave birth to Sofia, afraid the dog might attack the baby or infect it with a rare disease. Marco Timoleon had tried to dissuade her but in the end had to bow to her wishes and banish the dog from the island to a farm on the mainland. But he had not forgotten him. Until the end of Caesar's life, Marco would take the launch and drive to the farm where the dog was exiled to feed and play with him.

He had bought Soraya a year before the death of his first wife. A tall Afghan hound with a narrow black head, long neck and skin covered in thick hair, she roamed round the island with immunity, free to harass the farm animals, to trample over the flower beds, to gnaw the furniture, doing all that to the staff's despair while her owner watched with pride. She did no tricks, no matter how hard the servants had tried to teach her, and for that reason everyone assumed that she was deaf. She avoided humans, especially the guests, and until recently she was not allowed into Marco's bedroom. In retaliation, he never seemed able to find her when he wanted company on his walks. They met in his study where he went to read. As soon as she saw the lights go on, she would come upstairs and lie quietly on the rug next to the fireplace where Marco Timoleon would sit with a book and a cigar that perfumed the air with its smoke. After his son's death, when he began to spend more time on the island, he let her at last into his bedroom, and then the dog began to follow him on his after-lunch walks. They stopped at Saint Mark of the Cypresses to put fresh flowers on Daniel's grave and continued along the narrow paths that cut through the dense vegetation, returning to the villa a long time later, having circled the island.

Marco Timoleon abandoned his attempts to read and walked out on to the balcony. Soraya stretched, yawned and followed him. Watching his servant water the flowers, Marco thought of going for a swim before the Piaggio arrived but decided against it: perhaps after lunch when the water would not be as cold. He was contemplating the sea with a glazed expression when he heard a voice.

'I see you're still alive.'

He turned round.

'Score one for me, doctor,' he replied.

The doctor walked out on to the balcony.

'You proved your point. But don't make a habit of it. Draughts kill more people every year than tobacco,' he joked. 'You, of course, do both.'

He was a tall man, older than Marco Timoleon but in even better health. At his age, when eating and drinking was meant to be a vice, he no longer ate red meat but only fish and pulses and drank no alcohol. He did not mind. Unlike his friend, he had adapted to the changes of age without protest but with relief; physicality had always been a burden to him.

Comfortable and at peace with himself, he was happy to say that he looked forward to dementia, which he called 'my second childhood'.

A mother tongue was one of the few things Marco Timoleon and the doctor had in common. Aristide Patrikios was a man of science. He had studied medicine with the intention of pursuing an academic career, but idealism had got the better of him, and he had spent many years in South America before moving to New York for an easier life. Despite his advanced age, he still received patients two evenings a week. He would say: 'My patients draw great comfort from me not because of my abilities but from the fact that I will die before them.' He had specialised in surgery, and his years in some of the remotest parts of the world had brought him a vast range of skills, from brain surgery to jeep repair.

He had not allowed his dedication to science to affect his love of culture. He was on the boards of several museums and galleries around the world and a regular at exhibition opening nights, royal galas and classical concerts. Years before, he had introduced Marco Timoleon to opera and considered it his greatest failure that he had not managed to infect him with his own passion for it. He was at his happiest when he was walking around a museum, studying the artefacts of bygone times, listening to the sound of his heels on the polished floor and the dead talking about forgotten glories, another world waiting for him to join it under the cobwebs.

The two men had first met more than fifty years earlier at the Strangers' Club in Buenos Aires where Marco Timoleon had obtained membership on false evidence. A solitary figure dressed in his eternal cream suit, the doctor could be seen in the billiard room or the gardens, strolling alone and avoiding the other members, an attitude that had earned him the reputation of a snob. The truth was less horrible: at the time he had been pre-tubercular and did not want to infect anyone else.

'Did you have a chance to see the room?'

Marco Timoleon beckoned the doctor to follow him to the guest wing at the end of the corridor. At one of the doors, he took a key out of his pocket and unlocked it, let in the doctor first and locked it behind them. In the middle of the room was an operating table with stirrups, next to a large piece of electronic equipment with a monitor and plastic tubes. A set of powerful lights was hanging down from the ceiling. There were also a lit autoclave, a metallic table on wheels, a pair of stools and a glass cabinet filled with medicines and surgical instruments.

'Well?'

Dr Patrikios walked round with his hands in his pockets.

'It's all here,' he said.

Marco Timoleon nodded with satisfaction.

'The anaesthetist and the nurse?' the doctor asked.

'They're coming today. Just another couple invited to the party.'

They left the guest room, locking the door again and returning to the master bedroom where the doctor declined the offer of a whisky and soda. He watched his host making one for himself and pouring into it what remained of his previous drink.

'There's always time to change your mind,' he said.

Marco Timoleon was not prepared to reconsider. The previous evening the two men had clashed over the ethics of the matter. Dr Patrikios was a staunch defender of the moral necessity of abortion, which he saw as an unpleasant but essential demonstration of free will, but he doubted whether free will was going to be served on this occasion.

'I can always find someone else,' Marco Timoleon said.

The doctor felt insulted.

'No. I'll do it. But only because I love Sofia and don't want her to go under a charlatan's knife.'

He was one of the few people who were aware of Marco Timoleon's superstition that often led him to take advice from faith healers and miracle workers, and it was he who had to use all his skills to reverse the damage they caused to his patient. For a while neither of them spoke but stood watching the sea out of the french windows.

'I married Lucrezia Borgia,' said Marco Timoleon, sipping his drink.

Dr Patrikios knew that Marco and Olivia Timoleon had been living separately for some time. He himself had never married.

'Not all marriages are necessary.'

'I have decided to end it,' Marco Timoleon said. 'I want her out of my life *and* out of my fortune.'

He confided to his doctor that his lawyers had already begun the process of filing for divorce. Things had been put on hold until he knew how long the whole thing would take, how much it would cost him and also whether he could disinherit Olivia before the divorce came through.

'Your daughter will be pleased with the news,' Dr Patrikios said.

Marco Timoleon nodded. It was true that Sofia always thought of her stepmother as a gold-digger. He finished his drink and tapped his fingers on the heavy glass.

'Maybe I could accuse her of adultery,' he said. 'That would save me having to pay alimony.'

He must have meant it as a joke because it was he who had been a famous philanderer all his life. In spite of his best efforts, his wife was not unaware of the fact. Dr Patrikios raised his head to the sky and made a more accurate suggestion:

'We're fortunate. It seems the weather will be good tonight.'

THE SOCIÉTÉ DES CHEMINS DE FER OTTOMANS D'ANATOLIE
had been founded with the main purpose of building a railway
line that would link the Bosporus with Mesopotamia. When
Victor Timoleon, Marco's father, started working for the
company, he was a young man who had not yet given the idea
of marriage a serious thought. He was not against it in principle but believed that a family at that moment would have
interfered with his career ambitions. Then, on his first journey
out of Istanbul to Anatolia, where he was sent to supervise the
building of a branch of the railway line, he met his wife: this
would not be the only occasion in his life that things would not
go according to plan.

The project for which he was given full responsibility was
very demanding for a junior engineer, but he had welcomed
it because it was his opportunity to escape his desk. Like his
son after him, Victor Timoleon was short, with broad shoulders, a wrestler's neck and a vigour that could not be concealed
despite an affected nonchalance that had pursued him ever
since he had written a book of poetry that failed to find
a publisher. He dressed smartly, in formal clothes that toned
down his rough shape: black frockcoat, white shirt with winged
collar, black bow-tie and waistcoat, grey trousers and a
top hat that gave him a few essential inches in height. What

distinguished him from other men of his age was his hair, which had turned grey before he was even thirty, and a pair of muttonchops, which he insisted on growing even though they had long gone out of fashion.

Having saved himself from the torments of poetry, he had thrown himself into his job with more enthusiasm than was good for him. He began to stay late in the office, absorbed in his work, alone among the empty desks, the empty drawing boards, the open windows that let in the night breeze from the Bosporus, with only the company of the night-watchman, who appeared when the clock on the wall struck midnight to convince him to put down his slide rule and go home. It was less a passion for engineering than an all-consuming and endless search for meaning that he would pass on to his son.

It was around that time that he was introduced to what would become his lifelong passion for reading and collecting the classics, an expensive habit that changed his life but also threatened to ruin him until his wife took control of the situation. The seed of his collection was three volumes of Aristotle tied together with a ribbon, a birthday gift from his colleagues at CFOA. The evening he received them, he lay in bed, opened one of the books with the intention of reading himself to sleep but ended up reading all three volumes from beginning to end. In the morning he came to work with dark circles round his eyes, put down his briefcase and declared:

'All paid jobs absorb and degrade the mind.'

So said Aristotle. By lunchtime he had convinced his colleagues that philosophy not engineering was going to help humankind, and they had all better start reading the classics. By evening news of the mutiny had reached the management, and the matter was discussed by the board of directors. The next day he was asked to report to the director-general, a French banker who knew

Aristotle better than Victor Timoleon did and put the young engineer in his place once and for all:

'It is unbecoming for young men to utter maxims.'

Victor Timoleon was then told that he was to take responsibility for an important project in rural Anatolia that required his absence from head office for long periods of time. He was no less glad to leave his desk behind than the company directors were to see him go. Rather than making him change his mind, his secondment encouraged his interest in the classics, which became his raft in the lunar loneliness of his days off work. His collection grew rapidly with books ordered by post. He read all the time, from the moment he woke up until he went to sleep, in daylight and candlelight, standing up, sitting down and lying in bed, indifferent to the world around him. Without his guidance, the crew of workers worked blindfold, and the railway line meandered across the landscape, avoiding towns it was supposed to link to the network and passing instead through others that were not in the original plans. In some of those places, grand stations had already been built in anticipation of the tracks, and some of these are standing to this day, abandoned and crumbling and never used. In fact, on the platform of one such ruin in 1974, while researching his book, Marco Timoleon's biographer came across a man well into his nineties dressed in a CFOA stationmaster's uniform, complete with cap, flag and whistle, patiently waiting for the train that was by then seventy years late.

The classics were to blame. Victor Timoleon continued to read with scholarly passion until an order was delayed in the post, and he had the idea of paying the school in a neighbouring town a visit, hoping to borrow a few books. He arrived at midday, during classes. The school for girls was a single-storey building with yellow walls and an earthen yard with a palm tree in the middle, a providential vision in the eyes of a man lost in the desert. The classrooms were on either side of a long corridor with doors made out of mosquito netting through which Victor Timoleon could see rows of desks with little girls in long dresses sitting in silence and scribbling on slates with pieces of chalk. The same thing was happening in the next room and the one after that, and what struck him as strange was the fact that the classes were not supervised by an adult but by one of the pupils, seated at the teacher's desk. In one classroom he finally saw a young woman at the blackboard, but it was only a fleeting glimpse before the caretaker, armed with a broom, surprised him and informed him that he was trespassing. Then he escorted him to the headmistress's office to wait for her.

Miss Eugenia Pavlidi saw him at break time, greeting him with a handshake that was both welcoming and questioning. Before he had the chance to introduce himself, she explained, with the disenchantment of a defeat conceded a long time ago, that in addition to being the headmistress of the school, she was also its sole teacher because of lack of funds. She was just as poor herself. She wore a Victorian mourning dress with a high collar, long sleeves and a row of buttons down the front, an outfit that together with her simple hair, cut by her own hand, and her face powdered with chalk, made her seem like a nun. Victor Timoleon straightened his bow-tie and explained the reason for his visit. The woman listened with interest while he complained about the dullness of his job, the loneliness of his days and the lack of books, and when he finished, she invited him to follow her and showed him into the school library, a small room with empty shelves that reached the ceiling. Victor Timoleon counted five books in all, covered in dust, but resisted his impulse to borrow them all at once. He picked up only one, blew off the dust and read the spine with satisfaction.

'You have saved a man's sanity,' he said.

He returned the following week to borrow the next book. He did the same a week later, and the one after that, taking the opportunity on every visit to sit with the headmistress between classes and have tea from the porcelain service reserved for the visits of the regional inspector of schools. Out of politeness, Victor Timoleon offered her a cigarette and was surprised to see her accept it: a nun that smokes, he thought. By his fourth visit, he was feeling that time was running out. He picked up both remaining books, leafed through them and chose one, letting Eugenia know what she knew already, that he would be returning the following week to borrow the last. When the day came, she found him in her office, sitting motionless as if he were posing for his portrait and perspiring in his black frockcoat and top hat that were even more unsuitable for the Anatolian heat than her own black dress.

'We are a pair of mourners in need of a funeral,' she said light-heartedly.

Victor Timoleon sprang to his feet and took off his hat.

'I haven't come for Herodotus,' he said in deadly earnest.

So it started. Like him, Eugenia Pavlidi was a Christian and almost as much an outsider in the town as he was. She had accepted the post of headmistress unaware of the difficulties that lay ahead. She wanted to leave home, a town on the Black Sea where her parents had died within a week of each other, honouring the pact they had made on their wedding night that they would never leave each other. Her enthusiasm had drained away when she reached her destination and learned that she would be the only teacher in the school, but she had refused to be beaten. When Victor Timoleon walked through the door, two years later, the school numbered sixty-one girls in nine classes that Eugenia taught all at the same time, rushing from one room to the next. She had started new courses in home economics, sewing, cooking and French, but her greatest pride was the annexe, a timber-framed building that housed the school theatre, built with donations although the money had run out before they could buy the seats and build a stage. All this she gave up when Victor Timoleon asked her to marry him, a decision she would come in the course of time to blame on love.

She joined her husband in the caravan of workers that travelled across Anatolia in random directions to lay branches and extensions of the railway line, repair the damaged track and build bridges. The marriage did not make Victor Timoleon forget his passion. He continued to read the classics, which he collected poste restante in the fortunate towns that found themselves on the route of the railway line, not forgetting to place another order at the same time and paying in advance. The parcels that consumed both his time and salary soon began to worry Eugenia Timoleon.

'There is nothing else to do in this place,' he said. 'If it wasn't for reading, life would have no purpose.'

Her answer surprised him:

'You could try to make this place fit for a baby.'

For almost a year, they had been living in a canvas tent, which Eugenia had tried to transform into a home by laying rugs on the floor, buying bookcases to shelve Victor's growing book collection and hanging oil lamps that made the tent glow in the night like a lighthouse. It was there that Marco Timoleon was born in the summer of 1903. A year later the baby suffered a serious attack of croup that almost killed him. What would have lasted no more than a few days was made worse by Victor Timoleon's decision to take matters into his own hands. He gave Marco hot mustard baths and warm enemas, fed him spoonfuls of syrups, paregorics and emetics, and made him inhale chloroform and turpentine vapours that cured neither the baby nor Eugenia's fears.

'Have faith in science,' he told her. 'Medicines were invented for a reason.'

In the end Eugenia Timoleon carried the medicine cabinet outside and set it on fire with the surgical spirit. Then she stopped giving Marco anything but water and orange juice until his condition improved.

'I'm not living here another day,' she said.

It was the end of Victor Timoleon's engineering career. They moved to the port of Izmir on the Mediterranean coast where he became a tobacco merchant, a good trade that helped him prosper more than engineering would ever have done, but he never stopped reminding his wife: 'I sacrificed a promising career for you.' In the cosmopolitan city, he could indulge his passion for the classics, raiding the bookshops and returning home laden with books he read over the weekend, seated alone in the iron glasshouse in the garden where the sunlight shone through the glass misted over from the tropical plants.

The family lived in a large house that used to belong to the American consul and his wife, a childless couple who had returned home after many years in the East. There was a big oval table in the dining room where the Timoleons sat every Sunday to have lunch together. Marco Timoleon remembered it as an endless torment that resembled a Quaker meeting, the family sitting in a silence sometimes interrupted by a comment made by one of his parents that received a brief reply.

From the start Marco's relationship with his father was one of mutual diffidence that worsened with time. Victor Timoleon did not kiss his son, did not read him bedtime stories, did not play with him. When Marco came into his study to show him his school reports, his father would read them carefully before pointing at his enormous library and reminding him: 'All you need to know is in these books.' Then he would congratulate him with a firm handshake and reward him for his grades with one Ottoman lira.

Victor Timoleon loved his son but at the same time was terrified of children, a problem that two generations later would resurface in a different shape: not many people knew that Sofia had a morbid fear of dolls. His phobia caused Victor Timoleon panic attacks. He would be short of breath, his heart would start beating faster, he would sweat and sometimes vomit. He felt defenceless against the stares of children, their aptitude for disobedience, their mocking laughter, which he heard behind his back and was convinced was aimed at him, their defiance against punishment. On his solitary afternoon walks in the park, he changed direction if he spotted a class of schoolchildren ahead, lowering his hat over his eyes and hurrying to return to his office where he felt safer among his clerks. He often said with more desperation than humour: 'We are the slaves of our offspring.' There were worse implications. Victor Timoleon's unreasonable fear meant that he never attended Marco's school celebrations and sports tournaments. Worse still, the boy's birthdays passed without a party – just him, his parents and their maid round the big oval table.

At least he had a healthier relationship with his mother, who drew on her experience as a teacher and an only child to make up for the boy's lack of friends. Eugenia Timoleon knew what to do to fill Marco's idle hours, how to create fantasies that unlocked doors in his mind, how to nourish his imagination with tasks that demanded his concentration: notes concealed around the garden, treasure maps that led to buried biscuit jars, riddles that had their answers hidden in books.

Marco would have been horrified to discover that all this fun was actually teaching him something. School did not interest him much. For a while he got good grades with little effort but stopped short of distinction even though his teachers agreed that he could achieve it. He preferred sports instead, above all swimming, both in competition and for pleasure, a habit he kept throughout his life, helping him to maintain a healthy body. On his way to school, he often took a turn that led to a secret beach some distance away where he undressed and swam naked for several hours, far from the shore and always alone. Every winter the sea brought many things on to the beach. Marco Timoleon had found a rusty sextant buried in the sand and taught himself how to use it, so that he could tell from the position of the sun when school was out and it was time to go home. And he was there when, after a storm that had lasted two days, the sea had brought out a grand piano that sounded like a dying animal and the beachcombers, moved by its sound, had decided instead of selling it piece by piece to bury it in the cemetery, writing on its gravestone the date they found it and its name: *Steinway*.

The first signs of his business flair he showed at the age of fifteen. During a walk on the beach, he noticed a rusty funnel rising above the surface of the water and a mast where a bird sat. When he came closer, he saw that the bird was a torn flag flapping in the wind. The wreck was not far from the shore. Marco Timoleon stood at the edge of the water, put his hands above his eyes to shield them from the sun and tried to guess the size of the sunken boat. When he took the road home, he had already decided to raise and repair it.

It turned out to be a twenty-six-foot steamboat that had been abandoned as not worth the salvage costs. Marco Timoleon bought it from the owner with money he made by working and borrowing from his father, raised it and spent an entire winter cleaning barnacles from the hull and sanding it down. If a piece of the hull was rotten, he cut it out and replaced it, making sure the repair was watertight.

On Sundays he worked on the boat all day, stopping to have lunch in the shade of the tamarisks and wonder about the fate of the captain of the steamboat, whom he imagined standing at its wheel in his peaked cap, his epaulettes and long grey beard like the haunted figure of the Dutch mariner who sailed eternally about the Cape of Good Hope. When he finished with the deck, he began work on the wheelhouse, replacing the door hinges that had rusted away, putting new glass in the windows that had been smashed by the waves and varnishing the wheel. He only had to hire someone to repair the engine for him. The following summer he launched his boat and managed not only to cover his costs but also earn a small profit by chartering it, a success overshadowed by the fact that some time later the steamboat sank again in a sudden storm without, at least, loss of life.

It was not the only misfortune. One day Victor Timoleon came home and announced: 'There are no more books.' The possibility that he might run out of books to read *had* crossed his mind, but he did not expect it to happen so soon. He hoped that when it did, his eyes would be so weak from old age that it would not be a disaster but a blessing. Now the truth dawned on him. In the following days, he sank into deep melancholy, and no human or divine intervention could lift him out of the quicksand. Eugenia Timoleon tried to tempt him into reading other books, travelogues, encyclopaedias, even novels, but he flung them across the room after a few pages, complaining that they were merely descriptive when what one needed from a book was help in understanding reality and existence. His friends bought him subscriptions to foreign magazines, including the *National Geographic*, *Everybody's Magazine* and *The Strand*, but he used them to kindle the fire. Doctors examined him but found nothing wrong with him; the Orthodox bishop carried out an anointing, but neither his biblical readings nor his prayers nor the smearing with blessed oil brought the sick man any relief; the mayor presented him with the Key to the City, but Victor Timoleon misplaced it soon afterwards, forcing the mayor to change the locks of all the doors in town.

Victor Timoleon withdrew into himself, speaking rarely to his family, spending his time at the office where he paid little attention to the affairs of his tobacco business and sat staring out of the window. At home he locked himself in the glasshouse where he withered among the African plants he refused to water, and he slowly turned into a ghost in a frockcoat and pyjamas. One Sunday Eugenia Timoleon and her son came home from church and found a piece of paper in the study scribbled with a quotation from Marcus Aurelius: *The object of life is not to be on the side of the majority but to escape finding oneself in the ranks of the insane.*

They never saw or heard from Victor Timoleon again. In an attempt to avoid scandal, Eugenia Timoleon decided not to notify the police but pretended to carry on as if nothing had happened until a rumour began to circulate that she had murdered her husband and buried him in the garden. Then she was forced to tell the authorities the shameful truth, and they believed her, but only after they had dug up the whole of the garden and found nothing.

It did not stop the storm of gossip, which continued to spread across Izmir, forcing Eugenia to shut herself in the house, close the windows and plug her ears with cotton. News of the disappearance was reported in the local paper together with Victor Timoleon's photograph. Articles were written, speculating that he had been kidnapped for a ransom never paid; that he suffered from amnesia, which meant that he could not even recognise himself in the mirror; that he was a European spy whose cover was blown, and he had had to be recalled. Marco suffered the humiliation with growing detachment. It was then that he must have begun to understand the workings of publicity, which he would later court and try to manipulate. In any case, it took him a while to learn. Some time after the disappearance, a journalist had visited the house, asking for a reaction to the published theories about his father, and Marco had given him an answer that was quoted verbatim the next day: 'Victor Timoleon was an illegitimate father.'

The misfortune led him to invent a fierce anger behind which hid an intense despair that lasted for many years. To do this he had to banish every memory of Victor Timoleon from his mind, and none were more difficult to erase than those that did not fit his conviction that his father was born without a heart. One spring, he told his biographer once, when life had not come off the tracks yet, his father had taken a break from reading and made room in the glasshouse for his workbench and tools. He covered the glass walls with old newspapers, fitted the door with a heavy padlock and every evening after dinner retired there for several hours with a book from his collection of classics whose title Marco Timoleon could no longer remember, returning to the house only to go to bed, tired, covered in grease and refusing to talk about his work.

The truth was revealed later that summer when Victor Timoleon, sleeves rolled up, braces dropped and fingers smeared with paint, took his son to the glasshouse and showed him a strange contraption he had built him for his tenth birthday. Victor Timoleon had wiped his fingers on his trousers and shaken the boy's hand before letting him have his present.

'Next year we'll try to fly on the back of a griffin,' he said.

It was a drum made out of brass and big enough for a grown man to fit inside; in this way, Victor Timoleon said, the man could stay underwater for long periods of time. Recounting the story now, one cannot help but speculate that the book that had inspired Victor Timoleon was Aristotle's *Problematum* where it is mentioned that Alexander the Great had once plumbed the sea depths in a diving bell. Unfortunately, Victor Timoleon's version had little luck and the drum sank to the bottom of the sea where it still probably is, rusting away among the wrecks of other civilisations.

Whether all this did truly happen, it is impossible to tell, but his biographer believed that it was one of Marco Timoleon's fanciful stories. At any rate, it does say something about his relationship with his father at the time, the need to worship him, his failure to do so, the attempts of the older man to show affection, all of them as doomed as his mythical machine.

After Victor Timoleon left, Eugenia surrendered to darkness and suffered in silence, locking herself in her room and sitting on the edge of her bed for hours, trying to remember how life was before the young railway engineer had walked through the gate of the school for girls. Her shock did not last for ever. One day Marco walked into the study and saw the framed portrait of his father missing from the wall behind the desk. Soon he discovered that all his father's photographs had disappeared from the rooms, as had the family albums, even the silver locket Victor Timoleon had given his bride as a wedding present. That was not all. His shirts and suits were not in the closets, his coats and hats not on the wooden stands, his shoes not in their boxes. Later the same day, Eugenia announced that she was going back to teaching.

She accepted a job at the Christian Academy for Boys where instruction was in agreement with the gospels, but which also put strong emphasis on science. She had been offered a better position in the Izmir school Marco attended but had to turn that down because his bad academic performance would have embarrassed her in the eyes of students and teachers. Her starting salary was small, but she did not mind. She was happy to be among children again, resuming a career she had abandoned for the sake of love. In fact, it was not long before she proved her worth to the governing body of the school and began to rise through the hierarchy. She became headmistress after only three years, overtaking her male colleagues, who were both older and more experienced but not such good teachers. Her secret was her belief that teaching should be based on the needs and aptitudes of the child rather than the needs of society and the precepts of religion. She was the first teacher in the country to use the Montessori method not only for teaching young children but also for adolescents, letting them do by themselves the things that interested them most, within strictly disciplined limits of course, at a time when most of her colleagues continued to use the methods of the Spanish Inquisition. Because of her achievements, Eugenia Timoleon was later the first woman to be offered the presidency of the school, but she politely declined and retired instead.

She lived a quiet life and died the way she had lived: with dignity. The news of her illness took Marco unawares. Already rich by then, he would have brought the best doctors to examine her or flown her to the best hospitals if he'd known. Not only did she never ask for his help but she did not even tell him she was unwell. When he found out, he immediately travelled to Izmir to be with her. By that time no power in heaven or earth could help her. Marco Timoleon wanted to give her a funeral worthy of his fortune and his love for her, but she spared herself the indignity of being paraded about like a religious relic: before losing her reason, Eugenia had dictated a letter to Pandora, her maid, forbidding her son any extravagance that would have embarrassed her if she were alive.

She was an avid fan of the cinema from the day her young husband had taken her to see the fantasies of Georges Méliès, and together they had watched every film that played in town, but she lost interest when sound was invented, which she considered vulgar. During the last days of her life, Marco Timoleon paid the owner of a local cinema to organise for her a screening of *Gone with the Wind*, which he was certain she would like. One evening a cart arrived at their street with an enormous projector on the back, which the projectionist aimed on the wall of the house opposite. Marco pushed his mother's bed out on to the balcony and sat with her to watch the film, which the rest of the neighbourhood were watching from the street. Minutes after the film had started, Eugenia Timoleon, bedridden and confused as to where she was, asked her son for her coat and handbag.

'You can stay,' she told him. 'I'll be in the foyer.'

Those were her last words to him. A week later Eugenia Timoleon died quietly in bed. It was several years before Marco received a yellowed postcard, postmarked with the date after the historic projection but having travelled round the world several times before finally resting on his palm. Written in his mother's agonising but unmistakable handwriting, it simply said: *Thank you.* Then he forgave her for having kept him in the dark about her illness and allowed himself to return to the family house where her maid lived alone. He entered through the back door and wandered around, observing with sad eyes the devastation, the old furniture covered with dust, the curtains drilled by the moths, the thick cobwebs until he came into his mother's room and saw the bed where she had lain for more years alone than with the man she had married. The sight made his flesh crawl: the rats had gutted the mattress, scattering the wool all over the floor. Before leaving, he searched the drawers where Eugenia Timoleon had hidden one last surprise for him. Under her everyday clothes, he found an old photograph of her with her husband on the day of their wedding. It was this photograph that he gave an artist as soon as he returned to New York, asking him to paint the big portrait of his mother that would later hang, framed in gold, in his study.

At least, the day-to-day life of the family had not suffered after Victor Timoleon's disappearance because Eugenia had always been the ruler of the household. She looked after it with the help of Pandora, who knew the secrets of the house better than her own past: she was an orphan whom Victor Timoleon had won in the annual church tombola. At first Eugenia, not used to having servants, had not been pleased to have her in the house.

'Take her back,' she had told her husband.

He had shrugged his shoulders.

'I can't. She's a gift from God.'

They kept her, and as she grew older, she proved to be exactly that. Pandora became her mistress's trusted helper, a good listener when the master of the house began to lock himself in the glasshouse and Eugenia's invaluable companion after he left. She never went to school but had a natural intelligence that compensated for her lack of education: it took her several years, but she had eventually taught herself to read and write with the help of Marco's old language primer. She had been found on the steps of the church wrapped in a towel with a note pinned to it: *Help her live.* She was only nine years older than Marco, who always maintained that she was the first woman to seduce him and teach him the secrets of lovemaking. The truth was more ordinary: Marco Timoleon learned about sex in the brothels. Pandora, who outlived him by several years, was fortunate never to find out the lie he had been spreading about her in interviews he gave to popular magazines later in life, or she would have died of apoplexy. She had a strict sense of morality and must have died a virgin because she never married or had a known love affair, devoting her life to her mistress's needs.

After his father disappeared, leaving his family the wisdom of Marcus Aurelius to remember him by, Marco Timoleon began to play truant and wander the streets of Izmir and its harbour, which his father always considered to be the most beautiful in the world. At the entrance to the bay stood the old fortress bombarded by the British three years earlier, during the time of the Great War, and behind it spread the city, on the shore and up the slopes of a low mountain with another ancient fortress on its top. Facing the main promenade were two theatres, three cinemas, the best hotels, several consulates and the offices and houses of the most prosperous merchants. Marco Timoleon strayed into the depths of the city, passing veiled women and men smoking water pipes beside ancient fountains while in the shade of grapevines old letter-writers sat at tables and wrote love letters and heart-breaking missives. He climbed the steep passages where ramshackle huts made of tin, wood and tarpaulin stood anyhow, to reach the top of the hills that had the best views of the city: in the distant sea, he watched the iron steamers coming from Europe, and on the roads in the east the long camel caravans arriving from Baghdad and Damascus. On other days he walked through the Jewish or the Armenian quarter that smelt of food he had never tasted, or he took the train to the nearby towns where the descendants of British, French and Dutch merchants had settled a hundred years earlier in imposing houses fortified with rose gardens.

On rue Franque, the principal business street of Izmir, he was caught in the afternoon crowds that poured into the department stores, and he stole, out of boredom, anything that would fit in his pocket: fountain pens, key rings, combs and perfumes. Later, becoming bolder, he began to steal anything he could carry, from straw hats on sunny days to leather gloves and umbrellas in winter, which he got rid of on the way home where Eugenia Timoleon waited for him with suspicion. One day he found himself in the Grand Bazar d'Orient, one of the biggest stores, and he wandered aimlessly about, stopping briefly at the men's department to put on an expensive jacket. He then continued around the busy store, browsing for a long while before taking the stairs to the exit and casually walking out into the street. He had taken only a few steps when a hand grabbed him by the shoulder. It was a shop assistant slightly older than him, dressed in a tailcoat.

'Stop in the name of the law,' he said. 'You're under arrest.'

He had been watching Marco Timoleon from the moment he put on the jacket and had been following him patiently around the aisles, up and down the stairs, knowing he did not intend to pay from the moment he tore off the price tag but waiting until he walked out of the store in order to have the right to stop him. Marco Timoleon had been stealing from shops for several months but the probability of being caught had not crossed his mind. Standing in the middle of the road, he tried to come up with something to say.

'Fuck off,' he finally said. 'I'll sue you for slander.'

This was how Marco Timoleon met him, and they would never have become friends if the shop assistant had not let him go, taking back the jacket and making him promise to meet him the following evening in one of the cafés near the store. Marco went neither the next day, nor the one after that, nor any other, forgetting about him until one evening three weeks later the man came to the house with a bunch of roses. Pandora took the flowers and left him standing in the hall while she went to inform her mistress. It was a long time before she returned and showed him into the living room where Eugenia Timoleon greeted him with a stern expression. She had assumed that he was another journalist enquiring about the disappearance of her husband and was very relieved when she heard that he was not a foe. She offered him a seat; Marco was not at home, but he was expected. Her visitor removed his hat and paced the living room with his hands behind his back, stopping to examine the paintings on the walls, the books on the shelves, the bone china. Then he sat down, and the two of them had a long and interesting conversation about art and music before Eugenia Timoleon asked him how he knew her son. He replied without hesitation: 'We share an interest in fashion.' She approved of him. She liked the pallor of his face, his honest eyes, his manners that belonged to another age. She also noticed his good taste in clothes, which was up to date, not knowing that he had borrowed them from the Grand Bazar d'Orient without asking and had to return them in the morning. It was from him that Marco Timoleon would learn to dress in a fashionable and formal way, no matter the occasion, following the principle that says a man should dress not according to his means but his ambitions.

Marco Timoleon arrived an hour later. When he realised the shop assistant was not there to inform on him, his horror turned to anger. For the rest of the visit, Marco said very little but had the chance to speak to their visitor alone when he saw him to the door. 'Listen,' he said. 'You're wasting your time. We're so poor the maid is paying us.'

He did not have to worry. A better judge of character than her son, Eugenia Timoleon was right about the shop assistant's sincerity: he was a friend. And so she opened the door of their unhappy house to him, giving him the right to come and go as he pleased, treating him like a member of the family who had returned after a long time away until, with time, she changed the facts to suit her, as often happened with the Timoleons, and she began to tell everyone, even Pandora who knew the truth, that the shop assistant was a nephew of hers. The young man had no objection. He invited Marco to teas, dances, musical afternoons and evenings in the salons of rich locals, to the Sporting Club, the Greek Club and the Cercle de Smyrne, and Marco went along not only to please his mother but also out of curiosity about the lifestyle of the rich and famous, which he knew little about. His friend was not a member of those clubs, of course, but had connections among the waiting staff, the cooks and musicians, who smuggled them in through the back door and let them watch from the kitchen, the bandstand or the garden if they promised to talk to no one. Other times they played sports, got drunk or visited the brothels. One evening they headed for the red-light district but found the door of their favourite house locked. They tried elsewhere but it was the same. Refusing to admit defeat, they continued to roam the empty alleyways like lost souls, looking in vain until Marco Timoleon remembered that it was the First of April, feast of Saint Mary of Egypt, patron of reformed prostitutes: all brothels were closed for the day. They ended up, exhausted and drunk, in the shop assistant's room hours later where they collapsed on to the bed and continued to drink to forget their disappointment.

'Screw the whores,' Marco Timoleon said.

'Quite,' his friend said.

He began to undress. Marco looked at him through the daze of the alcohol.

'What're you suggesting?'

'To save us some money,' the other man replied.

That is what his biographer was told had happened. The man who told him knew both Marco and his friend and insisted it was true, swearing on the Koran. He also said that Marco's friend had choreographed the whole incident with great care, sensing for a long time that all that was needed was a spark: not seduction but deliverance, the conclusion of an affection that had developed over several months without intention and without a clue as to what it was leading up to. Marco Timoleon must have worried about the Christian sin he was committing, the risk he was taking in a provincial town where everyone knew everyone else and homosexuality was a crime, but worse was the burden of shame he said that he felt, which he overcame only with large amounts of alcohol – or so he wanted his friend to believe: one night his lover sat up in bed, reached for the bottle of raki that Marco Timoleon had been drinking and took a sip of the clear alcoholic drink, not knowing that he was about to expose the fraud: 'This is water with aniseed,' he said.

In later life Marco Timoleon would always deny the affair, choosing to hide behind an exaggerated sense of masculinity that stressed physical courage, virility, domination of women and aggressiveness: a macho man. But his biographer was convinced the affair did happen, and it lasted several months up until he left for South America. Eugenia never suspected anything, not because she was not suspicious by nature but out of a failure of imagination: it never crossed her mind that two men would like to do what, in her experience, a man and a woman did with little enthusiasm, out of reproductive necessity.

Not long afterwards war between Greece and Turkey broke out, and the city was overrun with troops awaiting deployment to the front. Early one morning the army came to requisition the house. When Eugenia Timoleon heard the noise of boots on the floor, the doors opening and closing, the rude voices, she jumped out of bed and confronted the soldiers.

'Get out of my house,' she ordered.

They retreated and waited for the General to come. An hour later he arrived in his yellow Packard, which he had shipped out to Anatolia together with his chauffeur, expecting the expedition to be a pleasant trip to the countryside. When Eugenia Timoleon looked out of the window and saw the General in his uniform, his medals and his pistol, she calmed down. She put on her widow's dress, which she continued to wear even after she had admitted to the police that she had not killed her husband, she combed her hair and rouged her cheeks. When she was ready, she sat in her armchair and said:

'He may come in.'

They became friends. Eugenia Timoleon offered him her room, but the General refused and chose instead to sleep in the attic that until then was used for storage. The soldiers cleaned it and brought in a bed where the General could dream his campaigns and a desk where he could plan them. He always slept until late in the morning and then bathed, shaved and trimmed his moustache, which grew an inch every night. He had lunch under the date palms in the garden, his orderly standing behind him with an open umbrella to protect him from the guano of the gulls, and left for his rounds as the town was shutting down for its afternoon rest. His passion was not war but breeding carrier pigeons, and he spent many hours every day feeding his birds, grooming and talking to them.

At first the campaign went well. News of battles won in the interior reached the town, and more ships unloaded supplies and troops that were sent east. A year after the landing of the expeditionary corps, the front had moved far from the coast, and the General had to leave town. Before climbing into his Packard, he kissed Eugenia's hand.

'I will write,' he said.

He kept his promise and wrote every week, letters marked *Top Secret* that army messengers delivered to her personally. As soon as she received them, she locked herself in her room and read them several times over, not revealing their contents to anyone, not even her maid. Once she had read them, she held them over a candle until the flame had burned her fingers, and then she scooped up the ashes and blew them out of her window. It was a strange ritual for a strange relationship. The General never visited the house again. Yet his letters continued to arrive, even when he happened to be in town for a religious festival, an evening ball or a military parade to celebrate another victory on the battlefront. One time Pandora, intrigued by the postal affair, had made a casual comment: 'He must be crazy.' Far from being annoyed at her impudence, her mistress had shrugged and replied with good humour: 'No. I have simply moved from a man who just read to one who just writes.'

By the beginning of the third year of the war, the letters were arriving less often, in creased, dirty or torn envelopes. Eugenia Timoleon still waited for them with hope. When she received one, she rushed to her room where she smoothed down the creases, brushed the dirt off and sat at the window to read it. If the letter was torn, she put it together like the pieces of a jigsaw puzzle. The war was not going well. There were no caravans of prisoners any more, but ships still brought soldiers, who were sent to the front together with mules, trucks and artillery. In the spring the army messengers stopped coming to the house altogether. For several weeks no letter arrived until, one afternoon, Pandora found a dead pigeon on the veranda with a metal capsule tied to its leg. She immediately took the bird to her mistress, who opened the capsule and read the small piece of paper hidden inside. Then she asked her maid to bury the dead bird under the palms in the garden. From that day on, she stood on the roof of the house, gazing for hours in the direction of the faraway columns of smoke that marked the battlefield, but no other pigeon ever came.

By the end of summer, the columns of smoke were at the outskirts of town. Marco Timoleon heard the noise of artillery that only stopped at night, he felt the house shake, he tasted the gunpowder and burned metal in the air and knew the end of the war was near. In the following days the evacuation began. Soldiers passed through town and boarded the ships waiting in the bay. The flow of men grew bigger and faster every day that passed until the retreat turned into an uncontrollable torrent that left behind it a horrific debris of dead animals, burned lorries and dismantled weaponry. Watching the departure of the expeditionary force on the promenade, Marco Timoleon saw the General for the last time. He rode past on a mule, dressed in his torn uniform but without his medals, without his belt, without his cap, unshaven and silent. Marco called out to him, but the General could see nothing because his eyes were bandaged. It was how Marco Timoleon would always remember him: tied on his saddle with ropes that held him upright like a sad wooden effigy.

That night he was lying in his lover's bed, and his friend said: 'This place is going to hell.'

Marco Timoleon was eighteen and until that moment the thought of leaving home had never crossed his mind. His friend had helped him find a job as a waiter in one of the clubs in town, and he had abandoned school only months before graduation, a decision that had shocked his mother who had stopped speaking to him: mother and son communicated now through

Pandora. When a few days later the war ended and a big part of Izmir lay in ruins, destroyed by fire, Marco Timoleon finally took his decision to leave.

The fact of the matter was that the Timoleon family had long been drifting towards bankruptcy, and the devastation left by the war only speeded up the inevitable: penury. After the dust of Victor Timoleon's disappearance had settled, Eugenia had sold the tobacco business for a good price and put the money in the bank. Every Monday morning, on her way to the school, she stopped to make a withdrawal for the week's expenses. Once a month she asked the cashier to calculate the interest and write it down in her account book. Their savings and her salary were not enough to support three people and also maintain the big family house, so Eugenia Timoleon had taken the decision to let out one of the rooms. But things had improved little. As time went by, she let out more and more rooms, offering full board and a weekly change of linen, but after a while the profit rather than increasing began to drop: 'It's the law of diminishing returns,' the bank manager had explained to her.

Still, Marco Timoleon's decision to leave was a blow to his mother, who refused to accept the reality of their situation. When he announced that he had bought a ticket to South America, Eugenia was in her bedroom, sitting in a chair that faced the window. The Sunday light on her tired, malnourished body made her look like a saint on her way to heaven. Pandora was also in the room, sitting on the edge of the bed and knitting. When Marco said he was leaving in the morning, his mother beckoned to her maid and spoke into her ear.

'She says, "Fine",' Pandora said.

It was a vow of silence that lasted six years and was finally broken by a telegram Eugenia Timoleon sent her son with the sad news that his friend, whom she still called her nephew, had died of diphtheria. From then on they stayed in touch by post but had no chance to speak to each other face to face until Marco Timoleon returned, twenty years after he left for South America, to care for his dying mother.

BREAKFAST WAS BEING SERVED ON THE TERRACE. THE doctor gone, Marco Timoleon was again alone in his bedroom. It was not a good start to the day; his conversation with Dr Patrikios had left him irritated. He called his servant on the phone to order a fresh pot of coffee and shut himself in his study to keep busy until the rest of his guests arrived. This room too was furnished with little taste despite Olivia Timoleon's repeated attempts to correct her husband's excesses: one of her habits was to hire interior decorators and take them on a world tour of the couple's houses and have them redecorate the rooms according to her taste.

It did not always work. One time she had tried to redecorate the *Sofia*, unaware that the yacht was her husband's holy of holies. Marco Timoleon, who had designed and furnished it himself, considered it the high point of his taste. His own state-room was divided into three spaces: a bedroom, a marble bathroom and a study with panoramic views of the sea. Olivia Timoleon had the king-size bed with the Venetian linens removed because it reminded her of a deathbed, she had the Baccarat-crystal lighting taken down, the wood-panelled walls of the study painted orange and the floor fitted with a carpet. Only the lapis lazuli fireplace escaped her fury but only because she could find nothing to plug the big hole it would leave in the wall. She bought furniture made of black leather, chrome and glass that was then in fashion and a round waterbed so big that one needed a nautical chart not to get lost in it. She often took decisions without considering the circumstances or the consequences, relying on her good taste and charm to overcome the opposition, but that time she had overstepped the mark. Marco Timoleon would later dub his reaction *The Battle for the Furniture*. When he saw the changes, he flew into a rage that threatened to dissolve the marriage just months after the honeymoon. In the event it did not, but the incident caused one of many cracks that would slowly bring down their relationship although the couple never formally divorced. He began a search for the old furniture, going from cabin to cabin until he found it, safe and sound, in the ship's hold, packed and ready to be sent to Asian bazaars where someone was bound to appreciate its ornate splendour. He then demanded that everything be put back in its exact place, that the walls be repainted, the carpet removed, the waterbed sold to an aquarium. He held the crew responsible, refusing to pay their salaries for two months, but the greatest punishment he had reserved for his second wife: he had declared that from that day on, his yacht was out of bounds to her.

The smell of breakfast coming from the open window did not distract him. He sat at his desk, lit a cigar and drew on it several times before picking up the phone. A moment later his servant entered with the coffee pot, placed the silver tray on the desk and turned to leave. Marco Timoleon lowered the receiver.

'Where's the Englishman?'

Told that he was having breakfast with the doctor, Marco Timoleon nodded and returned to his phone call. The way he spoke to his subordinates was rude and direct, using the expletives of the boatmen of Izmir, who could shoot a bird from the sky with their profanities. He spoke clearly but fast, so that those who listened could follow only if they paid attention. While he spoke, the sun moved, and the shadows of the furniture on the floor grew shorter. On the other side of the room was a projector directed at the wall, next to a stack of film cans. The last film he had watched was *The Godfather*, one of his favourites, which had come out three years earlier, and he had seen it thirteen times so far. He watched films late at night when everyone else had gone to bed, alone, savouring the brief truce: no footsteps, no voices, no phones ringing. The last time he had watched the film, drinking several glasses of whisky, a slight sense of boredom had come over him either from having seen it so many times already or from the alcohol or from something else, and he had switched off the projector and stayed in the dark until dawn, staring at the darkened wall.

Still talking on the phone, he poured himself a cup of coffee, adding three spoons of sugar. On the walls were pictures of ships from the commercial fleet he had built over the last half century, among them the first real ship he ever owned, an ageing dry bulk freighter he had intentionally sunk soon after buying it in order to collect the insurance. He sipped his coffee in slow gulps, stopping to puff at his cigar or listen to the clatter of cutlery and the voices from the terrace where his guests were having breakfast.

He was pleased he was not alone but did not feel like joining them. Sitting at his desk and working, he experienced a sense of contentment that somehow reminded him of his younger self: for a moment the clouds had parted and the sun was shining through. It did not last long. There was a knock on the door, and he gave permission for whoever it was to enter. When he raised his head, he saw that it was the Englishman. Marco Timoleon returned his greeting with a single word: 'Sit.' He made several more calls, putting down the phone and picking it up again, dialling number after number without having to look up any of them and surprising the person at the other end of the line with an immediate salvo of questions about business matters. Finally he put down the phone and did not pick it up again.

'They're crucifying me, Mr Forster,' he said. 'And what do my staff do? Useless as the Disciples.'

He told his guest about the problems he faced with his businesses as if he were talking to an old friend, and then moved on to offer his opinion about the end of the Vietnam War and the beginning of the one in Cambodia, but what he wanted to discuss more than anything else was the fascinating story in the news recently about a Japanese army officer who had emerged from the jungle with his rifle and ammunition intact thirty years after Japan's surrender.

'You know what his first words were?' Marco Timoleon asked. '*I am sorry I did not serve my emperor to my satisfaction.*'

He stood up and walked to the window where he looked out with his hands clasped behind his back.

'He didn't serve his emperor to his satisfaction . . .' he repeated pensively.

His guest looked at him but did not speak. Marco Timoleon turned away from the window.

'And how are you today, Mr Forster?'

Ian Forster, Marco Timoleon's biographer, was a tall man not older than thirty, whose conservative way of dressing owed more to his lack of money than his taste. They had first met in London after the Englishman had been stalking him for months around the hotels and restaurants of the capital where Ian Forster was denied access. He had written countless letters asking the tycoon for an interview, but all he ever achieved was getting himself on the mailing list of Timoleon Enterprises, Inc., which meant that every Christmas he received a card with a printed wish. He had tried calling but was always redirected to public relations officers, who listened to his proposal for an authorised biography politely and then turned it down. He had not given up and had finally cornered Marco Timoleon at Annabel's nightclub in Berkeley Square, the tycoon's favourite shelter from his insomnia. Dressed in black, Marco Timoleon had been sitting on a sofa with a young woman who was not his wife. Before the bodyguards had time to stop him, the Englishman offered his hand.

'Who the hell are you?' asked Marco Timoleon.

'Your future biographer.'

Marco Timoleon did not shake his hand but waved his bodyguards away. He asked how long he had been trying to see him, and when he heard the answer, he chuckled.

'The drops of rain make a hole in the stone,' he said.

Ian Forster added: 'Not by violence but by oft falling.'

'You know your Ovid.'

'Lucretius,' the Englishman corrected him.

'Of course,' Marco Timoleon said. 'But if you want my help, you also ought to learn flattery.'

When he had first had the idea of writing Marco Timoleon's biography, Ian Forster was still a freelance journalist who contributed to lifestyle magazines and was paid by the page. Unable to afford the costs of the research he would have to do, he had tried to find a publisher to finance him, but they had all turned down his proposal, warning him about its flawed premise: it was a story readers had read many times already. Then in an act that was born as much out of inspiration as desperation, Ian Forster had decided to ask his subject himself to support him.

Seventy at the time, Marco Timoleon had been the subject of several biographies over the years, none of them authorised.

His life had attracted the attention of many good journalists, some better than the Englishman, who had all approached their subject with a combination of suspicion and awe. He declined to collaborate but put no obstacles in their way, saying that he respected the freedom of the press, safe in the thought that, sooner or later, the hacks would lose their bearings in the various inventions about his life. He was not the only source of untruths about himself. He would say: 'I have no more control over my past than my future.' It was not an exaggeration. Obsessed with facts rather than the truth, the journalists would twist their findings to fit their argument but in the process create more riddles than they solved, and their prey would slip through the net.

Marco Timoleon made fun of those attempts while reaping the benefit of the free publicity they generated until he reached the age when mortality comes knocking, and then he was forced to think about it. He took down photo albums, blew off the dust and studied the fragments of the past of a man who could not have been himself. Dr Patrikios had asked him once why on earth he wanted to help the young biographer when the tycoon had so many secrets to hide, suggesting that it was perhaps the unreasonable but irresistible hope of a serial criminal to be caught. Marco Timoleon had surprised him with the simplicity of his answer: 'I want to know the truth.'

So, he had said yes, and Ian Forster had found himself travelling first class by air, sea or land, staying in five-star hotels and eating in gourmet restaurants, waiting for the phone call that would summon him for an interview that usually took place late at night in one of Marco Timoleon's offices somewhere across the world.

Two and a half years had passed since the Englishman had ambushed Marco Timoleon at Annabel's, and the biographer was more determined than ever to finish his book and make public everything he had discovered. He would wake up in the middle of the night and sink into his flood of old books, letters and articles, reading through interviews, business reports and social commentaries, making notes of names, dates and locations that he would have to investigate further, cutting out photographs and pasting them above his desk. He travelled continuously, finding himself in Oriental markets, city libraries and public record offices, interviewing people who claimed to have known Marco Timoleon, searching for clues to the mystery of the man who paid him but did not really help him, until he began to suspect that the tycoon had no intention of seeing his biography in print and that it was all an amusing pastime to satisfy his curiosity, which would end as soon as Ian Forster typed his last word. His fears had grown after his search unearthed an unexpected piece of information: as a young man, Marco Timoleon had had a love affair with another man. The Englishman had told him about his discovery, expecting him to fly into a rage, but not for the first time he had been surprised by his subject's reaction. Marco Timoleon had sucked his cigar and said simply: 'It never happened.'

A week earlier in London, Ian Forster had received a first-class flight ticket in an envelope that also contained an invitation: *Mr & Mrs Marco Timoleon request the pleasure of your company on the occasion of Miss Sofia Timoleon's 25th birthday.* He had come to the island hoping to find the opportunity to interview Marco again for the book after not having met him in a long time, and that morning he knocked on the door to ask whether they could talk. He had caught him at a bad moment. Marco Timoleon paced round his desk.

'They want to ruin me,' he said.

He reached over the pile of magazines delivered the previous day and held up one with his picture on the cover. Inside, an article revealed that his empire was in irreversible decline.

'Am I a dinosaur, Mr Forster?'

The Englishman leafed through the article, which was not news to him. He put the magazine back on the desk.

'You didn't use to worry about a bad press,' he said.

He was right. Marco Timoleon took great pleasure in the exaggerated stories that described him as a dubious character with an unpredictable mind and a criminal past, stories which did so neither with pity nor ridicule but always with a certain degree of awe. But it was also true that he was slowly beginning to lose the war against his competitors, the way he was losing the battle against time: since the death of his son, he had been growing older at a rapid pace. Every morning new wrinkles appeared in his face and his eyes sank ever deeper in their sockets. He also seemed absent-minded – at least it was not dementia: he talked about the distant past as if it were yesterday.

'You have to help me write a reply,' Marco Timoleon said. 'We have to deny their claims and threaten legal action. These lies cost me dearly.'

Ian Forster felt disappointed.

'I was hoping you'd have time for us to work on the book.'

'That will have to wait.'

The young man left the room and returned with his type-writer. Marco Timoleon sat in the leather chair, lit another cigar and poured himself more coffee. His fighting spirit was invigorating him. He dictated with the cigar in his mouth, speaking in the heavy accent that his biographer still found difficult to understand after so many interviews. He began by letting out a torrent of abuse, none of it publishable, but slowly calmed down, regaining some of the reason that had made him one of the richest men in the world. What he liked more than anything was winning an argument, which he did with a combination of flattery, intimidation and sophistry. He would say: 'Even truth has to lie sometimes.' They worked for a long time, revising the letter, retyping it, changing it again until they lost track of time. Suddenly Marco Timoleon asked:

'What do you think of Sofia, Mr Forster?'

The Englishman did not know what to say. He put his fingers on the keys of his typewriter as if he would rather type his answer.

'I can't say that I know her very well.'

'From what you know.' Marco Timoleon propped his glasses on his forehead and read the letter. 'Based on your professional skills. Aren't you a biographer?'

'I like her,' Ian Forster said.

Marco Timoleon nodded. He made a few corrections to the letter and handed it back.

'Good. I like her too.'

It was a brief incident that seemed to have no significance, but that evening the Englishman would remember it. Carried by the afternoon wind, the faraway noise of an aeroplane travelled in through the open window. Marco Timoleon recognised the sound of his son's death: it was the second Piaggio. He lowered his glasses to his eyes, relit his cigar and dismissed his biographer. The young man put the cover back on his typewriter, collected the sheets of paper and left the room. The cigar smoke hung heavily halfway between the floor and the ceiling. Marco Timoleon's coffee had long turned cold, but he sipped a little to cool himself. The air conditioner in the wall was silent: after his previous night's dream, he had ordered all the air conditioners switched off except for the ones in the guest rooms. It was a warm afternoon, and he walked to the window where he stood in the shafts of sunlight. Watching the Piaggio coming in to land, he could not avoid a pinch in his heart. The sky was calm and bright, and the shadow of the plane, moving in a straight line, rippled on the surface of the water. The seaplane touched down gently and approached the jetty where servants were already waiting to catch the rope and let down the gangplank. Moments later the door opened, and despite the distance Marco Timoleon recognised, at the head of a small crowd of friends, his second wife, dressed in a white midi dress with a shirt collar, a pair of sandals and a brimmed hat. Olivia Andersen Timoleon, a woman with a nice body but no longer young, still carried herself with the same confident manner that had once impressed him but that he now thought of as a forgery. He waved to her from the window of his study, and Olivia saw him and waved back before turning to supervise the unloading of her luggage on to the jetty.

They had first met six years earlier at a charity gala in New York where no one had to introduce them because they were already familiar with each other by reputation. Marco Timoleon could still remember how she looked when he first laid eyes on her: tall and elegant, with black hair cut to neck length, dressed in pink, a pearl choker around her neck, moving across the Grand Ballroom of the Waldorf-Astoria as if she were skating on ice. Their meeting had been the result of a series of coincidences. Marco Timoleon had only decided to attend the gala at the last moment after a long and difficult day at the office that had ended well. He would have liked to idle away the rest of the evening in the company of friends, but for once no one was available. The event was in full swing by the time he arrived: a band played dance music that made the glasses rattle, the guests chattered in black tie, the waiters rushed about with large trays lifted in the air. At once he regretted having come. He turned to leave, but at the door he was held back by a sudden storm. Watching the rain lash against the windows, he told the liveried doorman not to call his limousine after all, and he returned inside. It would take one more providential event that evening to bring Olivia and him together. She was in charge of the raffle where he won third prize, a trip for two to Venice, complemented with a kiss on the cheek from her that sealed their fate.

They could not have been more different. The only daughter out of six children, Olivia Andersen was descended from New England aristocracy and had grown up in a family that believed in God and commerce in equal measure. The family enjoyed a high standing in society thanks to her paternal grandfather's ingenuity. Back in the 1920s, he had published privately a genealogy which traced his ancestry back to a sixteenth-century European nobleman, a deliberate fraud that took advantage of a surname that was not unusual. He then sent his pamphlet to every library, every archive and every learned society in the country. In truth, the Andersens were descendants of an ironmonger who had arrived in America a century earlier. Cornelius Andersen, Olivia's father, was four years younger than Marco and an old-style businessman, who ran his affairs from the two-storey Victorian family house which faced the Atlantic. Gladys, her mother, was a skilled painter, with her own studio in a converted outbuilding of the house, who had taught her daughter the importance of art and music from an early age. Olivia Andersen spoke French without effort, having learned it at the same time as English, a good thing because Marco Timoleon considered it the sexiest language in the world. Her father, for whom Olivia was his favourite child, did not want her to leave home, saying that she did not have to go to university to receive a good education, but she did. In New York she studied journalism and met her first husband, and there she continued to live after her divorce. When Marco Timoleon met her at the charity gala, she was thirty-two years old and he sixty-six.

They became friends at a time when Olivia Andersen needed to turn over a new leaf, which was something that her old friends could not help her with. Despite their presence, the truth of the matter was that her divorce had left her bitter, exhausted and stranded on a desert island. She had put all her efforts into trying to make her first marriage work, promising herself afterwards that she would never do it again, not suspecting that a few years later she would be doing exactly the same in another doomed relationship. Perhaps it was her religious upbringing, perhaps it was kindness or stubbornness that stopped her from jumping ship before it sank, perhaps it was greed. More likely, it was a combination of reasons, some known to her and others not, that made her what she was and attracted her to Marco Timoleon, with whom she stayed for better or for worse, an attitude that led him to dub her *Saint Olivia the Martyr*.

A failed marriage was one of the very few things they had in common. More importantly, her stamina in listening was as good as Marco Timoleon's was when it came to talking. He could discuss anything apart from art, which did not interest him at all. Olivia made it her purpose to get him to like music, literature and theatre, fighting the battle that Dr Patrikios had lost years before. For a while Marco did accompany her to the opera, to concerts and art exhibitions, but when the wind dropped and their marriage slowed down, he began to ask others to go in his place. The doctor was glad to do so.

Standing at the window of his study, Marco Timoleon gazed at the crowd on the jetty where the servants were unloading the luggage and the guests recovering from the flight before braving the steep steps to the villa. He had not seen his wife in several months. More than a year before, he had suggested they spend some time apart in order to reconsider the future of their marriage. He smoked as he watched the guests follow Olivia up the stone steps to the villa, while further behind the servants, dressed in their white uniforms with the gold buttons, carried their suitcases. Then he waited for the knock on his door, and it was not long before he heard it.

Olivia Timoleon was tired from the journey that had started the day before in New York, but there were few misfortunes bad enough in life that could not be put right with rouge and lipstick. He kissed her on the cheek and pulled up a chair, then sat at his desk and picked up the phone to order refreshments.

'How was your journey?' he asked.

Olivia had left her friends in the care of the servants with specific instructions to show them to their rooms and attend to their needs, and she had gone to see her husband in the hope that things were the way she expected. His phone call had come at a time when she was already convinced that their marriage had no chance of surviving. Her friends had advised her to seek the help of a good attorney and had, in fact, found one for her, a successful New York lawyer who specialised in war reparations. Olivia Timoleon had gone to see him reluctantly, and he had suggested filing for divorce immediately on the grounds of adultery, habitual drunkenness and impotence. She refused to do it. That afternoon she arrived on the island hoping that Marco's wish to have her next to him at his daughter's birthday party was his attempt at reconciliation.

Marco Timoleon poured her a glass of juice and filled his own with Scotch and ice. Sitting behind his desk, he drank slowly, taking the glass from his lips to ask his wife about her journey. She had travelled via Paris where she had enough time to visit the city before boarding the next plane for another comfortable flight, but in the Greek capital her friends and she had to squeeze into the old Piaggio for the final leg of their journey. Marco Timoleon listened in silence, refilling her glass before it emptied.

Meeting her parents had been the first bad incident in a long history of bad incidents. Marco and Olivia had arrived at the house in the middle of the night after a flat tyre far from anywhere had delayed them by several hours and were greeted by an old couple in nightclothes who were not happy to see them. They took them into the living room, offered them milk and biscuits, and then Cornelius Andersen had shown Marco into the library where he said:

'Let's cut to the chase. I do not approve of this relationship.'

Five years had passed since, and his feelings for Olivia had waned but not his memory: he had not forgotten the angry disagreement he had with Cornelius Andersen about whether he had the right to date his daughter in view of their age difference and the pain of a recent divorce that affected her judgement. Marco Timoleon used the argument of love to convince him, but Olivia's father dismissed it with a single sentence: 'You and I are old enough to know that a marriage built on love is a sandcastle.' Then he said that he was familiar with the tycoon's reputation as a man who did not play by the rules whether in business or anything else. Marco Timoleon had never sought anyone's permission to do what he wanted to do, but Olivia had a great love for her parents. To make matters worse, she had been a devout Roman Catholic from a young age and had preserved this spiritual dimension in her later life. In the end Marco Timoleon found an ally in Gladys Andersen, who did not like him any more than her husband did but knew her daughter better than both men. She took Marco into the kitchen, shut the door and filled his glass with Scotch until he had stopped shaking.

'I would marry her tomorrow,' Marco had told her. 'But I don't think one should marry out of anger.'

Gladys Andersen advised him to visit Father O'Malley, the

priest who had christened Olivia and still played an important part in her life. Once a month she met him for tennis and confession. Father O'Malley was the only man in the world who could wield influence over Cornelius Andersen, with whom he had fought in the Pacific. A few days later Marco Timoleon had visited him, ready to use his charm to persuade the priest that he would make a good husband.

A tall thin Irishman with a pale face and hair the colour of carrot, the priest received Marco Timoleon in his office, making it clear from the beginning that he did not like him either. He said: 'I know who you are.' He was in the last years of his office and was looking forward to retirement. For more than forty years he had served an affluent parish and not a day had gone by without his wondering whether his parishioners asked for his advice out of faith or habit. Marco Timoleon took a seat.

'*To abstain from sin when one can no longer sin is to be forsaken by sin, not to forsake it,*' he said.

Father O'Malley felt weary of the words he had heard so many times that they meant little any more.

'Bless Saint Augustine,' he sighed. 'He's made a difficult job even harder.'

They talked for a long time. Marco did not manage to convince him that he would be a good husband to Olivia or anyone else. But Olivia had secretly implored the priest not to be an obstacle to her happiness, and he felt a lot of affection for her. In the end not only did he give his consent but he allowed the wedding to take place in the Orthodox church of Saint Mark of the Cypresses on the tycoon's private island. Marco Timoleon was pleased. He kissed the priest's hand, a foreign custom that made Father O'Malley frown.

'I hope you are not the Antichrist,' he told him.

Marco Timoleon shrugged.

'I'm only a king who makes his jester laugh, Father.'

The couple married four months later. Cornelius Andersen, whose dislike for Marco Timoleon would never subside, refused to attend, sending his daughter off with a brief blessing: 'Good luck. But you're crazy.'

Sitting at his desk opposite her on that August afternoon, Marco Timoleon had to admit that his father-in-law had been right: the marriage had not lasted. He took a sip from his drink.

'We have problems,' he said. 'But nothing we can't work out.'

Olivia Timoleon nodded, not looking directly at him.

'I think so too.'

'We've been together for some time,' said Marco.

'Six years.'

He smiled and his teeth showed even whiter against his tanned face. Then he raised a finger.

'Six years, five months and three days,' he said.

Slowly he turned his chair towards the big windows, and his smile disappeared from Olivia's view. She could not help but wonder whether her husband was still smiling while staring out where the afternoon sun burned.

'But the last year has been bad for us,' she said.

'Nevertheless, I'm very glad you are here.'

The ice in the bucket was melting. Marco Timoleon dipped his fingers in the water and dropped a few cubes in his glass before pouring more whisky. Some time passed in silence that made it harder to speak again. He lowered his glass.

'Yes, I'm glad you came,' he repeated. 'Because I need your help.'

'You were always a generous host but not very patient, Marco. You and I can make this a great party.'

'No, not that.'

Olivia Timoleon waited quietly to hear what he wanted to

say. There was an air of dignity about her, Marco Timoleon had to admit.

'This is something very important,' he said.

Then he told her about the pregnancy. He said that he did not yet know whether Sofia intended to keep the baby, but he needed Olivia's help to persuade his daughter to agree to have an abortion. It was a mistake, and besides it went against what he had in mind for Sofia. Ever since she had come of age, he had been introducing her to the sons of his business rivals, with the ambition of creating a joint empire, but she turned them all down after the first date. Marco Timoleon had also tried, without success, the sons of members of parliament, government ministers and aristocrats with titles but no fortunes.

'I know who the father is,' he said. 'And he's very unsuitable.'

'There are certain rules even you don't have the right to violate,' Olivia said without anger.

Marco Timoleon stared at the cigar that had long gone out in the ashtray.

'Under different circumstances I would agree. But this is serious. I need your help.'

'I don't know. I have to think about it.'

'It's the right thing to do. If this was a serious relationship, the father would have come forward.'

She agreed with him on that. But even if she did not approve of the affair, she had no power over her stepdaughter.

'I don't think Sofia likes me.'

'It has nothing to do with you,' Marco said. 'She worshipped her mother.'

Sofia disliked her stepmother from the moment the latter had entered Marco Timoleon's life and never missed the opportunity of reminding her: she reminded her at the dinners where Marco brought the two women together in an attempt to broker a ceasefire, she reminded her with her silences at the Sunday brunches where Olivia invited her stepdaughter to make friends, she reminded her with her glacial stare on the couple's wedding anniversaries.

'Let me speak to her,' Olivia said.

'It would help.'

'I will speak to her.'

'Good,' Marco Timoleon said. 'Because me, I can only talk numbers.'

From the study Olivia went to their bedroom, but her luggage was not there. She did not ask the servants but searched herself until she found her suitcases in one of the guest bedrooms. The windows faced the sea but not the same sea that her husband watched from his room; the sea in this direction was dark and rough because it was deeper. Olivia rummaged through her handbag until she found her cigarettes. She lit up and smoked standing with her arms folded across her chest. Not for the first time, Marco had made her promise to do something she did not want to.

In the wardrobe she found, brought over from the master bedroom, her summer clothes, her shoes, her hats and sandals. Folded neatly in the drawers were her swimsuits and underwear. On the bedside table was the book she had been reading two summers before, when the clouds had not yet gathered over her marriage, with a bookmark where she had stopped reading. From the window she saw a man dressed in a cream suit walking down the paved path that led to the villa. When he came closer, she was pleased to recognise Dr Patrikios. She always believed that the only thing that stood between them becoming good friends was his loyalty to her husband. The doctor passed under her balcony, unaware of the eyes observing him. Suddenly, the idea that he could well have been invited to the birthday celebration to carry out the medical procedure crossed Olivia's mind. It was a grim possibility that she did not want to think about. She felt the beginning of a headache. Before putting out her cigarette, a white sailing yacht appeared on the horizon: more guests were arriving. She opened the window, and the fragrance of the lemon groves began to cleanse the stale air of her room. She came out on to the balcony to watch the yacht anchoring in the bay, but her headache was so bad that she had to return inside and lie down, covering her face with a towel sprinkled with cold water. Some time later she was awakened by the noise of the new arrivals being shown to their rooms and made out, not without apprehension, her stepdaughter's laughter.

BUENOS AIRES LAY ON THE WESTERN SHORE OF THE
shallow estuary: a sombre city of gold-seekers and contraban-
dists built on the other side of the world that forever suffered
from nostalgia for the ancestral land. The ship entered through
an artificial channel, ploughing through a fleet of steam dredgers
hoisting mud from the riverbed and scattering the small fishing
boats with three blasts of her horn. Before the new port was
built, the ocean liners had to anchor several miles off the coast,
and passengers were ferried ashore on tenders, but when Marco
Timoleon arrived on the *Pesaro*, vessel of the Lloyd Sabaudo
Steamship Company that made the passage from Genoa to Rio
de la Plata via Naples, Las Palmas and Rio de Janeiro, most ships
tied up at the port. As they came closer, he saw the distant
derricks on the wharves, tall and grey, with black smoke rising
from their funnels, he heard the swearing of the stevedores
waiting for the liner to dock, he smelt the air of the harbour,
full of soot and decay, and for a moment the dream of a happy
life in the southern hemisphere seemed to turn into smoke too.

They were coming to the end of a long and difficult voyage.
The third class could accommodate fewer than six hundred
passengers, but by the time the ship left Majorca, more than a
thousand were crammed into the shared cabins below decks
where living conditions were not good. Marco Timoleon found

67

out for himself as soon as he climbed down the ladder leading to his quarters, which were filled with noise, smell and smoke from the coal-fired boilers of the engine room just one level below. There were few portholes, and the only light came from a few light bulbs in the passageways where seasick passengers wandered like lost ghosts.

Just days after leaving port, an unofficial order had been established below decks. There were dogfights, cockfights, card games and boxing matches where the immigrants bet their savings, there were improvised kitchens that sold cheap food of bad quality and a profitable brothel in a storeroom near the stern that began life at a chance encounter between a deckhand and a passenger. Conditions worsened after a week at sea when a typhus epidemic broke out and the captain ordered the third class quarantined. Marco Timoleon could not stand it. He decided that if he wanted to save his life, he had to move. Eugenia Timoleon had allowed him to take whatever money was left of his inheritance with a view to it lasting him for a few months until he had settled into a job, and he spent it to escape the squalor of third class not for a second-class cabin but a first-class stateroom, which he moved to after bribing the guards, who enforced the quarantine with loaded rifles.

The voyage lasted twenty-five days. The luxury of his new quarters, the abundance of food and the attention of the stewards seduced him, but what fascinated him more than anything were the first-class passengers whose languages were as foreign to him as their attitudes. He observed them in the ballroom as if he were spying through a keyhole. He watched how they kissed the air one inch from each other's cheek, how they sat at the table with backs and necks straight, how they danced as if floating on air. Above all he admired their confidence – none more so than that of the ruined aristocrats who had lost their fortunes in Europe and were now on their way to South America, without the slightest doubt that there they would rise from their ashes. Marco Timoleon saw it in the way they enjoyed themselves by paying with money they did not have, by signing promissory notes or accepting the generosity of others, their predicament not seeming to dent their armour. Loud and apparently happy, they all, men and women, attracted attention to themselves without effort, whether it was the adoration of other passengers or the dislike of crew members, to whom they complained constantly. Marco Timoleon observed the merchants, the senior clerics, the wealthy tourists, the diplomats, the engineers and doctors, soon coming to understand that he could buy if not their friendship at least their curiosity with flattery and improbable stories about himself: those were the formative years of his wild imagination that would blur the line between reality and fantasy and cause Ian Forster countless headaches when he was researching the book more than fifty years later.

More than company on the long journey, he was after knowledge. He had known from early on what he wanted to do in life, perhaps ever since the modest financial success of the salvaged steamboat, but his father's disappearance and the war had pushed him off course. His plan to succeed in business, which he had shared with no one, not even his lover, was always in his mind, and he was adding to it from time to time, sorting out various problems, thinking several moves ahead in a game of chess that had not yet begun. He had come to realise that what he lacked was not so much specialist knowledge, that was the easy part, but knowledge of people: the way they thought, the way they behaved, their histories and habits. So he set out to learn about them, how to interpret their words and actions, how to predict their reactions, and in time he became an expert at manipulation whether it was of the stock market, the media, politics or his own private life. Still, things would not always go according to his plans because he allowed for everything in life except one: failure.

No one taught him more on board the *Pesaro* than the Baronessa, a small Italian woman whom he met at dinner a week before they arrived at their destination. Their friendship had started with an innocent question:

'First time in Buenos Aires?' Marco Timoleon had asked.

'No,' she had replied. 'Twenty-sixth.'

And she explained that she had been living on the steamship for the past seven years, in a comfortable cabin she had leased for life with the proceeds of the sale of the family palazzo. When Marco Timoleon had asked her why, she had shrugged and answered:

'Because my house didn't float.'

She was in her mid-eighties, with blue eyes, thick white hair and the gait of a wounded animal. Her slight limp was the result of a leg operation that had been, according to the surgeon, seventy-five per cent successful, prompting Marco Timoleon to call her affectionately, but behind her back, *The Three-Quarters Woman*. She used a walking stick with a hint of shame, which meant that she sought to sit down whenever she could even if she were not tired. She regarded food as the excuse to engage people in conversation and drink her daily glasses of Tuscan wine, which were the secret of her longevity. She loved to talk, but unlike most people, only if she was listened to. Feeling a maternal affection for Marco Timoleon, she decided to teach him how to act rich without the means, a skill that he later used to gain entrance to the élite circles of Buenos Aires. 'Remember,' she would tell him, 'that truth is no more than a consensus of generalised opinion.' He believed her, and by the time the ship arrived at Rio de la Plata, he had become an accomplished liar.

It was during the long voyage that Marco Timoleon also learned about ships and shipping, the technology, the running costs and other aspects of the business that would make him rich and famous in the future. He introduced himself to the captain, a quiet man with sad eyes and a grey beard who spoke English with a heavy accent, explained to him his fascination with the sea and expressed his wish to learn more about his profession. Amused by his eagerness, the captain agreed to take him on a tour of the ship that started from the bow and ended at the stern several hours later. He told him her history in detail, when she was built and where, what her journeys had been, he gave him a complete list of her specifications and the number of crew, and then made him plug his ears with cotton before taking him to the engine room where he explained the purpose of the various machines, raising his voice above the noise. Later, in his cabin, over tea with a shot of brandy, he showed Marco Timoleon their route on the chart, he revealed to him the secrets of Atlantic navigation and answered as simply as he could the many questions put to him.

Marco Timoleon was captivated. He made intelligent enquiries that not only demanded careful thought but soon became so specific that the captain had to call in the first mate to help him give the answers. Marco Timoleon wrote down everything in the small notebook that he would keep in his pocket all of his life, in countless reincarnations, the talisman and code of his success. In its pages he did the simple sums that helped him create and expand his business empire, a fact that was as unbelievable as it was true.

Before they arrived in Buenos Aires, he had to endure, in addition to his impatience with the slow progress of the ship whose propellers turned with the speed of the previous century, the punishment of a big storm that caught them off the South

American coast, forcing the captain to change route, which delayed their arrival by two days. The storm convinced Marco Timoleon that he was a coward. From the moment he saw the lightning in the distance, the stewards folding up the deckchairs and chaining them together, the first drops of rain falling heavy and warm on the wooden deck, he started to shudder. He had never been in an ocean liner before and was unprepared for the violence of the sea that hit the ship before sunset. He took to his stateroom and lay in bed, convinced the ship was going to sink at any moment, until the torrential rain eased off, the strong winds dropped and the waves turned back into a ripple.

In Buenos Aires his days of comfort finally came to an end: he had spent most of his money on board. After trying to persuade the Baronessa to come ashore with him, which she refused to do, he said goodbye to her with a bow and a kiss of her hand and stepped off the *Pesaro*.

He would never see the Baronessa again, but later would hear the legend of how her longevity turned out to be her misfortune. A few years after Marco Timoleon had walked off the *Pesaro*, the ageing steamship had made her final voyage across the Atlantic to a dry dock where she was to be scrapped. But the Baronessa refused to leave the ship, brandishing her lease at the dismantlers, who had come to ask her to gather her belongings. Finally they had to give way. They used their saws, their blowlamps and hammers to cut off her cabin, and they carried it, walls, floor and ceiling, plus all the furniture, to a corner of the shipyard where the Baronessa lived for many years afterwards, watching the world from the porthole of her cabin and refusing to go unless Death came and asked her himself.

In Buenos Aires Marco Timoleon found a small apartment in one of the poorest neighbourhoods, on the fifth floor of an old tenement where other immigrants also lived, and began to apply for jobs, a difficult task because he did not speak any Spanish. He paid people a few coins to write application letters for him, he scanned the newspapers for job offers that he translated with a dictionary, he called in on shops and offices, but no one wanted to employ him. The last of his money quickly running out, he began to spend more time at home where, saving on gas, he moved between the unheated rooms in the dark like a sleepwalker. When he was out, he mostly went to the parks where his mournful appearance, his silent walk, his dusty overcoat and muddied shoes were the cause of a rumour that a ghost was haunting the city.

Yet, he refused to admit defeat and return to Izmir. He had the opportunity when a merchant ship sailing to Europe needed extra crew, and Marco Timoleon, in a lapse of hope, put his name down. By the end of the week, when the ship set sail, he had changed his mind. Having stopped trying to find a job with a local business, Marco Timoleon concentrated his efforts on foreign companies that had offices in Buenos Aires. He spoke passable English, which had been taught at school back home, but it was not enough. He tried Harrods and the shipping and insurance companies but was turned down even for menial jobs because of his pauper's clothes and starving-man's breath.

Later he would remember that time with fondness, not mentioning his struggle in order not to admit that he, too, was a poor immigrant like anyone else. It would take a second visit to the city in 1970, forty-seven years after his time there, to acknowledge the truth and see himself the way he had been then: a blindfolded immigrant who could have died of cholera, tuberculosis, malnutrition or homesickness if it were not for his strong constitution, his small inheritance and a great amount of luck. He dreaded to think what his life would have been like had the coin landed on its other side, the way it had done for so many young men who were cleverer than him, more hand-some than him, much kinder than him. At a formal dinner in his honour at the Strangers' Club during his second visit to the city in 1970, rich and famous then, he gave a speech where he talked about all this with great humility, which was unlike him, and ended by raising his glass and saying: 'Underneath our dinner jackets we're all naked.' His audience had not understood but had laughed and applauded all the same.

It was, in fact, soon afterwards that he took to nudity, and there exist countless grainy photographs in magazines of him going about his daily life without clothes: on his island, on the sofa in his Paris apartment, even at his antique desk in his London office, talking on the phone. The world misunderstood him, of course, assuming it was a pervert's habit, imagining sexual orgies and autoerotic secrets, but what attracted him to it was the honesty of nakedness, the fact that one look in the mirror was enough to remind him how defenceless he too was in face of the passage of time.

The man who finally saved him in Buenos Aires was Colonel Stanley Nicholls, director-general of the Eastern Telegraph Company, whom Marco Timoleon went to see without an appointment. The retired colonel agreed to see him for a few minutes. A compassionate Quaker who had spent several years in the Middle East as a young army officer, the Englishman had developed a great respect for the character of Levantines. One look at the young man was enough to make him take pity on him. Far from discouraging him, Marco Timoleon's stubble, his uncombed hair and his soiled shirt humbled the Colonel. The young man seemed to be in a state of trance: it was the result of malnourishment.

'You seem like the Ghost of Christmas Future,' the Colonel said.

He ordered cream tea and sat back in his chair. Colonel Nicholls prided himself on being an excellent judge of character. He based his judgement not on intuition but phrenology, the long-discarded science that assumed abstract qualities such as integrity or depravity were associated with the bumps and ridges of the skull. Just before the tea arrived, he briefly examined his visitor: Marco Timoleon had the skull of a clever and ambitious man.

Stanley Nicholls gave Marco Timoleon the chance to become the man he wanted to be. A soulful bachelor who stood by his decision not to marry but had very much regretted not having children, perhaps he saw in Marco his chance at fatherhood. He dressed in regulation tweeds, but this was as far as his imitation of a true gentleman went. He took off his tie as soon as he sat at his desk in the morning and immediately lit up not a pipe but several unfiltered cigarettes made from Turkish tobacco that stained the fingers, which he left burning in various ashtrays across the room to purify the air. He was tall, with a body that despite his sixty years still displayed the benefits of army training, and he was balding without a chance of reprieve. He had accepted the directorial job of the Buenos Aires branch of the Eastern Telegraph Company not because of career aspirations, of which he had none, but simply because it had helped him to flee an England which after so many years away seemed like a foreign country to him: what he feared more than death was retirement in the Home Counties.

It had not taken the Colonel long to learn Spanish because his ears were attuned to foreign languages. It allowed him to strike good friendships with local people of both sexes and all walks of life, reserving his snobbery for the members of the Strangers' Club, the haunt of European expatriates on San Martín Street, which he reluctantly visited only if he had to dine with an important client of the telegraph company. After work, which involved planning telegraph and telephone links across the continent and co-ordinating the repair of lines damaged by tropical storms, he spent the rest of his day in the cool garden of one of his friends' houses, playing chess or discussing everything from literature to science and religion but never politics because their anti-colonialism made him ill at ease.

After examining Marco Timoleon's skull, the Colonel served tea and sat at his desk to talk to the young man about a position that did not yet exist, but he proposed to create especially for him: junior assistant to the private secretary of the director-general. Colonel Nicholls was impressed by the young man's energy that it seemed could power a train, he was carried away in the torrent of his Mediterranean speech that was full of persuasion, but above all he was amused by his earnestness. In the course of their discussion, Marco Timoleon casually announced:

'I intend to get rich soon.'

'Patience is more important than intellect in going about it,' the Colonel said.

'No. Money is.'

In a way he was right: money breeds money. Colonel Nicholls took him under his wing at a time when no one else would come near the stocky young immigrant with the dark features that had already earned him his eternal nickname: the Turk. Having earned his employer's favour did not mean, however, that he had to work less hard to prove his worth. From his first days in the office, Marco Timoleon discovered that enthusiasm was not enough to make him a useful employee of the Eastern Telegraph Company. He had convinced the Colonel, or so he thought, that he knew how to use a mimeograph, that he could type fifty words a minute using only one finger, that he was a competent draughtsman, that he was familiar with the laws of electricity and the principles of telegraphy, without expecting that he would sooner or later have to prove all this. He failed. But Colonel Nicholls forgave him and offered him the chance to learn what he claimed to know already, taking a personal interest in his education.

During working hours, he taught Marco Timoleon the essentials of bookkeeping, the Morse code and general office manners that were appropriate for an employee of the Eastern, then left him unsupervised to figure out the details of his duties by himself. He was not disappointed by the young man's ability to learn. Colonel Nicholls also introduced Marco Timoleon to the life of the rich expatriates by inviting him to the Strangers' Club not only because he enjoyed his company but because he saw him as an ally against the boredom of the bar: a reformed alcoholic who had not had a drop of gin for eleven years, the Colonel still struggled with the memory of his habit. It was in the Club that Marco Timoleon first met Dr Patrikios, a fellow countryman of his who had arrived in Argentina two years before him. Even though they maintained a nodding acquaintance, they did not become true friends until much later, under different circumstances.

In the meantime Marco Timoleon managed to obtain full club membership through Colonel Nicholls's enthusiastic recommendation and a letter from an important local merchant, whose signature he forged without hesitation or fear because the man had suddenly died a few days earlier and could not unmask the deception. In memory of the deceased, the committee welcomed Marco Timoleon to the Club. Without needing the Colonel to accompany him any more, he began to visit the Club almost daily and make friends with the other members, who never imagined that he was a mere assistant secretary at the Eastern Telegraph Company. He stayed up late, drank a lot and played cards, getting to know the people who would later help him fulfil his business ambitions. He returned home only in time to bathe, change clothes and catch the tram to work.

Sustained by his excitement and the stamina that only abandoned him at the very end of his life, he could balance the life of a clerk against that of an insatiable socialite without effort. At first he sought his entertainment anywhere he could find it, in nightclubs, variety shows, harbour brothels, still behaving in the indiscriminate ways of his Izmir days, but as he started to become more recognisable, he also came to understand the importance of appearances. He soon saw that there were many opportunities open to a man new to the city, whom no one knew and who could, therefore, assume any identity. This was the period when he abandoned the shadows and came into the light, introducing himself as a wealthy businessman, keeping a conversation about his imaginary activities going all night, giving and taking advice, quoting numbers and forecasts and discussing his future plans. He paid for his social life with money he made on the side by running an illegal betting scheme in the Eastern where his colleagues could gamble on horse racing, football and pelota matches. It was a good racket, but he ran out of luck less than a year later when Colonel Nicholls found out about it from a clerk who had lost everything on the horses. His military pride wounded, his belief in his judgement of character shaken, the Colonel called Marco Timoleon into his office.

'The only reason I'm not dismissing you,' he said, 'is because I would be admitting *my* incompetence in having hired you.'

He then announced his decision, namely that Marco Timoleon was to be reassigned to the repairs department with immediate effect, and sent him off with the hope that he would do better in his new post.

'Good luck,' he wished him. 'You can still cause damage but, at least, no embarrassment.'

Marco Timoleon felt no shame at his demotion but did worry that his new circumstances would disrupt his social life: his new post demanded his frequent absence from the capital. As soon as he completed his technician's training, he was sent out on urgent assignments to repair the ageing network of the telegraph company anywhere in the country, driving a van loaded with spare parts, tools and instruction manuals. The job was not without its perks. In remote telegraph stations, which no one had visited in years, he was hailed as a messiah because he sold old editions of newspapers and magazines, which he bought in Buenos Aires for nothing as they were about to be pulped but that were invaluable to his colleagues who had not read the news in more than a month: another simple way to make a profit.

His journeys beyond city borders must have revealed to him hidden worlds that back in the 1920s were still ruled by nature: forests of trees weighed down with unknown fruit, winds that cried like humans, heavy rains that stopped as suddenly as they began. He passed through villages of silent Indians who had survived Pedro de Mendoza's conquistadors, teams of workers with spades and pickaxes who built new roads inch by inch, slow buses that scared the grazing cattle with their backfiring exhausts. More than anything else, his time in the countryside reinforced his superstition, his belief in fate, in magic and miracles.

Marco Timoleon repaired transmitters, telephones and cut wires, put back telegraph poles uprooted by the storms, erected new ones made from trees he had to cut down himself. He chopped off their branches, coated them with tar and lifted them into place with the help of the local representative of the Eastern Telegraph Company and a group of Indians. He had been doing the job for several months when he was struck down by dysentery. The disease forced him to take shelter in a small village that was not on the path of the telegraph line. His condition worsened day by day, but no one could help him. After a week, convinced he would die, he set off a pair of flares that he found in the back of the van and watched them light up the night sky as they drifted to the ground. He felt little hope. He passed blood several times a day and suffered from cramps and strange hallucinations. When the pain would suddenly wake him up, he saw the flies circling above his head, attracted by the pool of his own filth where he had sunk, he saw the shadows of people coming and going, he heard their whispers until he would slowly lose consciousness again. It was a day later, or perhaps two or three because he had lost his sense of time, that he opened his eyes and saw a man with rolled-up shirtsleeves leaning over the bed and studying him. The stranger raised his hat.

'The repairman from the Eastern, I presume,' the man said.

He was a doctor. He took charge of the situation without delay, asking the locals in their native tongue to throw away Marco Timoleon's clothes, bury his excrement and bring him fresh water. Then he bathed his patient and hung a mosquito net over his bed. Marco Timoleon submitted to his care without questions, drank without complaint the bitter solutions the doctor prepared for him and slowly began to recover. As the fog in his eyes dissolved, he had a feeling he knew the man that looked after him. One day, writhing in agony, he managed to ask him:

'Have we met before, doctor?'

The stranger gave him a morphine shot.

'Not in real life. At the Club.'

Then Marco Timoleon recognised Aristide Patrikios, the distant doctor who was not often seen in Buenos Aires because he worked in the jungle and who even when he was in town preferred to spend his time at the theatre, the opera or the national library, stopping by the Club only to collect his post. A man with remarkable powers of observation, which were honed by his solitude, he had not for once been fooled by Marco's invented identity of a wealthy businessman but had not betrayed his secret because he did not want to interfere. It was part of a private code of ethics he never violated, sticking to his favourite response, which he delivered tirelessly, time and again, with a shrug of his shoulders: 'I am sure he had his reasons.' That was who Dr Patrikios was. He had the ability to accept others the way they presented themselves to him even when they happened to lie. He was not insincere in his feelings. He voiced his disagreement but did not challenge or try to change other people's minds, only to cure their bodies, he said.

In that, he did a remarkable job. He had introduced modern medicine into a world where doctors without degrees still diagnosed imaginary diseases like humoralism. He was astonished to see in the twentieth century his colleagues practise medieval theories on helpless patients: purgatives to evacuate the bowel, diaphoretics to induce sweating, emetics to bring about vomiting, blisterings to rid the body of its poison. Dr Patrikios helped put an end to the black magic, and was, in fact, so successful in his mission that for a while he had to sleep with a loaded revolver under his pillow. He started campaigns against hookworm, he eradicated animal diseases in the provinces he passed through, and even had time to pen a scientific paper that attempted to prove a link between the tango and the spread of tuberculosis.

Related to Ian Forster by Marco Timoleon himself, the incident in the Argentine jungle has all the hallmarks of a story well told: drama, romanticism, a happy ending. His biographer had failed to verify it, and despite his repeated attempts, Dr Patrikios refused to confirm or refute it. The story bears a strong resemblance to the famous encounter between Dr Livingstone and Henry Stanley, and if Ian Forster later related it in his book the way he heard it, he did so because he believed that everything one says, whether true or false, tells something about you that is often more significant than many facts.

In any case, the story goes that the doctor was in a neighbouring village when Marco Timoleon's emergency flares lit up the sky. He checked that his revolver was loaded, threw it into his medical bag and set off on his mule, marking the beginning of a friendship that lasted more than fifty years, despite the many disagreements between the two men. If not always sympathetic to Marco Timoleon's views, Dr Patrikios was more than trustworthy. He offered his opinion whether Marco asked for it or not and looked after his friend as if he had created him himself from the dust of the earth, not unaware that people mistook his devotion as well as his reserve as a clue to an undeclared homosexuality.

After the incident in the jungle, Marco Timoleon would not forget him. The next time Dr Patrikios came to Buenos Aires, Marco, who was already on the way to becoming rich, gave him an envelope filled with banknotes to thank him for saving his life. The doctor opened the envelope and glanced at the money.

'You have a high opinion of yourself,' he said and gave it back. 'No man is worth that much.'

Marco Timoleon did not give in. A year later he offered to build a hospital wherever the doctor thought it was most needed, an offer Dr Patrikios could not turn down. Marco Timoleon not only stood by his promise to pay for the materials and builders but also paid for the furniture and equipment. Yet, despite Dr Patrikios's persistent requests, he refused to open the new hospital himself in a ceremony arranged to honour him, and he never visited it. It was the first deed of a constant stream of benefactions to individuals and good causes throughout his life, from penniless students from his homeland to war refugees, research institutes and the tramps who managed to elude his security guards and walk into his office, begging his charity.

Acute dysentery was Marco Timoleon's first serious illness but would not be his last during his time in South America. His travels across the country soon turned into a catalogue of woes that ended only when he left Argentina. Perhaps those diseases ultimately armoured his body, for he rarely fell ill in later life. During those years he finally learned Spanish, which he never forgot and spoke with the diction of the Indians, telling those who tried to pin down his intriguing accent, 'I learned it by infection.'

His life changed for ever when he happened to overhear a conversation while repairing the switchboard at the telephone exchange in Buenos Aires. The information led him to borrow as much as he could from loan sharks and buy shares on the stock market that tripled in value within a month. The profit he made he did not invest but used as a deposit on an apartment in an ornamented building on Avenida de Mayo, one of the best addresses in the city, where he moved while still working for the telegraph company. It was a strange decision that only he could have made, an ordinary technician living in an expensive neighbourhood among bankers and diplomats, but more than an impulse, it was the calculated first step of a shrewd businessman.

He pressed for a permanent post in Buenos Aires, so that he could resume the life he had been forced to give up when he began to travel. He managed to get it on health grounds thanks to Dr Patrikios, whose reputation had reached the capital, earning him the respect of, among others, Colonel Nicholls. From the day he moved into his new apartment, Marco Timoleon resumed his life of the fake rich expatriate. He went to listen to Carlos Gardel, he went to dance halls where he stayed until dawn, he went to pelota matches, the casino and the racetrack not so much to have fun or bet as to make friends with the prominent citizens of his adopted home. It was not long before people began to recognise him in the street although no one knew exactly who he was, where he came from or what he did for a living.

Among the houses built in the style of the French renaissance and weighed down with decoration, there still survived in the city many of the old colonial buildings: single-storey houses with flat roofs, parapets, one or two courtyards and barred windows into the street. When he did not go to the Strangers' Club, Marco Timoleon wandered around the nicer neighbourhoods, the plazas laid out with flowers, shrubberies and shady trees, the Recoleta and the Paseo de Julio on the riverfront or took a stroll along the footpaths of the great park at Palermo with its lawns and lakes, but if he happened to have more time, he much preferred to visit the suburbs of Belgrano and Flores to admire the big country houses and their gardens, the way he used to visit the suburbs of Izmir a few years earlier. He slept with women he met at the Club, women he met in the cheap restaurants where he ate his only meal of the day in order to save money, women he came across in the park or the street, building a reputation among those who were in the know as being discreet, tender and giving. Those were good times for him.

He always changed out of his technician's overalls at the office and returned to his apartment dressed in a suit. He had a short rest before bathing, putting on clean clothes and then leaving for the small restaurants that were far from the Strangers' Club and other places where he might come across people who knew him. He sat at dinner alone but rarely finished it without company. He invited strangers to join him, ordinary men and women who were often immigrants like him, and enjoyed the informality. Those transient friendships lasted as long as his meal, but they were precious to him. He discussed the political situation in South America and elsewhere, he talked about sports, the rumours that went round the city and the latest crimes of passion, but what fascinated him most were his acquaintances' opinions on the economy, on commerce and their particular line of work whether it was mining, shipping, retail or anything else. He listened attentively, making brief notes in his notebook, insisting on picking up the bill and charging it to his account, which he settled once a month. The information that he gathered, he painstakingly cross-checked against the opinions of others he came across in his perpetual roaming across the city, and then he distilled everything into invaluable knowledge that helped him put whatever little money he saved in good investments. It was a simple method, but not before long his capital began to grow faster than he could spend it. This was the time of the Argentine boom of the 1930s when the wealth of natural resources gave the country one of the highest incomes per capita in the world. Marco Timoleon finally left his job at the Telegraph Company six years after he had joined, handing in his resignation to Colonel Nicholls at a brief but sentimental ceremony that sealed their friendship with a lingering handshake.

Having resigned from the telegraph company, Marco Timoleon did not have to hide any more. He bought a black Bugatti convertible, the first car of its make to be seen in the streets of Buenos Aires, and invited friends and strangers on drives around town and the suburbs. He had many affairs during that time. He bought his lovers presents, took them to restaurants, the theatre and the cinema, to nightclubs and dance halls, and paid for everything. There was only one place he disliked going and would always try to dissuade his girlfriends from taking him, saying: 'Love ends at the steps of the Opera.'

Yet, it was on those very steps that he fell in love. He was waiting for one of his casual lovers. The performance had already started, but she had still not arrived. Marco Timoleon declined the usher's suggestion that he wait in the foyer; even when it started to rain and he had no umbrella, he chose to face the weather because he could not stand the music. He was already soaked to the skin when the doors opened and someone ran down the steps to flag down a taxi. Then he returned inside and escorted a woman to the waiting car with a big umbrella. Marco Timoleon looked at her walking carefully down the slippery steps, dressed in a fur coat and high heels. When she turned and glanced at him, he raised his hat.

'A very wise decision,' she said. 'Better than having to sit through all that caterwauling.'

Then she got into the taxi and disappeared before Marco Timoleon had the chance to agree. It had only been a moment, but no amount of rain that day would have made him forget her. For a long time afterwards, he tried to find her. He went back to the Opera many times, waiting outside for hours on end, he went to fashionable restaurants in the hope of coming across her, he searched up and down the parks on Sundays to no avail. His desperation had given her an uninspired name: *The Rain Woman*. Marco Timoleon wandered in the fog for months, trying first to find her, then to forget her until he almost convinced himself that she had probably never existed, and then he opened the newspaper and saw her photograph.

Her name was Flor Alcorta and she was seventeen years older than Marco. The wife of a government minister who was tipped as a future president and mother of his three children, she had sacrificed a career in the theatre as she was starting to become famous not only in her country but abroad too. Her husband had hoped that she would become a valuable political asset, but she had turned out to be a source of embarrassment to him: she was banned from the presidential palace because she outclassed the President's wife; she was not allowed on the platform where the officials stood during military parades because the troops fell out of step; and at religious celebrations, she was exiled to the furthest rows of the cathedral because the bishop disapproved of her dresses.

She had abandoned her career in order to marry Hipólito Alcorta only three months after meeting him for reasons best known to herself and had stood by her decision ever since even though she never fully reconciled herself to the idea of being a housewife. The older she became, the more difficult she seemed to find it to control her temperament: the day that Marco Timoleon saw her picture, she was again in the news, this time for having insulted a foreign ambassador.

Marco Timoleon found her address and began to send her flowers, making sure that the bouquets were delivered late in the morning when Flor Alcorta's husband was at the Ministry and signing himself *The Man in the Rain*: not romantic coyness but a sensible precaution. What he did at the time with sincerity would later evolve into his trademark method of seduction, which he summarised in the words: 'Beautiful women can't stand moderation. They need an endless supply of excess.' He sent her flowers every day for a month, always without his real name or address, and then he began to wait outside her house. The opportunity came one afternoon when he watched her leaving alone and followed her at a distance down the street hidden behind a newspaper, trusting in the silence of the siesta that the sound of her heels would show him the way. She led him to the cemetery where, instead of visiting a grave, she started to feed the cats. It was a sombre sight: a woman in black sitting on a bench, surrounded by cats eating in silence. Marco Timoleon approached her.

'You look like you've come back from the grave,' she told him.

'*No*,' Marco Timoleon said. '*Soy el hombre en la lluvia.*'

'*¿Qué?*'

'The . . . man in the rain.'

She began to laugh.

'That explains why you're so wet,' she said.

He was dripping with sweat. Flor Alcorta made him blush even more when she told him that she had seen him many times from her window, standing there across the street. That afternoon she had, in fact, decided to give him the opportunity to explain himself. The quiet cemetery was the best place to do this, and the mourning dress was her necessary disguise.

'In this city, even the dead gossip,' she said.

Their affair began on that bench among the dead and continued for a long time afterwards in secret meetings that took place every Tuesday at a different corner of the large cemetery. They did not stay there long. Marco drove her to his apartment where she never let him open the shutters in case someone might see them. He was not Flor Alcorta's first infidelity, all of them brief and bloodless, but he was the first one who did not know that he was not the first, and she had decided not to ruin his delusion because she quickly noticed his jealousy, which endeared him to her almost to the point of pity.

The apartment where Marco Timoleon lived faced the *avenida*, but it was on the fifth floor and the noise and the fumes from the street barely reached it. He always left the tall windows open, day and night, winter or summer, latching the shutters for ventilation and coolness, a habit that reminded him of his home town where the winters were never very cold. In the apartment all there was were a big brass bed built a century earlier, a writing desk with a phone on top and a dining table with a pair of candlesticks. Marco Timoleon fed Flor Alcorta grapes and plums, served her pancakes filled with *dulce de leche* to accompany their cups of tea and coffee, opened bottles of excellent wines. His behaviour strengthened her suspicion that he was probably a criminal. 'What a scandal,' she would say light-heartedly. 'The wife of the trade minister sleeping with a black marketeer.' Marco Timoleon refused to say what he did for a living not because it was illegal, although some of his dealings were exhausting the patience of the law, but out of vanity: he always looked up to gangsters, imitating the way they dressed, the way they walked, the way they talked. As a result people began to assume that he had more to hide than he actually did, inventing impossible conspiracies to accuse him of anything: presidential assassinations, military coups, bloody revolutions and big earthquakes.

In return for his attentions, Flor Alcorta treated him with affection. She filled the big enamel bath for him to bathe, she rubbed his back for hours, she cut his hair, and she would have shaved him too if it did not make him nervous to put his life in her hands. There was only one thing she never did: go out with him. Marco Timoleon begged her to go to a restaurant, go to the theatre, hell, go to the cinema where the darkness would hide them, but Flor Alcorta always refused, afraid she would be recognised by people who knew her husband.

What complicated their relationship even more was the fact that Marco Timoleon had not stopped seeing other women. One afternoon they were sharing a cigarette in bed when he asked her how many men she had been with in her life.

'More than Virgin Mary,' she replied.

He insisted that she tell him, but she continued to refuse until he revealed to her that *he* slept with other women at least once a week. Then she gave in, partly to free herself from his harassment but also to even out his unexpected revelation, which had disappointed her. Her frankness hurt his pride.

'I wasn't expecting a whore's tally,' he said.

'Maybe you thought you were fucking your mother.'

He slapped her face, the first time he would hit anyone, she brought the phone down on his head, and the fight was over before more blood was spilt. No one mentioned the incident again, and the affair continued, intermittent and clandestine, for several more months. Then one night Flor Alcorta, who always slept at home, was woken up by her husband crying in his sleep. She watched him in the dark, in silence, sensing that she was watching an omen. At the breakfast table, she asked him whether he remembered it, and Hipólito Alcorta nodded from behind his newspaper.

'It was strange,' he said. 'I dreamed that you killed me, and then you took me to the cemetery not to bury me but to feed me to the cats.'

He had known for a long time, the way he knew about all her previous affairs from the Intelligence Service reports he received every month. But this time things had gone on for too long, and he was starting to fear that his wife would leave him. The truth was that their passion for each other had died a long time before, but their marriage had survived thanks to their Christian faith and a sibling-like affection that was stronger than pride. The same afternoon Flor Alcorta dispensed with the masquerade of the mourning dress and went to the cemetery in her normal clothes. Marco Timoleon immediately knew something was wrong.

'This can't go on,' she said. 'We're hurting my husband's ambitions.'

Marco Timoleon neither argued nor asked for an explanation. He had brought flowers as he always did, but instead of giving them to her, he laid them on the gravestone of a stranger and walked away without saying goodbye. It was years later, but he still felt great joy when he happened to read in the papers that Hipólito Alcorta had failed to be elected President of the Republic – a result, he hastened to reassure his biographer without him having asked, he had nothing to do with.

FROM THE WINDOWS OF HIS STUDY HE SAW THE TRIM white shape of a yacht sliding towards the bay, and wondered whether Sofia was on board. Moored at the jetty, other boats moved up and down with the pattern of the sea. It was late afternoon, and so far a small flotilla had arrived, bringing guests for that evening's celebration, but his daughter had not come yet. Marco Timoleon was beginning to worry that she might not come, perhaps because she knew that he knew her secret and would not dare face him – or simply because she wanted to embarrass him in front of his guests: a reason that seemed more likely.

The announcement of the birthday party must have been as much a surprise to her as to everyone else because it was interrupting after only twelve months the three-year mourning period he himself had declared following his son's accident. He had kept his promise until now, having given no parties, or even celebrated his fifth wedding anniversary. He had also turned down invitations to public functions, opening cere-monies and presidential inaugurations as well as a rare chance to be blessed by the Orthodox Patriarch in Istanbul. He continued to go to his favourite nightclubs after work where he did not sit with friends but chose a table as far away from the dance floor as possible, cordoned off by his bodyguards.

Sometimes he asked his biographer along, him and only him, knowing that the Englishman would jump at the chance not because he had any true sympathy for him but because he desperately wanted to finish the book that would make him rich and famous.

On the face of it, that seemed to be all the effect Daniel's death had had on him: a small change in his daily routine. But to someone who knew him well, there was no doubt that the accident had transformed Marco Timoleon. The boy had meant a lot to him. Over the years Marco Timoleon had made great efforts to mould his son in his own image, an impossible task because the two of them were opposites by nature: he taught him to swim, but Daniel lacked his father's physicality; he gave him the classics to read, but Daniel had no interest in literature; he encouraged him to go out with girls, which Daniel did but not in the abundance that would have made his father proud.

Still haunted by the ghost of his own father, Marco Timoleon had meant to be to his children what Victor Timoleon had not been to him: tolerant, lively, open-handed and, above all, there. He thought he had started well, but with age he came to realise that he was beginning to resemble his father, a reluctant but unavoidable transformation that continued until one day, while dressing in front of the mirror, he saw his old man – no black frockcoat, no top hat, no muttonchops but definitely him – looking back at him with a frown. Marco Timoleon was disappointed. He started again, promising to be there when his children needed him, to advise them, to play with them, to show an interest in their interests. By then it was too late with Sofia: she had grown up. But he had a brief period with Daniel because he was younger and also a boy until the scales tilted with him too, and the father needed the son more than the son the father.

He could remember the exact day it had happened. It was September on the island, and the two of them were playing poker on the veranda. All afternoon Daniel, fifteen years old but already a consummate player, had been guessing his father's hand. In the evening he stood up to leave, bored by a game he was winning without much effort, and then his father, bare-chested, in shorts and flip-flops, touched him on the arm. 'Stay,' he said. 'I don't like patience. It's a game for old people.'

But the boy had gone away, and Marco Timoleon had been left to face the melancholy of the autumn evening alone, playing patience while the sun sank in the sea, the roses released their mournful smell and the birds flapped in the dusk like bats. Thinking about it now, he could not suppress a deep loathing for the world which carried on spinning while his son lay buried behind Saint Mark of the Cypresses, above all for the risk-takers who stuck two fingers up at life but survived every time. Heavy smokers like him, for example, puffed like loco-motives all their lives but were speeding towards their eightieth birthday: there was much luck to go round in the world but little fairness.

Out in the bay, the crew of the arriving yacht lowered the sails and let a rubber dinghy into the water to ferry the passengers ashore. Marco Timoleon's pessimism intensified: his daughter was not among the first group to make the trip to the jetty. He took out his handkerchief, wiped his forehead and folded it in slow movements. A moment later there was a knock on the door. The servant walked in, carrying a broom and dustpan. He told him that the band had cleared customs, and he began to sweep the floor.

Marco Timoleon searched through the drawers of his desk until he found his binoculars. On the yacht more people were stepping into the rubber boat with the help of the crew. Looking through the binoculars, he breathed out with relief: a young woman in a big soft hat was sitting at the front of the dinghy. Before lowering the binoculars, Marco Timoleon saw Sofia turning and looking in his direction. Despite the distance, he was not convinced that she could not see him. He walked away from the window in a hurry, putting the binoculars back in the drawer.

Sofia Timoleon had given him enough reasons to disown her over the years, but he had shown a leniency to her he had not shown her brother. Things had gone wrong from the start. Her mother, Miranda Timoleon, Marco's first wife, had suggested they name her after her mother, but Marco wanted to give his daughter his own mother's name. In the event they christened her with both names, and for a few months her mother called her Anna and her father Eugenia until they finally agreed on a third name, which they gave her by deed poll: Sofia. At least there had been no disagreement when the couple's son was born. Marco Timoleon, who only much later in life forgave his father for having abandoned his mother and him, had no objection to giving the baby his father-in-law's name.

The problem with Sofia Timoleon was that she was closer to her father in temperament, a fact that both pleased and exasperated him. In fact, the thought had crossed his mind even before Daniel's death that it was *she* who should be running his companies after his retirement and not the boy. Now she would have to: she was his only heir. What worried him, though, were her mood swings, sudden and unpredictable and, since the accident, more frequent than ever. He tried to make light of the problem by saying: 'At least they prove she's really my daughter.'

It was a joke that hinted at an old but not forgotten story.

A magazine had once claimed that Daniel was not Marco Timoleon's real child, a claim simply made on the basis of his appearance – his auburn hair, his thin lips, his small nose – which owed a lot more to his mother than to his father, and his shy personality that was the opposite of his father's. The absurd claim had hurt Marco Timoleon. Far from ignoring it, he had paid his lawyers to prove the truth beyond doubt, and they had done so with the help of blood tests, cranial measurements and birthmark comparisons, which offered good statistical correlation with those of his parents, taking into account the age difference. In the process the lawyers were also able to pinpoint with accuracy the day of conception: an overnight stay at Hotel Splendido in Portofino.

It was a bitter victory. The incident had drawn attention to the fact that Miranda Timoleon did sleep with other men, the way her husband slept with other women. Her excuse was that he had started it long before she did, and she was only doing it to even things out. It was in that marriage that Sofia Timoleon had grown up to become the woman sitting that evening on the rubber prow of the dinghy that was speeding towards the jetty. She had witnessed the growing hostility between her parents, from their slow drifting apart to their bitter hatred of each other, trapped in no man's land while the war raged round her. Neither her father nor her mother made any attempt to hide the collapse of their marriage from the children, just as they had not restrained themselves in front of their friends and guests.

The first great argument that Sofia remembered was the one her father, with his fondness for labels, called *The Battle of the Portraits*. Later to hang in Marco's study, Eugenia Timoleon's portrait was first placed above the fireplace in the living room of his villa on the island, with smaller portraits of Marco,

Miranda and the children on either side. Once a year the holy icon was taken down and carried in procession to the church of Saint Mark of the Cypresses where Eugenia Timoleon's bones were kept in the ossuary. Marco Timoleon had brought them over from Izmir himself, wrapped in silk, and every May on the anniversary of his mother's death he invited the archbishop from the capital to perform a memorial service. It was the most important event of the year for Marco Timoleon when the island disappeared under a fog of frankincense and silence that did not dissolve for seven days. Then the portrait was hung again back in its place on the wall, the winds carried the holy smoke out to sea and life resumed.

One day Marco Timoleon had come into the living room and seen Daniel Negri's portrait hanging next to his mother's. His father-in-law had been a famous shipping tycoon long before Marco had joined the game. Never the best of friends, the two men had fallen out over Marco Timoleon's treatment of Miranda. Later Daniel Negri lost most of his wealth in the storm of a bad investment that he was convinced his son-in-law had brought about, but he died without being able to prove it. Marco Timoleon had studied the big portrait above the fireplace that dwarfed his mother's and had not held back.

'This is out of place,' he said.

His wife, who was also in the room, playing the piano and waiting for his reaction, ignored him. For a few days, the portrait continued to hang above the fireplace without further comment from her husband, but Miranda Timoleon knew him well enough not to celebrate her victory yet. Sure enough, one morning she came downstairs to find the portrait hanging in a corner of the hallway. Immediately she asked Marco to put it back.

'Out of the question.'

'He was my father,' Miranda said. 'I have every right. You know how much I loved him.'

'He was a failure,' said Marco.

Miranda Timoleon was incensed. Without another word she walked to the fireplace, took down Eugenia Timoleon's portrait and threw it into the fire. Marco saved it from the flames before it was damaged, but no one could save Miranda from him. He chased her around the villa, shouting at her, and when he caught her, he tore her clothes and punched her, and when he tired of hitting her, he went on to smash her porcelain collection piece by piece as her ultimate punishment. Finally, an hour later, he walked out of the living room, sweating, puffing and shaking, and saw little Sofia hidden under a chair in the hallway. His expression changed in an instant. He had said: 'Let's go for a dip, sweetie.'

In later years, whenever she felt the desire to dislike her father, Sofia Timoleon would remind herself of that moment. His sweaty face, his heavy breathing, his knitted brow: the face of a criminal. But even *she* had to admit that back when she was a child, she had found it difficult to dislike him because he was good with children. When Marco Timoleon invited guests to the island, he insisted that they brought not only their children but their children's friends too and treated them all as his guests of honour, behaving in silly ways that made them laugh. He jumped in the swimming pool from a great height in defiance of Dr Patrikios's warnings, he gave them ice-cream, carbonated drinks and sweets against his dentist's advice, he bought them expensive presents, and in the evening he gathered them in his study to read them Aesop's fables in his heavy-smoker's voice from an old book of his father's. Life was too staid for his taste, and children shared his view: 'The world is not sick but in permanent sedation.' Children loved

Marco Timoleon for his reputation as a pirate with a parrot on his shoulder. He liked to think that he rebelled against decorum, which he fought with a vulgar sense of humour.

Miranda Timoleon, on the other hand, found it hard to relate to children – hers or anyone else's. She was only twenty-one, and perhaps not yet ready for motherhood, when she gave birth to Sofia. Daniel was born four years later, but Miranda was still struggling with her role, despite the help she had from the servants who changed nappies, filled milk bottles, bought toys and stayed up at night while she slept. Not that she had not tried to fathom the mystery of motherhood. She had bought Dr Spock's *Baby and Child Care*, already a big best-seller, and pored over it for days on end, ignoring Daniel who cried in his cot somewhere in the house, ignoring Sofia who wanted to show her her paintings and ignoring Marco Timoleon who begged her to turn off the light so that he could get some sleep. In the end she lost patience and tossed the book across the room, complaining: 'It's all too theoretical.' Dr Spock taught her little but did bring to the surface her appetite for children's literature, and she began to reread the *Mary Poppins* books, which she had first read as a child and not liked. Miranda Timoleon had died, under peculiar circumstances, only two months after the film of the book came out in 1964 but had seen it already seven times, three with her children, two with her mother and twice on her own, praising Julie Andrews's performance and insisting that Marco invited her on their yacht the following summer.

Its motor switched off, the rubber dinghy slid gently towards the jetty. Before the stewards had tied the rope, Sofia Timoleon jumped ashore and strode towards the villa, pressing down her hat that flapped in the wind. On the terrace where the umbrellas, anchored in the concrete, swayed in the sudden gust, she stopped to greet the guests who had already arrived. On an old deckchair facing the sea, next to a table with a jug of lemonade, Dr Patrikios sat dressed in his cream suit, with his hat lowered over his eyes and his hands crossed on his chest. Sofia was surprised to see him because she knew that social engagements bored him unless they had to do with art or medicine. She bent down and kissed him on the cheek.

'Is my father well, doctor?'

Dr Patrikios raised his hat and opened his eyes. For a moment he seemed unsure where he was.

'That is a matter of doctor-patient confidenti—' Then he recognised Sofia. 'Oh, I'm sorry, dear,' he said. He put his elbows on the arms of the deckchair and rose slowly. 'He's fine. Your father is too busy to get ill.'

He took Sofia's hands and squeezed them with tenderness.

'Then you're here for my birthday,' she said. 'What an honour.'

The doctor nodded.

'Your father was kind enough to invite me.'

Sofia Timoleon looked at the familiar face and noticed a troubled benevolence. The doctor straightened his jacket, which was wrinkled from his nap.

'Are you well, doctor?'

He nodded with a hint of sadness.

'Doctors don't fall ill,' he said. 'But they do fall asleep.'

Sofia Timoleon poured him a glass of lemonade, and he drank it in slow gulps until he was fully awake. The sun was still above the sea, but the day was already getting colder. The servants came and went, bringing blankets for the guests who wanted to watch the sunset. Dr Patrikios refused one.

'The older I get, the more I wish I had studied paediatrics,' he said. 'Only now I realise how much old men are like babies.'

'Will you be staying long?' Sofia asked.

'A couple of days, maybe.'

'Then we'll get to talk a little. Everyone else is here for the cake.'

'Not true,' the doctor said. 'The champagne too.'

She kissed him again and continued towards the villa, greeting friends on the way. More guests came to watch the sunset. The launch from the mainland, carrying the food and wine but not the orchestra, broke the spell of the evening with the plop-plop of its motor. Sofia Timoleon entered the villa and saw her father, dressed in casual clothes, at the top of the stairs. Next to him Soraya was wagging her tail.

'Get dressed,' Sofia said, climbing the marble steps. 'Your friends seem hungry.'

The Afghan met her halfway. Marco Timoleon watched his daughter play with the dog and felt a current of warm air blowing through the villa. But a moment later it went out through the open window at the far end of the corridor where the voices of the guests admiring the sunset were coming from: to forgive her now would be noble but impractical. He took the cigar from his mouth and opened his arms.

'Happy birthday.'

'Not yet,' Sofia said, glancing at her watch. 'Still six hours to go.'

'At least you're here.'

On top of the stairs, she gave him a light kiss. Marco Timoleon held his daughter in his arms and kissed her on both cheeks.

'I have to get ready,' she said.

'It's going to be a great party,' said Marco Timoleon.

'Is *she* here?'

'Olivia? In her room. Last one on the left if you want to say hello.'

Sofia Timoleon went towards her own room, in the opposite direction. Marco Timoleon puffed at his cigar, watching her go.

'You two are my only family,' he called after her.

Sofia did not turn.

'And tonight we are gathered here to celebrate the fact,' she said. 'Is Miss Rees coming?'

'I invited her, but unfortunately she couldn't make it.'

The truth was that he had not invited her, afraid that she might interfere with his plan. Miss Abigail Rees, a prim tall woman with a small face who dressed in a matron's uniform – the job she had left for a career looking after children – drank tea and pronounced her name as if it were a military rank, had been Sofia and Daniel's governess. Miranda Timoleon had hired her because she needed someone with the mettle she herself lacked to bring the children under control. Miss Rees had proved her right but done so without authoritarianism. Her self-assurance was her way of letting everyone know that she was not married and was never going to be because she had chosen to dedicate her life to the children she taught. She believed in her mission with all her heart, and life had left her alone, with only one man during her lifetime ever regretting her vow of chastity: Dr Aristide Patrikios.

She had an awful singing voice, she disliked sports, she drew as if she had no fingers but had endless patience. Like Eugenia Timoleon she was an excellent teacher because she taught the children not the things that she knew but those she did not. She would say: 'A good teacher renders herself superfluous.' If this were true then she was a bad one: she was with the Timoleon family for ten years. She stayed in touch with the children afterwards through letters they sent her several times a year, to which she replied with postcards in her beautiful handwriting. Every Christmas Marco Timoleon did not forget her present, a subscription to *Life* magazine until it ceased publication in 1972, leaving Miss Rees inconsolable.

She managed to teach a large curriculum without ever appearing in a hurry, which showed not only in the way she did her job but also in the way she carried herself, moving quietly about the house without making any noise and speaking only if spoken to. When Dr Patrikios had first come across her, he had walked on without either of them saying a word. He had found Marco Timoleon in his study.

'There's a ghost in your living room,' he informed him.

'Something worse,' Marco said. 'A spinster.'

The next time the doctor saw her it was afternoon, and she was teaching the children how to swim not in the swimming pool because she could not swim herself but by explaining Archimedes' principle of buoyancy on the blackboard. Dr Patrikios fell for her that instant and had kept falling for her every time he visited the Timoleons since, having failed to rid himself of her invisible charm in the meantime. The ripple on his solitude made him reconsider the decision he had made when he turned fifty to stop hoping for love, and he decided to pursue her without knowing exactly how: when it came to love, he was an amateur. He began to visit his old friend in London, where the Timoleons lived at the time, at every opportunity. He visited on birthdays, on anniversaries, for christenings and parties, despite his deep-seated dislike of social gatherings, but all these opportunities were wasted because he could find neither the confidence to approach Miss Rees nor the right words to say to her. Then Marco Timoleon, who had understood the doctor's intentions from the beginning, came up with the idea of the imaginary diseases: he pretended to be sick so that his friend could be in the house even more often. Nothing changed.

Unaware of the conspiracy, Miss Rees finally broke the stalemate herself by asking the doctor for medical advice. They used Marco Timoleon's study for the examination, the first time they had ever been alone since their first haunted meeting. Terrified and unsure, Dr Patrikios delayed her physical examination, asking every relevant and irrelevant question he could think of and writing down the answers until he used up all of Marco Timoleon's stationery. Then he took Miss Rees's measurements with a tape measure as if he were going to sew her a dress but sooner or later had to face the inevitable. He started with her hands although she had complained about her legs and moved carefully until he summoned the courage to reach the root of the problem on her lower back.

'Nothing to worry about,' he finally said. 'A little pressure on the nerve.'

'At my age, doctor,' said Miss Rees, 'nothing is always something.'

He advised her to have a few days of rest until the swelling went away, not to lift weights or use the stairs and always to remember to sit down when there was no reason to be standing up. The governess was unhappy.

'Impossible. What about the children?'

'I declare the rest of the week a school holiday,' the doctor said. 'The Feast of Saint Sciatica.'

Marco Timoleon endorsed her sentence and encouraged the doctor to visit her. Dr Patrikios took his advice and came almost every day, neglecting his other patients. He knocked on Miss Rees's door, waited for a reply, then knocked again to confirm he had heard well and walked in with solemnity as if entering a church. He always found her in bed but suspected she had rushed back when she heard him coming, because there was a mischievous glint in her eye: she had probably been with the children. He did not challenge her but left his hat and leather case on the stand and then examined her, asking her to move her legs this way and that to check the progress of her recovery. Then he sat at the foot of her bed, and they had a few precious minutes of friendly conversation, she in her matron's uniform, he in his well-pressed cream suit, talking about art, music and other matters that caused no offence although they did get into a serious disagreement once when the doctor, knowing that Miss Rees liked to read, lent her a novel published in two volumes that year in Paris, titled *Lolita*, telling her that he was convinced it was destined to become a classic. She did not like it. On his next visit, she gave him back the two volumes, saying that if she had not known him so well, she would have forbidden him from coming anywhere near the house and the Timoleon children again.

Two weeks after forcing her to take time off, Dr Patrikios was still trying to dissuade Miss Rees from leaving her bed although she was by then in good health. Then she began to suspect the truth.

'I'm fifty-four years old, doctor,' she said with meaning.

Dr Patrikios understood but did not lose his courage.

'Your argument is not valid,' he said. 'I'm a year older.'

'Then you ought to be wiser.'

She explained to him that she was in love with her job, the children and no one else and thanked him for his medical advice and his feelings that flattered her, but she could not reciprocate. Dr Patrikios felt a mortal embarrassment. He stopped visiting the house altogether, stopped speaking to Marco Timoleon, did not return his phone calls, sent back his letters unopened and left his practice through the back door to avoid meeting him. The situation continued for six months until Marco Timoleon pretended to be ill in order to force the doctor to come and see him. As he expected, Dr Patrikios arrived the following day, walking into the house as sad as the day he had declared his love for Miss Rees.

'Are you dying?' he asked.

'Not me, doctor,' Marco Timoleon replied. 'Our friendship.'

Dr Patrikios had admitted his fault, apologised and restored relations with the Timoleon family, visiting the house from then on several times a year although he continued to feel like an intruder until Miss Rees's resignation ten years later.

Walking down the corridor, Sofia Timoleon wished her governess were there that evening. As soon as she entered her room, she hurried to open the windows. The cool air blowing from the sea cleared the dust that had settled on the furniture, the bed linen and the carpet. She had not visited the villa since the previous autumn, which was the last time she had let in the maid. Her visit had been cut short by an angry confrontation with her father that had erupted after dinner when he questioned her about her love life. 'I will not live for ever,' he had said. 'Someone has to take care of the business. If it's not going to be you, then you have to help me find someone else. I don't know whether *you* need a husband or not, but *I* certainly need him to help me.'

It was his constant complaint since the accident. Not long before his tragic death, Daniel Timoleon had reluctantly agreed to shadow his father in order one day to succeed him as chairman of the board. But Sofia was interested in business even less than her brother was. She had struggled through boarding-school, graduating only thanks to a generous donation from Marco Timoleon and refusing to continue to university despite her father's pressure and the pleas of Miss Rees, whom Marco had asked to mediate knowing the retired governess still wielded influence over his daughter.

These days Sofia passed her time travelling with an ever-growing group of friends, who depended on her generosity and agreed with everything that she said before she said it. They stayed at exclusive hotels where they demanded the best rooms without having made reservations. Marco Timoleon's reputation and money meant that foreign dignitaries in curlers, half-shaved ambassadors with lather on their cheeks and honeymooners in bathrobes were asked to vacate their suites with the excuse that a mistake had been made in allocating their rooms. Sofia Timoleon spent summer in the northern hemisphere and winter in the south, interrupting her permanent holidays to visit her beloved Miss Rees or attend a family gathering if her father threatened to sever her monthly allowance.

The world in the morning was an unknown planet to her: no matter when she went to bed, at midnight or at dawn, she woke up in late afternoon, usually with company, having inherited her father's sexual energy. She had lunch in bed, naked, letting her ephemeral lover feed her, and then took a long bath, not to cleanse herself of sin, for she believed neither in sin nor retribution, but to give the stranger time to dress and leave the room. Not caring about social class, she slept with waiters, bellboys and security guards as long as they had a nice face and a good body. Afterwards, she sent them on their way with a wad of banknotes in a sealed envelope stamped with a lipstick kiss, a gesture that had no other purpose than expressing her gratitude. She would stay in the bath, listening to music until she heard the door click shut, and only then would she stand up and shower and dry herself, with as much a sense of contentment as relief. She would observe her ghost in the bathroom mirror, misted over from the vapours of her scalding bath, and then would return to the bedroom where the only thing left to remind her of the night before was the smell of cigarette smoke.

She always maintained that she took more pleasure in departures than arrivals. It was a clue to her depression whose first symptoms had appeared in her teenage years, but the only person who had recognised them in a house ruled by Marco Timoleon's temper was Miss Rees, who had spent more time with Sofia and her brother than both of their parents put together. The governess had first appealed to Miranda Timoleon, whom she had found in the conservatory of their London house, quietly reading a children's book next to the gas fire. It was a cold morning without much light, but the glass roof and big windows allowed the woman to read without a lamp. For several seconds, enough to make Miss Rees feel unwelcome, Miranda Timoleon did not raise her eyes from her book, leaving the governess standing at the door. Then she folded back the page, shut the book and asked:

'Is it already the end of the month, Miss Rees?'

On the last Friday of every month the two women met in Marco Timoleon's study to discuss the children's progress. In the course of time, Miss Rees's responsibilities had expanded beyond the children's purely academic education to include sports, entertainment and even food and drink, a tacit agreement between the governess and the parents whose busy lifestyle left a void in the children's life. Miss Rees did not mind because she had grown very fond of the children. That day in the conservatory she told her employer that it was not the end of the month, but it was imperative to talk about Sofia's growing unhappiness.

'The best strategy is to ignore her,' Miranda Timoleon said.

'This you do perfectly, madam,' said the governess. 'But sometimes it is perhaps advisable to seek professional help.'

She knew that Sofia locked herself in the bathroom where she sank in the bath, smoked cigarettes stolen from her mother's handbag and read books that were not good for her. At fifteen she had already read, among other works of literature and philosophy, Camus's *The Outsider* and *The Myth of Sisyphus*, Schopenhauer's *The World as Will and Representation* and Nietzsche's *Thus Spake Zarathustra*, which she did not understand but still told her governess that they were preparing her for the absurdity of life. When reading did not offer her consolation, she just lay in bed, staring at the ceiling or cutting herself with a razor blade, suffering from the headaches she had inherited from her mother, which would torment her for ever.

It was clear to Miss Rees that Sofia needed help, but Miranda Timoleon was not prepared to admit that her daughter suffered from an illness that carried a social stigma. After Miranda, Miss Rees had spoken to Marco Timoleon. He listened patiently to her before saying:

'Her problem is that she has no problems, Miss Rees.'

'It's not that simple, sir. The girl's sick.'

'If you had children of your own you'd be more patient,' Marco Timoleon said.

His comment angered the governess.

'I have stayed with your family longer than I should have,' she said.

She offered her resignation, but Marco Timoleon did not accept it. He begged her to change her mind, admitting he was wrong to say what he had said and offering his apologies, and she agreed to stay for another two years. She finally retired with a generous gift of a central London apartment where she spent the rest of her life forever disappointed that she had failed to save the Timoleon children from their fate.

In the years that followed, Sofia's mood improved, but she never managed to escape her depression completely. She accepted its presence in her life like a shadow, pacifying its intermittent episodes with food and pills, which she discovered in time. Her weight fluctuated depending on her mood. In the frenzy of her hunger, she would eat everything, but as soon as her passion subsided, she would go on a diet until the next time something caused her to despair, and the cycle would start again, month after month, year after year.

The way she reacted to love was not as impulsive as some thought. At twenty-three she met a man more than twice her age, a divorced millionaire without children, and married him three months later in Las Vegas not because she looked forward to a long and happy life with him, but because she knew her father would be furious. Marco Timoleon learned the news when she rang him the following day from California, and although he felt angry, he was not surprised. 'Stay where you are,' he told her. 'A lawyer will contact you for the annulment.' His daughter had signed the papers.

Sofia Timoleon kicked off her shoes and inspected her room. Everything was in its place. Naturally: she always kept her room locked and forbade the staff from entering without her explicit permission. She dropped on to the bed, folded her arms behind her head and listened to the humming of the refrigerator in the corner – it was filled with Italian ham, boxes of chocolate and soft drinks: her staple diet. She was addicted to cola drinks, flying several cases of diet cola every month by private jet from America at a cost of three thousand dollars a case because it was not available in Europe. Having discovered that even in the can the drink lost its freshness after a month, she refused to buy in larger quantities. She would drink up to twenty cans a day and was able to tell not only whether it was the real brand but also the factory where each can came from. Across the room a record player was weighed down by several Linguaphone records from an Italian course she had never completed. Next to them was a stack of diet books, which she had read from beginning to end several times.

At the moment she was not overweight after a six-month diet that she had carried out with determination and the help of three tapeworms she had swallowed alive. A full-length mirror was facing the wall where she had pushed it the last time she had looked at herself the summer before. She jumped out of bed, turned the mirror round and undressed. For a long while, she studied the reflection of her trim figure with satisfaction. Of all the items in her room, the empty cheap birdcage was the most poignant. It used to hold a songbird Sofia had captured herself on the island with a small wire trap Miss Rees had showed the children how to make, so that she could teach them about bird migration. Every year in spring, the island was overrun with birds that stopped there on their way back from Africa. For a few days, their deafening song made it impossible for anyone to sleep, irritating Marco Timoleon. Then Sofia, only thirteen at the time, had made his torment permanent by keeping the bird inside the villa where its song dissolved the silence that reigned over the final years of Marco Timoleon's marriage to Miranda Negri. One day her father, in a fit of anger, finally took the cage out to the balcony and set the bird free.

'You can't keep birds and husbands in the same cage,' he told his daughter.

From the window of her room, Sofia Timoleon contemplated the big yacht that was named after her out in the bay. As children, her brother and she had spent many holidays on it, but she did not go aboard any more. It was on that yacht that she had met some of the richest and most famous people in the world, film stars whose names meant nothing to her back then – Monroe, Garbo, Taylor – politicians, businessmen and a striking as much as inscrutable young woman whom her father introduced to her as Her Serene Highness, the Princess of Monaco. It was on the yacht that Daniel and Sofia had witnessed their parents' affairs with other people, and the yacht had also been the setting for a strange incident, so odd that Sofia still wondered whether it had truly happened or if she simply imagined it.

It had happened without warning. In the early hours of one morning in the summer of 1964, only days after Miranda Timoleon's death, Marco woke up the children and asked them to get dressed in a hurry and follow him to the jetty where the launch was waiting with its engine running to take them and Miss Rees to the *Sofia*. From the shore Sofia could see the crew of the yacht in a state of alert, filling the tanks with fuel, storing supplies, winching the Piaggio on to the deck. They weighed anchor before the sun had risen and travelled at full speed until they could see land no more. All morning Marco Timoleon stayed on deck, watching the horizon with worried eyes and clutching the gunwale while his cigar blew more smoke than the funnel. In the afternoon a helicopter appeared and circled above the yacht for a long time, and only when it left did Marco Timoleon calm down. They did not return to the island or come into any port, not that day, the next or for a long time afterwards, but instead they travelled without haste, without purpose, without a destination, stopping every few days to refuel and load the yacht with supplies in what must have been waters beyond areas of national jurisdiction. Marco Timoleon gave his children no explanation for the sudden trip, shutting himself in his stateroom, talking on the phone all day, coming out briefly and only late at night when the children were in bed. Only Miss Rees seemed to understand the seriousness of the situation, but she did not challenge her employer.

She did what she was hired to do: look after the children. Inspired by Jacques Yves Cousteau's famous adventures, which the children knew from his documentaries, which Miss Rees had played many times for their ichthyology class, she came up with a fantasy to justify the endless voyage of the *Sofia* and make it enjoyable: the yacht was on an oceanographic mission. Daniel, who was only ten at the time, believed her, but Sofia was fourteen, too old to like fantasies. Refusing to take part in Miss Rees's fairy tale, she stayed in her cabin until the monotony of the journey defeated her stubbornness, and she agreed at least to come up on deck a few hours a day to catch the sun.

Rather than taking her mind off her mother's sudden death, the voyage exacerbated Sofia's sadness and doubts. The death had been suspicious: the couple had had frequent fights; the incident had happened on Marco Timoleon's island; the death certificate had attributed the cause to pulmonary oedema without an autopsy. These facts were enough to convince many that the woman's death was either suicide or, more likely, murder: Marco Timoleon had killed her in a fit of rage.

The first weeks of the voyage were quiet and uneventful. There was a gentle breeze, enough to cool the cabins but not to rock the big yacht, which cut speed to conserve fuel as it continued its aimless journey across the Mediterranean. In the evening the children had dinner with Miss Rees under the canopy at the stern, and afterwards the governess worked with Daniel on their oceanographic game until the captain, at the woman's request, signalled bedtime with two blasts of the yacht's whistle. In the fourth week, the wind dropped and the heat became unbearable, forcing everyone to take refuge in their cabins, which were kept cool by constant air conditioning. One afternoon, after several days of stupor in bed, Sofia

Timoleon was on the empty deck when she heard gunshots coming from the bow. She went to investigate and saw her father, alone, naked from the waist up, a cigar in his mouth, shooting seagulls. One after another the birds plunged into the sea where several more were floating with their wings open on a glistening layer of blood and feathers. The mindless violence sickened her, but she did not dare ask for an explanation; she just stood there, motionless, watching in silence. When there were no more birds in the sky, Marco Timoleon emptied his shotgun and began to clean it. Suddenly he caught sight of his daughter and smiled at her.

'So that I don't blow out my brains, sweetheart,' he said.

It was the first time Sofia had seen him kill anything, at land or at sea, even though she had seen him fire the shotgun before on their annual cruises: one of his fondest pastimes on board was showing off his marksmanship by shooting clay pigeons. For a long time afterwards, she would be haunted by that incident, which she could not explain. She would hear in her mind the noise of the shots in the afternoon, see the birds flapping their wings and splashing about in the water; above all remind herself of her father's inexpressive face. From then on she spoke little to him, avoided sitting at dinner with him and turned down his invitations to go to his stateroom, saying she had a headache.

In autumn the weather began to change, and Marco Timoleon decided to take the yacht to the Caribbean. They left the Mediterranean behind and set course for the Bahamas on a journey the *Sofia* had done several times before, carrying Marco and his guests on summer cruises to the West Indies. But it was now late October, and the first storms soon turned the ocean into an ordeal for the passengers. Sofia Timoleon was the one most affected: the weather exacerbated her headaches and started a tempest in her stomach that continued even while she slept. She stopped eating in order to stop vomiting, which made things worse, and spent a long time in the lavatory trying to empty her empty bowels. When it was not seasickness, it was horror of the waves threatening to break the yacht in half. Only Miss Rees remained calm throughout it all even though she was the one person on board who could not swim. She did not panic. All that she did was ask for a life jacket and put it on under her oilskin, and then she carried on, ignoring the waves, the gale-force winds and the rain, going from bow to stern and throwing back in the water the fish that the storm washed up on deck. When the captain expressed his admiration, she told him that she was a descendant of Captain James Cook. Whether it was true or one of Miss Rees's humorous remarks delivered with a deadpan expression, the fact remained that never once was she seasick. The voyage lasted three days before they reached the safe haven of the Caribbean waters.

Sofia never found out the truth about their abrupt getaway in the middle of the summer. For a long time afterwards, she could not help but suspect, always with a shudder, that it had something to do with her mother's death. One would never know. But the incident could well have been related to her father's perpetual attempts to avoid paying taxes, attempts that were inventive but rarely legitimate: perhaps he had to lie low after some fiddle. For his part, Marco Timoleon always denied the drama of the whole incident, dismissing most of what Sofia remembered as the imaginative creations of a child.

During that voyage Daniel Timoleon discovered his love for flying, which his father, not suspecting that it would turn into a fatal passion, encouraged because it relieved the boy's boredom on board. The beginning was a flight to search for whales, the result of Miss Rees's having persuaded Marco Timoleon to play along with her oceanography plot. During a lull in the storm west of the Azores, they lowered the seaplane into the water and took off on their mission. They flew for a long time, travelling from north to south and east to west, covering a large area round the yacht, which was a mere white dot surrounded by storm clouds. They saw tankers ploughing through the ocean, some heading for Europe and others for America, and Marco Timoleon recognised through the binoculars one of his. The pilot put down the seaplane, and a launch from the ship carried them on board for an unexpected visit. The spectacle of the crew lounging in deckchairs in their underwear made Miss Rees blush. The captain, who was more embarrassed than her, took her by the arm and led her away, explaining that these days there was little to do during the interminable voyages: the crew was mainly needed when the ship came into port. They had a lunch of fresh fish at a table laid hastily on the bridge. After many days on the yacht, this chance meeting with people who respected him restored Marco Timoleon's mood. He drank wine and joked, then had a tour of the tanker, listening carefully to the captain and making notes in his notebook before the launch took them back to the Piaggio, a short trip during which they came across a school of flying fish, which for a moment engulfed them, sparkling and noisy, enchanting the children. Their flight would have ended without success in their original mission if Miss Rees had not spotted a tall spout of water shooting up from the surface of the sea. Marco Timoleon asked the pilot to circle the whale so that his son could take photographs, but Daniel seemed more fascinated by the controls of the plane than the aquatic mammal. In high spirits, his father allowed him to take the controls briefly under the pilot's supervision: fate began its game.

When Daniel and the pilot could not fly because of the weather, the boy passed the time reading the flight manuals until he learned the function of every switch in the cockpit. His father was impressed. At the Bahamas everyone else was happy to step on dry land except Daniel, who stayed on board to study aeronautics. Marco Timoleon had bought the two Piaggios only a year earlier, in 1963. By the time of the accident in 1974, the two seaplanes were in poorer condition than their age suggested, after thousands of hours of flight, a shortage of spare parts and the effect of salty water, which was corroding their hulls. Daniel was always telling his father to sell them and buy a Learjet or a helicopter instead, a decision Marco Timoleon kept postponing not because of the cost but with the secret hope that Daniel would sooner or later lose interest in the old seaplanes and stop flying altogether.

That is why at first he had blamed himself for his son's death, despite the experts' reports that attributed the accident not to the age of the seaplane but to pilot error in difficult weather. Then he began to believe that it had been an attempt on *his* life that had gone wrong. His investigator searched for a long time for the proof that was never found, but Marco Timoleon remained unconvinced that chance alone could have changed his life with such cruelty.

But in 1964 all this was in the distant future. The strange voyage from the Mediterranean to the Caribbean and back would change the relationship between the children. Before they had set sail, Daniel and Sofia were closer to each other than ever before, but by the time the yacht returned to Europe, dropped anchor in Monte Carlo and the Timoleon family disembarked, the children were drifting apart. Both of them had been born in London where the Timoleons had lived for fifteen years, but after the cruise Marco moved with them to

Paris where he bought an apartment on avenue Montaigne. There, Sofia Timoleon watched, with mixed feelings, her younger brother change body and soul. She admired his transformation from a shy child to a confident aviator, but still felt nostalgia for the little boy who was no more. Slowly his eyes lost their curiosity, which was replaced by a world-weariness that could not have been genuine because he was too young to have much experience of anything, and his torso grew thick and rigid until one day Sofia noticed, to her unease, a layer of dark hair on his chest showing through his open shirt.

Unlike him, she had found nothing to dedicate herself to wholeheartedly, apart from being Daniel's confidante and adviser. For many years they had slept in the same room, not for lack of space, of course, but because Miss Rees demanded it. The governess believed that children should spend as much time as possible together to build up their social skills and teach each other things no one else could teach them, and Marco and Miranda Timoleon had no objection. The children continued to share the same room after their mother died and after Miss Rees left the family until Daniel Timoleon, aged eighteen, decided that he needed privacy. Sofia Timoleon was hurt. She had always helped him overcome the difficulties he faced while growing up, particularly in reading, a problem probably caused by dyslexia. For many years Sofia had sat with him after their lessons with Miss Rees, to read together, making him repeat words into a tape recorder, which she then played back for Daniel to learn from his mistakes until he improved.

Standing at the window of her room, Sofia Timoleon looked at the small church on top of the island. Daniel was buried there, in the yard of Saint Mark of the Cypresses, next to his mother and his grandmother Eugenia, in a plot intended for his father. It was on the island that Sofia had lived both the best and worst moments with her brother. It was there he was finally allowed to pilot the seaplane himself at the age of seventeen and a half before he even received his student licence. Sofia Timoleon had watched from the veranda of the villa, her heart beating fast, standing with her father and most of the staff as Daniel took off on a perfect summer day for a circular flight around the island that lasted sixteen minutes, every single one the last of her life. He landed in the water, not far from where some years later he would kill himself, and came slowly towards the jetty where everyone had rushed to congratulate him. Marco Timoleon shook his hand, kissed him and presented him with a gold wristwatch engraved with the date and place of the historic flight before promising to do everything in his power to get him his pilot's licence.

And so Daniel Timoleon's appearance began to change, to suit his newfound adulthood. He grew taller, his shoulders broadened, his face shed its adolescent pallor. Only his voice reminded Sofia of his old self, a voice trapped in childhood that would not change despite his heavy smoking and world-weariness, leaving his transformation into an adult somewhat incomplete. One evening not much later, Daniel came into their bedroom, gathered his things and moved to a room across the corridor, never to sleep in the same room with his sister again.

After his son's death, Marco Timoleon had ordered the servants to empty Daniel's room of everything – furniture, clothes, magazines and photographs – and store them in the basement. Then he ordered the floors hoovered and the windows left open until there was no smell to remind him of his sorrow. When this proved not enough, he told them to scrub the walls with caustic detergents, convinced that he could see Daniel's shadow stamped on them, and finally he locked the door, hid the key in his desk and did not set foot in the room ever again.

The sun had long set. The air was cold when Sofia Timoleon shut the window and checked the time: soon her birthday celebration would be starting with a formal dinner. She could not wait. Not for the party to start: she left her room, walking quietly towards the guest wing, past the landing, past her stepmother's room, until she found the door that she knew was the right one without having to ask the servants. She looked both ways down the long corridor and, satisfied that no one was coming, she knocked lightly a couple of times and walked in without waiting for an answer.

A STRANGER AMONG STRANGERS, MARCO TIMOLEON arrived in New York only months before the start of World War II. He had left Argentina just as he was beginning to feel at home, obeying his business intuition which was telling him the imminent war would offer rare opportunities that would otherwise pass him by. The fact was that Buenos Aires was an outpost in the world of commerce and shipping for a man of his determination. He left in a manner that was typical of his attitude at the time: he donated his wardrobe to the Strangers' Club for their annual bazaar, keeping only one suitcase of his best clothes. He sold his Bugatti and the furniture to pay for an extravagant party the night before his departure, and in the morning he sailed away on a luxury cruise ship, leaving no forwarding address with his friends or his creditors.

In New York he detested the cold, but even worse was his difficulty in making himself understood. It had taken him a little less than two years to learn to speak Spanish, another one to be able to read it and three more months to start to write with confidence, having learned not with a teacher but simply by talking to people, reading everything that fell into his hands and copying newspaper articles to memorise the rules of syntax. He could already read and write English, but its pronunciation still defeated him; only Colonel Nicholls could understand him completely because of his years in the East. Thirty-six years old and busy running a growing business, Marco Timoleon had neither the patience nor the time to wait for things to fall into place, and so he decided to seek help. His elocution tutor was Mrs Sylvia Frank, a retired opera singer, who for years had been singing a more dramatic repertoire than she had been trained to do. One evening her voice had finally cracked in the middle of a Wagner aria, doing damage so great that despite the remedial exercises she did she could have returned to the stage only as a concert artist but never as an opera singer. It was a career that did not interest her, and she had chosen instead to lock herself in her small apartment on the third floor of an inconspicuous brownstone on the Upper West Side where she received students three evenings a week, making just enough to cover her rent and basic expenses. She was separated from her husband – a well-known impresario, who left at about the same time as she lost her voice, her career collapsed and the money stopped coming in – but she had not divorced him and still kept her married name. Marco Timoleon came to her on Wednesdays, always bringing a bouquet of yellow roses, which she put in a vase before their lesson began. 'Don't worry, Mr Timoleon,' Mrs Frank would say. 'Few people talk the way language is meant to be spoken. You just need time.' But despite her best efforts, Marco Timoleon's voice would never lose its heavy Mediterranean accent. It had suited him perfectly when he spoke Spanish, but his English would forever be weighed down with the leaden vowels which added to his notoriety: a gangster.

He tried everything. Inspired by the Greek orator Demosthenes, who according to legend had learned to talk with pebbles in his mouth and recited verses while running along the seashore over the roar of the waves to improve his elocution, Marco Timoleon stuffed his mouth with cotton, pinched his nose with a clothes-peg and did his voice exercises for hours, pacing the room. He studied the movement of his lips in front of the mirror and listened to the radio late at night, trying to imitate the American voices like a parrot, but nothing worked. Mrs Frank was at a loss to know how to help him. After one of their lessons, she dropped into her armchair, exhausted.

'It would be easier to teach New Yorkers your language,' she said.

It was more or less what ultimately happened: Marco Timoleon would become so famous that his distinctive voice would be immediately identifiable, and slowly it became understood across the world, thanks to countless radio and television interviews, as well as cameo appearances on comedy shows and in cinema films where he always played himself. Sylvia Frank eventually refused to take more of his money, and she sent him off, wishing him good luck and hoping that time would polish off the edges of his voice, which she herself could not improve. Impressed by her persistence in teaching him and her dedication to her job, Marco Timoleon asked her to come and work for him. He had to try hard to persuade her because she had never worked in an office and, besides, liked her job, but in the end she accepted thanks to a very generous pay offer. As his private secretary, she would become one of the persons closest to him, her loyalty never in question although it would take her some time to adapt to his way of doing things. When she was first faced with a difficult situation at work, he did not advise her to persevere but suggested, with a wink, that she use the skills of a burglar:

'If the front door is locked, Mrs Frank, try the garden. As long as no one is watching, you'll be fine.'

She understood but disagreed. Her family came from Tsarist Russia, and she herself had been brought up on the Lower East Side, an overcrowded neighbourhood abounding with butcher shops and bakeries, traditional synagogues, charitable societies, Yiddish newspapers, Yiddish theatre and religious schools for children. She was not a practising Jew, but when faced with her boss's shady suggestions, she would defend herself with tractates from the Talmud. She never became like him, but Marco Timoleon's forcefulness did eventually sap her morality, and in the end she obeyed most of his instructions without judging them, which was the way he wanted his subordinates to behave. Few knew that she influenced him too, by introducing him to her private passion: astrology.

Occult sciences always appealed to Marco Timoleon, who had grown up in a place where the boundaries between the real and the imaginary were defined only by degrees of faith. When he was a child, Pandora had infected him with her own superstition through the stories she told him at night before putting him to sleep. When Ian Forster met her in 1974 for their one and only interview. She was a terse eighty-one-year-old with a face carved out of driftwood and a brain full of natural wisdom that could not perceive a random world, the way the eye cannot see more than three dimensions. As far as she herself was concerned, she believed that everything in her life had gone according to plan: she was born to be an orphan; Victor Timoleon was born to win her at the tombola; she was born to live a certain number of years (it turned out to be ninety-six). All facts nothing she could do to change even if she jumped off the roof. When Ian Forster challenged her, perhaps impolitely, about the element of chance in life, she answered him with one of her mistress's favourite aphorisms: 'Coincidence is the god of those too lazy to go to church on Sunday.'

Pandora had opened a box full of superstitions that both fascinated and terrified Marco Timoleon as a child. Convinced that he lived in a world ruled by spirits, headless highwaymen and the evil eye, he locked his door at night and hung his bed with crosses and charms. Eugenia Timoleon did not encourage him but turned a blind eye because she believed that fairy tales helped the boy develop his imagination. One night he was woken up by the squeaking noise of the hand pump they had in the garden, and when he looked out of the window, he clearly saw a tall man in a formal suit filling a bucket. The same thing happened every night for a week until Marco came across an old photograph and recognised the man as the American consul who had lived in their house before them and had since returned to America. He made the mistake of telling his father, adding: 'There are certain things science can't explain.'

Victor Timoleon, who was not only an engineer but also a devoted materialist, curled his lip. He believed that all existence could be resolved into matter or effects of matter, down to the phenomenon of consciousness, which he was certain one day would be explained by changes in the nervous system. He bitterly opposed idealism, which affirmed the supremacy of mind and considered matter merely an aspect of thought. To prove what he believed to his teenage son, he pricked the boy's finger with a needle.

'Convince yourself that this didn't hurt,' he said.

Despite his father's disapproval, Marco remained quietly sceptical of the real world. Over the years his faith in the supernatural continued to grow from the seeds sown by Pandora, out of a need to explain every coincidence that happened to him and an ignorance of modern science. It was not without its occasional uses: in the storms of his life, he found refuge in his intuition, which helped him make quick decisions without thinking. To anyone who dared question his beliefs, he would tell how a few years after the ghost in the garden the Great Fire that destroyed big parts of Izmir had missed the Timoleon house by only a few feet: Marco Timoleon was convinced the ghost of the American consul with the bucket had saved them.

So when Sylvia Frank had talked to him about astrology, he gave her his full attention, fascinated by the effect the movements of stars had on people's character. Soon, the first thing he did every morning when he arrived at the office was to order coffee, sit back at his desk and drink it slowly in long noisy sips while listening to his daily horoscope read to him by Sylvia Frank. The incredible idea of using astrology in business was his. Despite her belief in the horoscopes, Mrs Frank was not convinced it would work. Marco Timoleon asked her to draw him charts that took into account the positions of all the planets on various dates in the past, and then he carefully studied how the markets had performed on those dates until he convinced himself that there was a relationship between planetary orbits and the movement of stocks and shares on the New York Stock Exchange. Armed with that information, he began to invest without fear. Before a month had gone by, he had already lost a sizeable amount of money, not too large to bankrupt him but big enough to shake his confidence in his business wisdom, and reluctantly had to abandon his plan.

In the end, his success came not from the stars but from his ingenuity, his talent for challenging tradition and his messianic powers of persuasion. For some time he had been involved in shipping, having bought two ageing dry bulk freighters, the first of which he sank to collect the insurance. He had converted the second to carry oil, but it was causing him headaches because it spent more time in dry dock than at sea. After a lot of thought, he decided that if he were to expand his fleet, he should be designing his tankers himself and having them built to his exact specifications, bigger and faster than anything on the market. And so he did. He passed many nights alone in his office, calculating every detail in order that his ships would satisfy the needs of the customers he wanted to attract. But there was one problem: he did not have the capital to build his tankers.

It took him only a few days to come up with the solution, which turned out to be so simple that no one else had thought of it. Before the keel was even laid, he found a customer to whom he agreed to charter the tanker when it was completed, and with the contract in hand he walked into the bank and asked for a loan to build the ship, a loan that would start to be paid back from the charter fees as soon as the ship was afloat. It meant that when the entire loan was paid off, Marco Timoleon would be the owner of a ship in which he had invested no money at all. At first his proposition startled the banks not only because it was something that had never been done before but also because Marco Timoleon was a stranger about whom little was known in New York, and he was thus not creditworthy. He made an appointment and was seen by a junior bank manager who did not wait to hear everything that Marco Timoleon had to say.

'Is this your idea?' he asked. 'Or Groucho Marx's?'

Marco Timoleon did not give up. He returned the following day and many more after that, insisting on seeing the general manager until they threatened to call the police. Then he changed tactics. He began to wait outside the bank and finally waylaid the manager in a quiet side street during his lunch break. The man looked at Marco Timoleon, who was stocky, had his hands in his pockets and whose unsmiling face showed absolute determination, and he misunderstood.

'Is this a hold-up?'

Marco Timoleon smiled.

'No, a loan application.'

He offered his hand, and the other man shook it hesitantly, still not believing that the stranger was not holding a gun. Then Marco offered him a cigar, lit it with his gold lighter and began to talk, drawing lines and doing sums on the brick wall of the alley with a piece of chalk. The manager liked his idea and agreed to help him achieve the unachievable, which also proved profitable for the bank: Marco Timoleon was on his way to becoming one of the richest men in the world.

At the time his offices were a single room on the twelfth floor of the Chanin Building, the buff-brick art deco tower on East 42nd Street. When work was slow, he liked to perch on the windowsill and smoke his cigar one hundred and fifty feet above ground, watching the pigeons fly through the fog of fumes from the street and imagining the sound of the horns of the ocean liners in the distant river, setting sail for Europe. Sitting safely at her desk, Sylvia Frank shuddered from vertigo just from looking at him. He was fascinated by heights and admired the high-wire artists lured to the city by the skyscrapers and suspension bridges, which were unlike those anywhere else in the world. Marco Timoleon paid the few coins to watch them succeed, and when they fell to their deaths, he contributed generously to the collection made for their widows, wondering what those poor souls were thinking on the way down. Partly because of bravado, partly out of curiosity and partly to escape from an unreasonable boredom which came from he knew not where, he once decided to perform his own daredevil act, but the umbrella snapped, and he landed hard on the pavement, breaking his hip. If he had jumped from a greater height, he would have been dead. Instead, he spent three months in hospital covered with a plaster cast, wrapped in bandages and threatening to sue the umbrella manufacturer for bad craftsmanship. When he was discharged, he promised his secretary that he would never try it again but remained unrepentant, declaring himself Son of Icarus.

In the hospital his ward was always flooded with flowers, brought in daily by delivery men in brown uniforms and peaked caps, to the despair of the nurses. Soon there were so many bouquets on every table, in every vase, in buckets on the floor that their scent covered the smell of antiseptic. The flowers, gifts from the many friends Marco Timoleon had already made, show how quickly and how well he had adjusted to living in New York. His natural talent for striking friendships and showing affection to strangers was what set him apart from most millionaires of past and future generations, who are uncomfortable in the lime-light, preferring instead to barricade themselves in their mansions, private members' clubs and offices. As soon as he lost the cast, he threw a party at the Stork Club on East 53rd Street to which he invited all the patients from his ward. Some were still in recovery, and the club owner protested that it would be inappropriate to have people in bandages wandering around like Egyptian mummies, but it took Marco Timoleon only a moment before finding the solution: 'Then we'll have to make it a costume party,' he said. He was building up his fame in tandem with his fortune, spending as much on investments as on public relations, a practice he would continue throughout his life with the justification that his celebrity helped promote his businesses too.

Soon New York was not big enough for him. He began to fly frequently to the West Coast where he hoped to enter the filmmaking business, attracted by the popularity of the cinema and its glamour. The studios welcomed his money but dismissed his ideas for feature films as too simplistic and brimming with sentimentality. Marco Timoleon was not deterred. He kept going back, supposedly to discuss possible investments in future productions but in reality to submit more of his proposals, diligently typed by Mrs Frank, proposals that disappeared in the files of jaded studio executives as soon as they arrived. His fondness for film had started by chance in Buenos Aires when he was caught in a tropical shower and had to take shelter in a nearby cinema. The film that was playing was *The Barbarian* with Ramon Novarro and Myrna Loy, the story of an Englishwoman arriving in Cairo to meet her fiancé only to fall in love with an Arab guide who takes advantage of rich women tourists. It was a plot that captured Marco Timoleon's imagination. For the next hour and a half, he sat in silence, his eyes glued to the screen, his hands clasping the arms of his seat until the film ended, and then he took out his handkerchief, wiped his eyes and began to clap enthusiastically. From then on he went to the cinema at least once a week, sitting close to the screen because he was already suffering from myopia, which a few years later would force him to wear thick glasses. He enjoyed all films, no matter how absurd the plot – *King Kong*, *Frankenstein*, *The Invisible Man*, *Flash Gordon* – but above all he liked the matinée melodramas, he would always freely admit, about fallen women, doomed love affairs, infidelities and unrequited love, films which in later life he would dismiss as utter drivel but still not deny the influence they had had on him.

In those films he must have discovered the spirit of adventure that daily life did not offer him. Success in business was something he was soon achieving, but the great emotions eluded him like fabled animals; he was beginning to think they did not really exist. He had set out on his journey with all the innocence of his age, the simplicity of mind, the ignorance about the sacrifices he had to make to achieve his purpose, namely to get rich, all of which had inflated his hopes, but slowly the balloon began to lose height. Only much later would he admit that he lived an interesting life, much more interesting and privileged than many other people's, and if his happiness was not greater than theirs neither was his sadness.

That was before Daniel's accident.

Inspired by the films that he saw, he started to write scripts, which he flew out to the West Coast to deliver by hand. It was in the waiting rooms of the film companies that he met the starlets he saw in those days, some of whom would later become famous and deny they ever knew him. The only important relationship he had at the time was with Rebecca Ramsey, a twenty-three year old who had come to Los Angeles from the East Coast determined to become an actress. They met at the offices of Columbia Pictures in the spring of 1940. That day Marco Timoleon had been waiting for four hours and was still refusing to leave despite having been told that the head of the studio was too busy to see him. Suddenly he folded the newspaper he was reading, smiled and told the secretary: 'If your boss wants to see her, then he'll have to see me first.'

The secretary looked at him in bewilderment: they were alone. But a few minutes later the door opened and a young woman walked in, asking if this was the office of the head of the studio. When she was told that it was, she sat opposite Marco Timoleon and picked up a magazine from the table.

'I knew you were coming,' Marco Timoleon said.

Rebecca Ramsey looked up from her magazine. It took her a while to understand his accent.

'A premonition?' she asked.

'No, your perfume.' He relit his cigar and sat back. 'Shalimar by Jacques Guerlain,' he said. He explained that his nose could detect the slightest smell from a great distance, a gift he was not exactly sure how he had acquired. Then he resumed sipping his coffee and smoking his cigar in alternate movements while observing the woman with quiet admiration. The sun slanting through the venetian blinds lit her like a stage light, as she sat across from him turning the pages of the magazine on her lap. Marco Timoleon was impressed by the relaxed way she sat, with her legs crossed but not revealing even an inch that should not be revealed, by her confidence and honest nonchalance, which it seemed nothing in the world could unsettle.

Having grown up in a dormitory town that died in the morning and was resurrected in the evening by the whistle of the commuter train, Rebecca Ramsey had not met anyone like Marco Timoleon before. A precocious tomboy with an insatiable imagination, she had exhausted the possibilities that her small town had to offer early on, and by adolescence she had been left with little to do. She read anything that passed through her hands, from fiction to history, from comics to Geological Survey maps and machinery manuals, and listened to music on the family gramophone. Her life had changed for ever when her father sold the sofa to buy a Catalin radio, a significant investment in the years of the Great Depression, and this was how Rebecca Ramsey discovered the theatre. In the evening she would listen to the plays of the Lux Radio Theater, the Cavalcade of America, the Mercury on the Air, which was run by Orson Welles, and afterwards she would re-enact them in bed, the actors' voices reverberating in her mind. After school she had attended the American Academy of Dramatic Arts in New York and worked on Broadway, where a talent scout had spotted her. She said she preferred the plays of the classic repertoire, and there was one role that she particularly hoped to play.

'Jane Eyre,' she explained.

Marco Timoleon took the cigar from his mouth and offered his hand.

'And I'm Marco Timoleon. From New York.'

She shook his hand, amused by his ignorance, and continued to leaf through her magazine. Their short conversation gave Marco Timoleon enough to think about. When he was done thinking, he put his cigar in his mouth to stop himself from speaking because he knew from experience that it was her turn to move her piece on the chessboard.

'What brings you to the West Coast, Mr Timoleon?'

'Curiosity,' he answered.

'I hope you'll satisfy it.'

It was all they said to each other that day. The next time they met it was at a cocktail party to which Marco Timoleon had asked the host to invite her. He arrived late, calculating that after being on her own among strangers she would be glad to see him, but was disappointed to find her surrounded by a large group of men hanging on her every word. He only managed to get her attention when he handed her a glass of champagne, and she surprised him with her good memory.

'Mr Timoleon,' she said. 'From New York. Right?'

For the next hour, she let him talk, listening without interrupting. Marco Timoleon spoke about his life and offered his impressions of America in the short time he had been in the country. He said that he was leasing offices at the Rockefeller Center – which was still under construction, but he said it to impress her – and described his life in New York as a ship lost in the fog that was looking for a lighthouse. Then he compared New York with Buenos Aires, which would always have a special place in his heart, he said, because there he had laid the foundations of his success. He also offered to teach her the tango, which – he said, trying to make her blush but failing – he considered the most erotic thing two people could do with their clothes on, before he went on to talk about the war in Europe: he was of the opinion that America should not take part. Then, without lowering his voice, he made the historic comment that would earn him a permanent place in the FBI files and cause him many problems later in business: 'A man like Hitler would be good for this country too. But he would have to be better looking.' How his admiration for Hitler could be reconciled with his having a Jewish woman like Mrs Frank as his most trusted collaborator is strange. His biographer asked him about it, but he waved aside his questions with irritation. After his death Ian Forster had the opportunity of asking Mrs Frank about it too, and she told him that in her opinion her old employer's anti-Semitism had been merely a Masonic hand-shake: he had wanted to show the social class he aspired to join that he shared its beliefs. She pointed out to Ian Forster that in 1938, only a year before Marco Timoleon had come to New York, Henry Ford, the famous industrialist and outspoken anti-Semite, had received the Grand Service Cross of the Supreme Order of the German Eagle, the highest honour of the Reich that could be bestowed on a foreign national.

In any case, Rebecca Ramsey did not agree with everything that Marco Timoleon said that evening, but like so many people in his life she decided that he was a man she liked to disagree with. When he told her he had been looking for her everywhere over the past days, his claim did not wash with her. She said: 'You were hiding from yourself, Mr Timoleon.'

A sudden shower of rain interrupted their conversation. The party had to move inside where a piano played the latest hits and the waiters continued to serve drinks. The fans on the ceiling checked the humid air creeping in from the glass doors to the garden and purified the atmosphere in the ballroom. Marco Timoleon invited Rebecca Ramsey to dance, and for a while they pushed their way round the room as if walking through mud while more people crowded into the house until it was not just impossible to move but also difficult to breathe. Marco Timoleon loosened his bow-tie and took deep breaths.

'If we stay here another minute, I warn you that I'll have a heart attack,' he said. 'And it'd all be your fault.'

He suggested that they go for a drive, and she followed him to his car without saying anything. They were silent throughout the trip, listening to the melodies on the radio and looking at the changing landscape as they left behind the city and headed towards San Bernardino County. The sun was setting behind them. Marco Timoleon rolled down the window, and the cigar smoke mixed with the smell of wild flowers. They went as far as the edge of the Mojave desert, passing ranches on the way where dogs chased after the car and lights went on inside houses, then they turned back because it was getting too dark and reached Los Angeles some time after midnight when there was little traffic in the streets. Neither inexperienced nor gullible, Rebecca Ramsey was still surprised when Marco Timoleon stopped the car in front of her house.

'I had a wonderful time,' he said, opening the door for her. 'Good-night.'

She did not believe his honesty that night but thought of his behaviour as a stratagem for impressing her with his sense of morality. It was not just that. All his life Marco Timoleon liked to confuse friends, associates and strangers who thought they knew him or knew what to expect from him. Whenever he did it, and they expressed their surprise, he would then say: 'Don't believe everything you read. A page has only two dimensions.' In Rebecca Ramsey's case, his intention was not just to sleep with her but make her fall in love with him, which he achieved slowly after dispelling her doubts one by one. It took him three months. What she did not know at the time was that his was an easy vow of chastity. As was the case with Flor Alcorta, Marco Timoleon courted Rebecca Ramsey while seeing other women too, with whom he believed he did not have to obey the same rules because he was not in love with them.

The way he set about charming Rebecca Ramsey followed his usual pattern of seduction. He began by sending flowers and boxes of chocolates with his card attached to them, asking for nothing other than her enjoyment of his presents. Delivery men knocked on her door at all times and more than once a day. Soon there were not enough vases for all the flowers, which began to wither among the armies of ants crisscrossing the floor to feed on the heaps of melting chocolates that no one ate. In the end she protested: 'You're trying to kill me with generosity.' Marco Timoleon did not end the siege but changed his gifts to more practical items that caused no health hazard: he bought her clothes, furniture, carpets and paintings to decorate the walls of her bungalow in View Heights, in south Los Angeles. He even paid a gardener to come by once a week, but when he offered to buy her an apartment in Beverly Hills, Rebecca Ramsey refused. He took her out to restaurants, film premières and weekend breaks to the coast, he gave her financial advice, introduced her to people in the film business and encouraged her dreams with enthusiasm. At last he had come to admit that he had no flair for the cinema or any other art, but with his remarkable powers of observation he quickly figured out how a screen actress must look and behave, and he helped Rebecca Ramsey learn the skills she needed to survive in the gladiators' arena.

This was the best time of their relationship despite Marco

Timoleon's strange habit of disappearing without warning and returning two or three days later laden with flowers and gifts but no explanation. One such time he returned and found a young man sitting quietly in Rebecca Ramsey's living room. The visitor was an actor too, with whom she was rehearsing a scene: tall and handsome, oiled hair, a perfect smile and a bespoke double-breasted pinstriped suit. Neither the explanation that the meeting had to do with work nor the young man's friendliness forgave his sin of putting Marco Timoleon in the shade. He did not shake the young actor's hand when he stood up and introduced himself, but sat in a chair opposite and watched the rest of the rehearsal with a stony expression. When the man left, Marco Timoleon offered his opinion: 'It was very bad.'

Rebecca Ramsey gave him a surprised look.

'Don't practise at home,' said Marco Timoleon. 'The conditions are not right – the sound, the lighting. Learn your two-bit parts here but only practise them at the studio.'

Rebecca Ramsey was hurt, even though she knew what this was really about.

'He's only a friend,' she said.

Instead of replying, Marco Timoleon stood up, opened the glass door at the back of the living room and dragged out into the garden the sofa where the two actors had sat earlier. Then he went to his car, came back with the petrol can, doused the sofa and watched it burn until only the metal springs were left.

It was the first incident in a violent stream of jealousy, which had gone unchecked since the days with Flor Alcorta. Over the next year, they fought several times – or, rather, he attacked her, and she tried to defend herself. He swore at her, chased her around the house, pulled her hair, punched her and kicked her, pointing out at the same time that he was not hitting her in the face because he cared about her career. Rebecca Ramsey never called the police, never told a friend, never went to the doctor but suffered in silence, refusing to admit to herself or anyone else that she had fallen for the wrong man.

In one interval of calm, she decided to solve the mystery of Marco Timoleon's abrupt disappearances. She did not need to hire a private investigator. She used her acting skills and enlisted only the help of a friend who worked at Columbia's wardrobe department and let her borrow any costume she wanted. She began to follow Marco Timoleon across town, hidden behind an inexhaustible combination of hats, scarves and dark glasses, morning and evening dresses, even uniforms if the occasion called for one: when she heard that he would be visiting a friend in hospital, she made sure she was there too, dressed as a nurse; when she heard he would be dining at a restaurant, she kept a close eye on him by posing as a waitress; when he went to the cinema, he did not suspect that one of the usherettes was her. The masquerade continued for several weeks until she discovered that, in fact, when he disappeared, Marco Timoleon did not leave Los Angeles but checked into cheap hotels across town where he spent the night in his room. She knew what all this meant: there was another woman. One night Rebecca Ramsey decided to confront him but was more surprised by what she found then than he was to see her. She paid the receptionist to give her the key to the room, unlocked the door, entered and found Marco Timoleon sitting upright in bed, propped up by pillows, smoking a cigar, drinking alcohol and watching a gangster film from a projector directed at the wall. He was alone. His secret was that he disappeared from the world to purify himself in solitude. Gregarious and outgoing most of the time, he flipped the coin and felt the desire to vanish, which he satisfied with these hotel stays.

He had an everlasting but impalpable disappointment about

life. He often said: 'There is no greater pleasure than starting all over again,' and the feeling seemed to grow stronger with time. For a while he daydreamed that he would do it. Every time he contemplated a beautiful landscape, every time he passed a dirt lane off the side of a road, every time he stood on the bridge of the *Sofia* in the middle of the ocean, he felt the temptation to leave behind a life damaged by ambition, which he had come to regard as a disease of youth. It was a romantic impulse; he knew he would never do it. Ian Forster asked him once why not, and Marco Timoleon did not have to think before answering him:

'Unfortunately, Mr Forster, life doesn't suffer from amnesia.'

When he had seen the woman at the door of his hotel room, he had not recognised her.

'I didn't ask for room service,' he had said.

Then he saw it was Rebecca Ramsey. He drew on his cigar and looked at her with untroubled eyes.

'This is an invasion of privacy,' he said.

He had refilled his glass and returned to watching the film, ignoring her presence. She left, and neither of them ever mentioned the incident again, but after that night, their relationship seemed to deteriorate. Now that she knew, Marco Timoleon stopped going away and ambushed Rebecca Ramsey more often both in her house and when she was out. He did what she had done when she had shadowed him, but *he* did not hide. He followed her to the restaurants and nightclubs where she went with friends, joining them at their table without being invited; he followed her to the studio where she worked, watching the filming from the shadows; he followed her to the swimming pool where she exercised three afternoons a week, swimming behind her like a shark; he followed her to the hairdresser, the bank and the shops until she lost all patience and told him: 'It is over.' He did not accept it, but then he had the bad luck to catch her in the Mayfair Club at the Biltmore with a big airman who beat him up and threatened to kill him if he ever saw him again. It put an end to the chase. With his business suffering from his long stays in Los Angeles and no access to Rebecca Ramsey any more, Marco Timoleon made the decision to return to New York.

It passes all belief, even when taking into account the morals of the time, that Rebecca Ramsay and he never slept together. Both insisted to Ian Forster that it was true, and he had no reason to doubt it because Marco Timoleon was never coy about sex. The more his biographer researched his life, the more he understood that Marco possessed a sense of morality that swung from conservative to libertine with the ease of a metronome. Many years later, when Ian Forster went to see Rebecca Ramsey, he asked her how their relationship could have been both passionate and platonic. Knowing about Marco Timoleon's impotence later in life, he asked whether this had also been the reason for the failure to consummate their affair back then, but Rebecca Ramsey looked at the biographer with contempt.

'The problem was not that he wasn't doing it, Mr Forster,' she said, 'but that he was doing it with everyone but me.'

After a long career in the cinema under a different name, she was by then a reclusive diva, playing occasional cameo roles in bad films in order to pay her rent and feed her seven poodles. She never played Jane Eyre. She lived in New York, surrounded by the memories of her long life, the ghosts of three dead husbands and the rusting reels of her films stacked against her bedroom walls and arranged in chronological order: she claimed she never watched them. She received Ian Forster dressed in a loose silk maxi-dress with a floral pattern and a white turban, very fashionable at the time, and talked to him for several hours about Marco Timoleon, before ending their interview with a medical diagnosis: 'He was a psychopath.' Bound by a confidentiality agreement at the time, the biographer knew that he would be forbidden from mentioning any of that in his book. It was disappointing: the affair would have been a sensational revelation even more than thirty years after it had happened.

After his return to New York, Marco Timoleon threw himself into work. While romance seemed to elude him, business success came easily. He stopped going out to clubs and restaurants, which was unlike him, and spent more and more time in his office, where he had his meals and often slept, on a camp bed he folded away in the morning. He returned to his apartment only to wash and pick up fresh clothes and then took a cab back to work. America's entry into the war, in December 1941, was the best thing that could happen to his shipping business. It was what he had predicted. He used his Argentine merchant fleet, safe from attacks of German submarines because Argentina was neutral, to transport goods across the world, including to Germany, while his American ships he leased to the Allies.

Work helped him overcome the grief of his separation from Rebecca Ramsey, but a greater sorrow was waiting for him. One evening he had fallen asleep at his desk after days of uninterrupted work when he felt a presence in the room. He opened his eyes.

'Yes, Mrs Frank?'

His secretary approached in the dark and handed him a telegram. It was from Pandora: *Mother ill, come quick.*

Sylvia Frank would always deny it was she who gave him the bad news, and indeed it is unlikely that she had: she always finished work at four o'clock in the afternoon, and Marco

Timoleon insisted that he received the telegram, which was never found despite a thorough search by both of them, late in the evening. What's more, Pandora insisted to Ian Forster that she had never sent a telegram, having promised her mistress that she would not tell her son about her illness. Eschewing the supernatural explanations that Marco Timoleon was so fond of, his biographer assumed that some neighbour had taken the liberty of telegraphing him the news. Whatever the case, Marco Timoleon left immediately for Izmir. To avoid the war, he flew first to South America, travelled by boat to Africa, took one plane after another to reach the Middle East and finally arrived in Izmir by train six weeks after leaving New York.

In twenty years he had kept in touch with his mother by writing to her frequently, but he had been postponing his return year after year because of the length of the journey, which would have left his business with no one in charge for a long time. He was pleased to find the house the way he had left it after so many years, in good condition outside, the garden tended and the branches of the date palms weighed down with fruit, but his satisfaction proved premature. He still had his key and used it, without much expectation, to open the door, but as soon as he entered, he saw that the house where he grew up was, in fact, crumbling from the inside. The plaster was peeling off, the doors were falling off their hinges, the plumbing made a haunting sound that echoed across the house, the floors were riddled with woodworm. Eugenia Timoleon had been refusing his repeated offers of money for many years, saying that she had more than she needed. When Marco finally ignored her objections and sent her an envelope stuffed with dollars on her sixtieth birthday, she returned them with a note that said: *If you want to give me a present deliver it in person.*

He took the stairs to his mother's bedroom and there she was, half asleep, covered in blankets and cobwebs, old and frail, breathing with difficulty but still commanding reverence. Marco Timoleon sat in a chair until she opened her eyes.

'Who the hell are you?' she asked.

Marco Timoleon had long been suspecting that his mother was suffering from dementia, but there was not enough evidence in her letters to confirm it. The truth was that Eugenia Timoleon had been aware of her own condition almost from the start, more than five years earlier, but she had been skilfully hiding it from her son with Pandora's help. It had begun with an episode of memory loss when Eugenia had asked her maid what day it was.

'Thursday,' she replied.

A moment later Eugenia Timoleon asked her again.

'Still Thursday,' Pandora said.

'Thank you.'

Not long afterwards her mistress asked her a third time. Pandora was now irritated and did not reply.

'Answer me, please,' said Eugenia.

'I've already answered you twice,' the maid said.

Eugenia Timoleon looked at her, puzzled.

'But I haven't asked you anything.'

Later she had begun to misplace things. Pandora would open the ice box and find the iron inside or would go to make coffee and discover her mistress's reading glasses in the sugar bowl. At first, these incidents amused Eugenia Timoleon, but one day she had to go to the market on her own and discovered that she could not remember the way back. She was fortunate that a neighbour recognised her and brought her home, but the incident frightened her so much that she stopped going out altogether, accepting the fate of her illness. A proud woman who up until then had resisted everything life had thrown at her, she began to feel ashamed of herself. She enlisted Pandora to help her hide the truth from Marco, telling her: 'I don't want my son to remember me like a scarecrow.' Her maid agreed. She would correct the spelling mistakes in her letters to Marco until Eugenia could not write at all, and then Pandora began to write the letters herself, double-checking the facts her mistress could not remember in the diary Eugenia Timoleon had kept ever since she was a child.

Sleeping in a chair next to the door that opened on to the balcony, Marco Timoleon stayed at his mother's side until she died. In the morning the noises from the street entered the world of the dead and lingered until evening, ignoring his grief, while Eugenia slept peacefully. In the brief moments that she was awake, she would try to speak but would forget the words or use them wrongly. Marco Timoleon's inability to understand her would cause her outbursts of anger. At other times he would notice a sparkle in her eyes, but no sooner would she unearth some memory from the sands of time than she would forget it for ever. One afternoon she woke up and smiled at him as if she had recognised him. Then her expression changed.

'Out of my house!' she shouted. 'Help! Thief!'

The events of the last few weeks of her life would affect Marco Timoleon deeply. He was always sad to have witnessed her mood swings and changes to her personality, her inability to recognise him, her struggle with language. His sadness was not lessened by the fact that at least she had not seemed to suffer any pain. Marco Timoleon knew that his mother always valued intelligence and judgement above anything else, and it was with her in mind that once he had told Dr Patrikios in all seriousness:

'Promise me, doctor, you'll pull the plug before I lose my marbles.'

The doctor had replied with equal seriousness:

'I'm afraid it's too late for that now.'

When Eugenia died, Marco Timoleon decided to leave the house to Pandora in addition to a large sum of money to pay for its full renovation so that it would be a lasting monument to his mother. While clearing her bedroom, throwing away the old clothes, the tarnished jewellery, the combs and brushes, he came across in a chest of drawers a bundle of letters tied with a yellow ribbon. He was surprised that she had kept within reach the love letters exchanged between his father and her. He could not resist reading them, now that he was older than the two people had been at the time they wrote them, and he undid the ribbon. He read for a long time, in silence, his face betraying no emotion, his fingers holding the paper that still smelt of perfume, his eyes fixed on the words, stained with tears, that preserved love like a prehistoric insect sealed in amber. They came as a revelation to him. His mother's behaviour all those years had convinced him that she had erased his father from her heart, and so the love letters felt then like a betrayal to him. Only with time would he come to accept his father's indelible mark on him. The letters were not the only discovery he made. In the attic he also found his father's complete book collection, which his mother had stored in sealed metal trunks to save from the rats. Marco Timoleon took them all back with him, and this was how his famous habit of reading the classics began.

He returned to New York almost a year after his departure, having left Sylvia Frank in charge of the business. He was pleased to find that she had done an excellent job. 'I would like to promote you,' he said. 'But the truth is I'm the only one above you.' Nevertheless, he raised her salary and appointed her head of operations of his expanding group of companies, a position Sylvia Frank held until his death when she was named executor of his will.

Eugenia's death took Marco Timoleon's mind off his everyday problems and sent it in other directions. For the first time, he began to question the meaning of life and the existence of God, suspecting that each human being is alone and completely responsible for their actions. He thought that the savage attack of age on his mother, the sanest person in the world, had been untimely and deeply unfair. He would say: 'My mother was a saint,' and by this he meant that not only had she helped innumerable children as a teacher for little in return, but also that she had suffered enough from the disappearance of her husband and the poverty that he had left in his wake: she deserved to have lived a longer and painless life.

Later his faith in God was restored. In fact in 1955 the canonisation of a nineteenth-century Orthodox monk, Saint Nicodemos of the Holy Mountain, led Marco Timoleon to approach the Ecumenical Patriarch in Istanbul and enquire about the possibility of canonising his mother too. Whether out of politeness or because they valued his generous contributions, the Patriarchate did not refuse him outright but indulged his whim, dragging out the process for several years: they gauged people's feelings about the pious woman in her home town and searched for evidence of miracles. In 1962 they even examined her remains before they were transferred to the island to be buried at Saint Mark of the Cypresses. They wanted to see whether the cadaver was well preserved or if the bones emitted a sweet fragrance, a sign the deceased has found favour with God (regrettably, she had not). But still they did not turn down Marco Timoleon's request, and the discreet negotiations were still ongoing at the time of his death.

The death of his mother opened up to Marco Timoleon a

fresh perspective on life at an age when ill health had not yet entered his calculations. Despite his cigar habit, his heavy drinking and rudimentary diet, he was still strong with a healthy heart and a firm body that was wrapped round him like armour. It was at this time that he asked his old friend Dr Patrikios to join him in New York. He wrote to him: *There are so many sick here that even Jesus couldn't heal them all.* Aristide Patrikios considered the invitation. He had been living in South America for two decades, constantly travelling the continent from Rio de Janeiro, where he was now based, and organising campaigns against yellow fever and malaria. He had helped eradicate diseases by setting up hospitals and laboratories that followed his procedures for diagnosis and cure, great achievements that had exhausted him but also given him the satisfaction that allowed him to consider a less active post. Finally, he agreed. He arrived in New York in the spring of 1943, six months after Marco Timoleon had written to him, and opened a general practice in Brooklyn, which Marco, living in Manhattan, thought of as a colonial outpost. At the opening of his practice, Dr Patrikios declared: 'I'm now officially retired.' He expected that it would be an easy job in comparison with his Napoleonic campaigns, but, as he told Ian Forster later, it was not long before he came to realise that suffering was the same everywhere.

Marco Timoleon showed his old friend the city. He took him on long walks, avoiding the tourist attractions and the crowds that flooded the streets, going to Central Park where they sat by a secluded corner of the lake and fed the ducks. Their discussions were endless monologues by Marco Timoleon on time, success, friendship and love, concepts he had never considered before. He talked about his inexhaustible impulse to become rich and famous, an ambition he would have fulfilled already if only he had not kept changing his definition of success. He had touched happiness many times but could not catch hold of it. He was trying to measure an intangible quality. One time Dr Patrikios, having listened to his usual rant, which he called *The Gospel According to Marco*, could hold back no longer. 'If I understand you properly,' he said, 'your dilemma is about choosing capitalism or existentialism.' In the middle of his life, Marco Timoleon had come to the place where the path forks, and perhaps the rest of the journey would have been happier if he had chosen not to continue with his dream of becoming the richest man in the world. Only in the last years of his life would he return to these meditations and pick up where he left off, but they would offer him only more disappointment.

One evening at El Morocco, the club on Second Avenue and East 54th Street, he came across Porfirio Rubirosa, the famous playboy and diplomat. Marco Timoleon had first met him in Buenos Aires, and they had struck up a friendship based on their shared love of the high life. When they met again in New York, Marco Timoleon's sadness at the death of his mother was almost gone. He was feeling a great sense of restlessness that kept him out of bed for days without getting tired, behaviour that would develop into a regular pattern and be with him always: one moment he was contented to the point of vanity, irritable and endlessly talkative, happy to squander his money and drink to intoxication, often aggressive and sexually insatiable, then the tide turned and he became sad and cynical, lost his appetite and was constantly tired, absentminded and withdrawn, showing no interest in his businesses or in other people. He talked about these things to Rubi.

'The doctors will say you suffer from depression,' the playboy had said. 'They'll stick a funnel in your mouth and pour pills down it for the next forty years. Do you think that's what you need? My advice is to get a good suntan and a rich heiress.'

Marco Timoleon followed his advice to the letter. He bought a tanning lamp as soon as they were invented and spent several hours every week under its green light, wearing a pair of goggles. He soon had the heavily tanned face he would always be remembered for even though he stopped using the lamp a few years later when he built his luxury yacht and began to spend more and more time on holiday, letting the business run itself. At about the same time that he bought the lamp, he walked into Mrs Frank's office and declared:

'It is time to marry.'

He was forty-one years old.

'I thank you,' Sylvia Frank said. 'But I won't make the same mistake twice.' When he explained that he did not mean her, Mrs Frank was mortally embarrassed. 'Good luck,' she said. 'Not to you. To the woman who would marry you.'

No single event was more important in the making of Marco Timoleon's business empire than getting to know Daniel Negri. Only seven years younger than Marco's father, his future father-in-law had left for America at the age of eighteen, as soon as he finished school, with a good knowledge of English, hardly enough money to last him the long sea journey and a distant relative's promise to take him in and help him find a job. But when he arrived in New York, no one was waiting for him. Despite searching he failed to trace his relative and found himself marooned in Manhattan without money or shelter. The year was 1895. His dream to travel on to California, lured by the gold mines he had read about in an old edition of *Encyclopaedia Britannica*, was cut short when he was found sleeping in a boxcar. He was thrown off the train and had to return to New York on foot, a punishing journey that took him eight months and three weeks, stopping every few days to work on a farm in return for a plate of food.

When Marco Timoleon first met him, Daniel Negri had for a long time been the patriarch of New York's expatriate businessmen. He had the largest fleet of freighters travelling the seas, strong political connections at home and abroad and an only daughter, who was still at prep school. Marco Timoleon knew him by reputation long before coming to New York from Buenos Aires and admired both his business wisdom and his refined manners, which betrayed nothing of his humble origins: behaviour Marco Timoleon would later copy but would never truly make his own. For a long time, his attempts to make friends with Daniel Negri did not go beyond a polite exchange of a few words in the clubs and restaurants where they ran into each other. Marco Timoleon, a well-known but still unimportant competitor in the international shipping business and with a bad reputation for using unconventional business methods, was not the sort of man Daniel Negri would show an interest in. But Marco would eventually sneak into his life through the back door, which Miranda Negri opened by falling in love with him.

Born when her mother was forty years old and her father well into his fifties, long after they had stopped trying to have a child, Miranda was considered by her parents to be God's blessing. They adored her. Marco Timoleon knew all this when he came across her at a charity auction at the Dominican Academy, the Catholic preparatory school in New York where she was a student. Miranda Negri was only sixteen and not yet taller than Marco, but there was no doubt that it was only a matter of time: when they married, three years later, she had to bend down to kiss him at the altar. She was slim, with auburn hair, grey eyes and a patrician disdain for food, which she never lost despite her two pregnancies. That afternoon at the Dominican Academy she was escorted by her mother, which was why her father, who was abroad at the time, would later hold Anna Negri responsible for the marriage. He would say, 'That man conned you out of our child,' and go on to repeat that *he* would have nipped the evil in the bud if only he had been there.

As likely as not, he would have been charmed along with his wife and daughter. At the charity auction, Marco Timoleon bid successfully for an antique mantelpiece clock, an item he had noticed Anna Negri examining carefully but ending up not bidding for. He had made sure to sit near the two women. After the auction ended, Anna Negri congratulated him on his buy.

'Unfortunately my husband is a very practical man,' she said. 'He doesn't like spending on decorative objects.'

'But time *is* money,' Marco shrugged.

They introduced themselves. His name sounded familiar.

'Aren't you the man they call the Turk?' Anna Negri asked without malice.

'It's not an insult,' Marco said. 'Simply an inaccuracy.'

They were talking in English. He informed her that he was a Christian, that Greek was his mother tongue, but he was also fluent in Turkish and Spanish while at present he was learning French and Italian. The following day he wrapped up the antique clock, tied it up with a silk bow and sent it to Anna Negri as a gift for the pleasure of having made her acquaintance. It was not long before he was invited to their house for tea and cakes, and he arrived dressed in a three-piece suit and a zoot hat, holding a bunch of white roses that he immediately presented to his hostess with an old-fashioned bow and a kiss of her hand: '*Enchanté.*' Daniel Negri shook his hand, eyeing him with suspicion. Then he gave him the bad news:

'My daughter cannot be disturbed. She's in her room, studying trigonometry.'

Marco Timoleon was not deterred. Later he excused himself but rather than going to the toilet found the girl's room and knocked on the door. Miranda Negri was at her desk, bent over a worksheet with a pencil in her mouth.

'Good afternoon,' he said.

Miranda Negri looked up and blushed.

'Hello, Mr Timoleon.'

He sat on the edge of her bed, pleased she had not forgotten him.

'I am sorry to interrupt you. I am lost.'

'Not as much as I am, Mr Timoleon.'

He glanced at her books.

'Plane geometry?'

'I hate it.'

'You shouldn't. It's possibly a sin. Plato said God was a geometer.'

'Then tomorrow I'll burn in hell.'

It was the first time they talked. From then on they would see each other often, in secret, managing to escape the close watch of the Dominican nuns in order to spend a few minutes together. At the same time, Marco Timoleon improved his relationship with Daniel Negri, who despite his suspicious nature knew nothing about what was taking place behind his back. It was a long courtship because Miranda was still at school. Finally, five months after her graduation, Marco Timoleon asked her father's permission to marry her, and Daniel Negri was forced to give his consent, a decision he would live to regret bitterly. The couple married in the spring of 1948 in the Greek Orthodox Cathedral of the Holy Trinity, on East 74th Street. Marco Timoleon was forty-four years old and Miranda nineteen.

WHEN IAN FORSTER BEGAN TO WRITE HIS BOOK, HE did not expect that there would come a time when he would have to choose. In the last two years, ever since Marco Timoleon agreed to help him write his biography, Ian Forster had learned more about the famous tycoon than any other person in the world, surprising even his subject, who would say: 'The Englishman is my nemesis.' Ian Forster knew that Marco Timoleon was not really worried. Before giving his permission and his money, he had placed in front of his biographer a confidentiality agreement: the book could not be published unless Marco Timoleon had personally approved it. Ian Forster had signed it; unable to finance his own research or get a publisher's support, he had no choice. The problem was that the deeper he delved into Marco's past, the more what had seemed like a big but uncomplicated project was growing into a torrent of truths, half-truths, errors and lies. Also, Ian Forster could no longer tell whether his own dedication had more to do with the pursuit of truth than with his dream of achieving wealth and fame through his work: the subject of the book was infecting its writer with his vices.

He was lying in bed with his eyes shut and thinking about these matters when a light knock on the door interrupted him.

He ignored it. All day the servants had been knocking on doors to ask the guests whether there was anything they needed. What *he* really needed was to rest if he were to last the night, which perhaps would supply him with material for his book. He was also hoping to persuade Dr Patrikios, one of his least co-operative interviewees, to answer some of the questions that had arisen from his research. There was another knock on the door. Ian Forster swore and covered his head with the pillow.

'Ian?'

'Mm?'

'Are you asleep?'

He lifted the pillow and opened his eyes. When he saw her standing at the door, he immediately jumped out of bed.

'This is damn foolish,' he said. 'What are you doing here? What if someone saw you?'

Sofia Timoleon locked the door.

'I missed you, Ian. Even though you're paranoid.'

Now that the door was locked, he relaxed a little, but he still frowned at her, annoyed she had taken a risk even if she did look beautiful in the yellow mini-dress and the pair of plat-form shoes that lifted her three inches above the ground and gave her the poise of an acrobat. Ian Forster had not seen Sofia Timoleon since June, when she had first told him she had missed her period. Later she had confirmed the pregnancy over the phone. He saw that her belly had not yet started to swell. Then he began to notice the things a lover ought to have noticed a long time before: the dimples in her face, the shape of her ears, a purplish birthmark on the side of her neck where he kissed her so often. Sofia Timoleon sat on the edge of the bed.

'Not paranoid,' he said. 'A month or two and the book will be done.' Then he remembered: 'Happy birthday.'

The previous week he had spent a whole day walking across

London in search of a present for her, from Liberty on Regent Street to Biba in Kensington, but found nothing she would have liked. Besides, a present from her father's biographer would have been noted, he now thought, looking on as Sofia stood up and went to the window.

'They might see you standing there,' he said.

She ignored him.

'This is a race against the clock,' she said.

'What is?'

'Your book and the baby.'

They had been seeing each other for more than a year, an affair that had begun after a series of interviews the biographer had done with Marco Timoleon's daughter for his book. The pair had first met in December 1973 in Monte Carlo where Sofia used to go whenever she needed a rest from the excesses of her lifestyle. Even her closest friends were not allowed to visit her in Monaco where she passed her days indoors, the curtains drawn day and night to prevent the journalists, who she supposed always lay in wait, from photographing her. She went from room to room in the twilight, barefoot, stepping on the pieces of giant, unfinished jigsaw puzzles, her favourite pastime, that were scattered over the floors. A few weeks later, she finally re-emerged, purified and indomitable and ready to face the world.

The apartment was in a modern building near Place du Casino. Ian Forster had arrived punctually for their interview but had to wait for two hours before Sofia would see him. A woman servant let him in and left the apartment as soon as she had served coffee, allowing him plenty of time to appreciate the luxury. The floor was laid with green marble that echoed his steps clear and loud. When Sofia Timoleon appeared, she did not apologise for her lateness but offered her hand and set the tone for the interview by saying: 'You're too young to be a biographer. Even Mickey Mouse's.'

It was not what he expected. They had never met before, but he thought he would have the upper hand in their interviews because he already knew a lot about her from his research. Far from being the defenceless heiress one read about in magazines, Sofia Timoleon was a tough opponent. She was of average height, had long dark hair and her mother's grey eyes, to which she had added a certain ambiguity that was probably a consequence of her addiction to tranquillisers. She held a tall glass filled with diet cola, ice and a slice of lemon, and despite the makeup, she gave the impression that she had just woken up. Ian Forster studied her studying him as she tried to decide just how much of his loyalty lay with her father. Then he nodded with modesty when she warned him that she would not tolerate any violation of her privacy.

'Unlike my father,' she said, 'I haven't sold my soul to the press.'

He thanked her for agreeing to see him and reassured her that he would not overstep the mark.

'My work requires your father's approval.'

Sofia Timoleon dismissed his reassurances.

'I don't trust him any more than I trust you.'

With the pleasantries out of the way, they sat down on either side of the coffee table where Ian Forster had already set a heavy Dictaphone. They talked about her family for more than an hour before Ian Forster realised that he had forgotten to turn on the recorder. Sofia Timoleon observed him scratching his head and grappling with the machine.

'You can't even pretend to be an impostor,' she said.

And before he had time to apologise, she dismissed him with a limp handshake and called her servant, who appeared a moment later to escort the Englishman out of the building. It took her several weeks to forgive him, but finally they repeated the interview and saw each other four more times after that, each interview a month apart. Ian Forster, this time sure his cassette recorder was on, asked Sofia about growing up in the Timoleon household, he asked her what she thought of her parents as a child and what her brother and her governess were like. Despite her initial hostility, Sofia seemed happy, almost thankful, to talk about her life, and she even let him read the diary she had kept since she was little, breaking, whether she realised it or not, the rules of privacy she herself had set in their first meeting. Only when the discussion veered on to her father's relationship with her stepmother did she lose her amiable mood; her face darkened, and she refused to answer any of his questions.

Their long discussions, each one recorded in a different location across the world, turned out to be invaluable to Ian Forster. They confirmed some of his presumptions, corrected others and brought to the surface new facts that no one had mentioned before. Since then the Englishman had played back the tapes of their interviews countless times, digging deeper into the gold mine, researching every revelation, every anecdote, every insinuation, and discovering good and evil truths in equal measure. At the same time, he could not stop worrying that all this was futile because his sponsor would almost certainly refuse him the right to publish them.

Their last scheduled interview took place in the spring of 1974 on Marco Timoleon's private island. Only the dog was there to greet him on the jetty, wagging her tail. Ian Forster ate on his own, sitting at the far end of the big dining table, which could accommodate more than twenty guests, listening to the sound of his fork and knife against the china plate. He was used by then to Sofia Timoleon's strange sense of hospitality. After dinner he strolled around the gardens, smoking a cigar-ette to aid digestion, and suddenly caught a glimpse of her in the lit window of her bedroom before she disappeared behind the heavy curtains. Their interview took place the following day after breakfast when Sofia Timoleon came to the veranda with a glass of diet cola in her hand and an air of happiness: she had lost weight.

'Good morning, Ian,' she had said.

It was the first time that she called him by his first name, and he did not understand why until later on, when the sun moved higher and they continued their interview under the lemon trees in the garden. Ian Forster asked everything he wanted to ask, mostly clarifications of earlier information she had already given him. At lunchtime he finally thanked Sofia for her co-operation and asked her if there was anything else she would like to add. Sofia Timoleon leaned over the table and pressed the stop button on the tape recorder.

'Tell me, Mr Forster,' she said. 'What is your marital status?'

This was how their affair began, with a direct assault under the lemon trees that took the Englishman by surprise. Since then they had met every few weeks, usually in London but never in Ian Forster's small flat: Marco Timoleon might have had someone watching it. Instead, Sofia checked in to a hotel, and he met her there late at night, coming up through the service entrance. It was a happy time for both of them. The morning after their first night together she woke up and told him: 'You surprise me. I thought all Englishmen made love with their socks on.' He had laughed, but then she had said something that troubled him: 'If my father knew, he'd kill you. Not so much because he's fond of me but because he's fond of you.' Ian Forster was not worried about his own fate but about his book's. He was afraid that if Marco Timoleon knew about the relationship he would end their collaboration and forbid him to publish not just the biography but as little as an article about him, according to the powers given him by their legal agreement. When the unplanned pregnancy happened, the Englishman's fears had reached the point of despair.

It was Sofia who had come up with the solution. Twenty-four years old and with a long history of failed relationships that had given her only disappointment, she seemed to have greeted her pregnancy as the only good thing that had happened to her in her life. To abort the baby was out of the question. But she had told him that they could deceive her father for both the baby's and the book's sake. It was now the end of August, and the baby was not due until February. If Ian Forster, who had almost finished his book, could submit the manuscript soon, then Sofia would help him press for her father's approval before the end of the year. Then there would be nothing Marco Timoleon could do to stop its publication. Also: when Sofia's belly started to swell, she could easily attribute the first signs to the frequent fluctuations of her weight that had plagued her all her life. Then she would simply avoid seeing her father until the birth.

'It's a perfect plan,' Sofia Timoleon had said. 'It'll work.'

Provided, of course, that her father remained in the dark about her affair with his official biographer.

Ian Forster stood behind her and looked out of the window. On the veranda the final preparations for the birthday party were under way. Servants were hurrying in and out of the villa, carrying tables covered with crisp white tablecloths and laying them with candlesticks, plates and cutlery. Other staff lit the orange lanterns hanging on the rose bushes until the garden began to glimmer. The sun had long set, but the launch had not returned. The chairs and the music stands on the small stage at the edge of the veranda stood empty: the Parisian orchestra that would be providing the evening's entertainment was now very late.

'I hate this party,' Sofia Timoleon said. 'Papillon had more fun.'

She was thinking of the film from the novel with the same title, which had played in the cinemas not long before: sentenced to life imprisonment in a French penal colony for a crime he did not commit, Henri Charrière attempts many times to escape until after thirteen years he succeeds. A gentle wind cooled the evening and white waves broke the surface of the sea. Far away the launch finally appeared, moving up and down under the moonlight.

'It'll soon be over,' the Englishman said.

Sofia Timoleon watched the arrival of the launch from the mainland with disappointment. Its delay had been her last hope that the party, planned to last all night, would be replaced by a brief dinner, a much less tormenting affair. Now she had to submit herself to a celebration that she had only agreed to in order to please her father: it was part of her plan to help Ian Forster get his book published. When the musicians stepped ashore, their white jackets, black trousers and shoes were soaked from the rough crossing on the open boat, the cases with their instruments were filled with water, and they were seasick. But they were there.

'I have to dress up,' Sofia Timoleon said.

Ian Forster still lay in bed.

'Don't try to escape now,' he said.

'Make the best of what we offer you,' she quoted from *Papillon*, 'and you will suffer less than you deserve.'

She left the room with a furtive kiss even though no one

could see them. Elsewhere in the villa, Olivia Timoleon had almost recovered from her journey. Finding herself alone in the unfamiliar surroundings of the guest room, where she had never slept in the six years she had known her husband, she dropped on to the bed, buried her head in the pillow and began to cry, putting into her tears all her disappointment about her marriage, all the humiliation of her demotion from hostess to one of the guests, all her anger towards Marco Timoleon and his daughter. Slowly she fell asleep and had a strange dream: she lived in a big house where suddenly the walls, the ceilings and stairs shrank more and more until she was trapped in a doll's house.

The dream upset her. She woke up and had a long shower that cleared her eyes, took three aspirins with a glass of champagne and dressed up in an evening dress sparkling with threads of silver, which was appropriate for the occasion and the humid weather. The late arrival of the orchestra had disrupted the tight schedule of the birthday celebration. Deciding to ignore her husband, she took control of the situation. She went to the kitchen where the cooks had mutinied and restored order within minutes, then gathered together the waiters and gave them specific instructions regarding the serving of the food and the wine. She collected the damp suits of the musicians and replaced them with clothes from Marco Timoleon's closets, which did not fit them well, and then she went to welcome the guests who were coming out to the veranda.

She always sought consolation in her duties as a hostess, a role that filled her empty days when Marco Timoleon travelled on, or on the pretext of, business. After their marriage the couple had lived in Paris, in the apartment on avenue Montaigne, until Marco Timoleon suggested they spend some time apart because things were not working. Olivia moved to their New York penthouse where at least she was close to home and her friends, and there she still lived, alone at the top of a steel-and-glass tower on Fifth Avenue, waiting for a phone call that was not coming. Arranged on two floors, the penthouse was a maze with high ceilings, wooden floors and white walls, which she chose not to hang with decorations. Wide windows of brown-tinted glass extended from floor to ceiling and did not open: the air in the apartment circulated through air conditioners working round the clock. Fifty floors above ground, the noise of the traffic faded into a gentle whisper that added to the solitude of the big rooms where Olivia Timoleon wandered in and out like a ghost, dressed in loose shirts and flared trousers. From the moment she woke up until the time she went to bed at night, she was constantly reminded of Marco Timoleon by his clothes and shoes, abandoned in the closets like the flotsam of a shipwreck, by the thick albums of their holiday photographs and a box of cigars in the dining room that gave off a heavy fragrance but which she refused to throw away.

She had put into her second marriage all her efforts, her imagination and good will in an attempt to make things work when everyone was predicting the opposite. She had forgiven Marco his infidelities, about which she was kept up to date by the glossy magazines; she had shrugged off his insults, often made in public; but above all she had endured his violent temper. At the same time, she had magnified his small acts of kindness – an occasional gift, a rare night of lovemaking, a letter arriving unexpectedly – and justified his behaviour to others. In fact, there seemed to be nothing that Marco Timoleon could do during the first few years of their marriage to drive her away, and it was widely supposed that Olivia was either too greedy or that she suffered from Stockholm syndrome: the victim becoming sympathetic towards her captor.

After graduating from college, Olivia Andersen had worked as a trainee journalist for an international magazine, a job that allowed her to travel first within America and later all over the world, writing about anything from sports and culture to politics and cooking. Cornelius Andersen disapproved. Her father wished that she would become a lawyer or company executive, a desk job that would have allowed her time to find a husband and then resign to look after her family. For this reason he refused to be impressed by her success, warning her: 'No one has found a spouse in the pages of the *Reader's Digest*.' She was already well known in New York circles as a journalist and socialite before meeting Marco Timoleon at the gala in the Waldorf-Astoria, but since then she had become famous across the world.

Now that she lived alone again she preferred to invite friends over than leave her apartment. There she could be a good hostess and have intelligent conversations that placated her loneliness, holding old-fashioned literary salons where writers and artists gathered to discuss their work and argue in loud voices that could be heard several floors below. Once she had also invited Ian Forster, who happened to be in New York at the time, but he arrived without knowing what to expect and froze in awe on the doorstep when he saw the famous guests. She had found it amusing. 'Come in, Mr Forster,' she had said. 'Literary lions don't bite.'

During the evening he had complimented her on her apartment, but Olivia Timoleon had dismissed his admiration:

'In truth,' she had said, 'I'm only a madwoman locked in an attic.'

It was true that her attitude slowly changed after Marco

Timoleon shut the door in her face and stopped returning her calls. She became bitter and her revenge was to spend his money on luxury clothing, antiques and entertainment. Once a month she posted him the receipts and invoices for him to pay, knowing very well how much he resented wasting his wealth on things that did not give him pleasure. She set off in her shopping campaigns at midday when a limousine picked her up from home and drove her across Manhattan where she plundered the best shops, giving her address and asking for the goods to be delivered later because she would have needed a van to do it herself. She bought everything that took her fancy: designer clothes and shoes, rugs and linen, antiques, cases of wine, furniture. When her apartment was filled with her purchases, most of which remained unopened, she hired a van to take everything to thrift shops across the Harlem River where Saint Olivia the Martyr was famed for her generosity. Marco Timoleon flew into a rage every time he heard that another consignment of luxury goods had gone to help the poor of the Bronx, but he paid up because if he did not, he would be admitting defeat. One time, seeing his friend fret over the exorbitant bills, Dr Patrikios had joked: 'You shouldn't be complaining. What she does is taking you with her to heaven.'

After several months of resisting her friends' urgings, Olivia Timoleon had finally agreed to file for divorce, but then the phone had rung: Marco was inviting her to Sofia's birthday party.

All the guests were on the veranda but not their host. Only four people had seen Marco Timoleon since their arrival on the island: his wife, his daughter, his biographer and his doctor. Those who had made their way up the stairs to greet him had been turned away by the servants before reaching the door of his study. Olivia Timoleon apologised on his behalf, inventing a business emergency that he had to take care of and trying to make up for his absence. She set the waiters in motion among the crowd to hand out drinks and canapés, instructed the orchestra to play louder in an attempt to cover up the murmur of discontent and introduced everyone to each other several times in order to buy time. She was in her element. Her nervousness only returned when Sofia joined the party and the guests rushed to offer her their best wishes. Olivia Timoleon wished her a happy birthday, and Sofia told her what she told the others too: 'It's not until midnight.'

'Then happy birthday for last year,' Olivia said. 'The last time I saw you, you were twenty-three.'

Olivia Timoleon complimented her stepdaughter on her Givenchy dress but reserved most of her admiration for the young woman's slim figure, knowing that it would be a short-lived victory in a war lost a long time ago. She was also intrigued to notice, the way only one who has been in a similar situation could notice, the young woman's calm confidence that could not simply be the effect of pills: Sofia seemed genuinely happy. There was a grace in the way she moved that Olivia had not seen before, as if her body was weightless, and that could only have to do with the secret of her pregnancy that was not secret. Olivia Timoleon took her stepdaughter's hands and repeated her amazement about her weight. Sofia shrugged off her comments.

'It's not important,' she said. 'I just don't have much appetite lately.'

Olivia guided her through the crowd, avoiding with great skill the guests who were trying to talk to Sofia. Across the veranda clouds of tobacco smoke rose up into the air like ghosts escaping the world of the living. The cool wind from the sea shook the glimmering lanterns on the rose bushes and the dark shapes of the trees beyond them, which were lit only by the moonlight.

'I have to talk to you,' Olivia Timoleon said.

They were standing at the corner of the veranda with their backs to the guests, who at last had left them in peace. For a while Olivia Timoleon talked about the preparations for the party, she talked about the food that was cooking in the kitchen, which she had had the chance to taste already, the many guests who had come from afar, the beautiful night they were having, which was fortunate because it was the end of the summer and the weather could not be trusted even in the Mediterranean, she talked about anything, apart from the matter she had promised her husband to talk to her stepdaughter about until a feeling of urgency came over her, and she risked a sombre comment:

'The truth is that you're your father's last hope of happiness.'

Sofia Timoleon looked at her and burst into laughter. She always thought that her stepmother was prone to histrionics, and it amused her to see her trying to control her temperament. It was malice, yes, but she also felt a certain consolation that she was not alone in the middle of the ocean without a lifebelt. She did not like to admit it, but it seemed to her that they were both her father's victims, and she thought about that now, leaning against the veranda rail. She felt the rust on the rail and the hardened salt from the cold winds that lashed the island from November to April when no one visited, not even her father. In winter the villa was boarded up and only a few guards remained, whose main task was to light the oil lamps on the three graves behind Saint Mark of the Cypresses.

'I thought *you* were my father's last hope of happiness,' Sofia Timoleon said with irony.

'He's a man of a certain age,' Olivia continued, enduring the comment. 'And his health, I hope I'm wrong, but his health is not as good as it used to be. The accident—'

'Because he can't get it up?' Sofia asked.

Her stepmother blushed.

'That's a lie,' she said.

'How would you know?'

A waiter approached with a tray of glasses. Sofia Timoleon asked him to bring her a glass of cola.

'So,' she resumed. 'My father's an old man. And I'm his last hope.'

The waiter returned with her cola. Sofia Timoleon took a long sip.

'And how do you enter into the equation?' she asked.

'I want to help,' Olivia said.

They could not ignore the guests any more. People came up to them to kiss their hands, kiss their cheeks, wish Sofia Timoleon happy birthday. The young woman let the stream of guests carry her away.

'Thank you,' she said. 'But I'm really not the one who needs help.'

Six months after Olivia Andersen had first met Marco Timoleon, he had proposed to her. A few days later, she was landing in Paris. Marco waited for her at the apartment, took her coat and showed her into the living room where a young woman in a soiled sweater and old jeans was lying on the floor, smoking and doing an enormous jigsaw puzzle. Sofia had begun putting the pieces together two days earlier and had still not finished, pausing only to go to bed or the toilet. She had not greeted their guest but continued to smoke, immersed in her pastime. Olivia Andersen had done everything she could to win her over that day, the next and every day afterwards until the break-up of her marriage. She sent her gifts, invited her to

New York and to her parents' house in New England, she took her shopping in London, gave her advice, but every time they met it was as if they were meeting each other for the first time. For a while, she held all this back from her husband, who was under the impression the two women had agreed a ceasefire. Then one day she told him:

'Your daughter hates me.'

Marco Timoleon had tried to reassure her.

'Nonsense. She hates everyone.'

Dressed in a borrowed dinner jacket, Ian Forster joined the party a moment later. He, too, was surprised by the absence of their host. The first thing he did was to stop a waiter, drink two glasses of champagne and take a third one with him, as he wandered among the famous crowd that was breaking up into smaller groups. Everyone was talking loudly and ignoring the music. He stood in a group of people chatting and looked for a long time at a short balding man with a moustache who spoke bad English. He recognised him as the Dictator, a good friend of Marco Timoleon, who had ruled the country for more than six years, but not any more: he was supposed to be in prison, serving a life sentence. He was in high spirits, joking with everyone and asking the women to dance, but they ignored him. Ian Forster, who had solved the mystery of the Mediterranean accent after many hours of interviews with Marco Timoleon, was the only one of the guests on the veranda able to understand him. Having found in him a sympathetic ear, the Dictator took him by the arm and talked to him about his intention to return to politics as the leader of a parliamentary party that one day would come to power. The Englishman watched him mopping his high forehead, watched his fixed gaze and the tense movements of his hands and did not reply, slipping away as soon as he had the chance.

Dr Patrikios was the only guest who had not changed for the occasion. His cream linen suit was crumpled from his having lain in the deckchair that afternoon, and his shoes were covered in dust from a long walk around the island he had taken to make the time pass until the party. Ian Forster was glad to see him.

'*A man hath no better thing under the sun than to eat and to drink and to be merry,*' the doctor said. 'Whoever wrote that did us doctors a great service.'

The weather was still pleasant. Perfumed by the roses in the garden, the evening breeze cooled the air and rocked the *Sofia*, which was anchored in the bay with its lights on. Urged by Olivia Timoleon, the orchestra played instrumental arrangements of pop songs of the day in no specific order, conducted by a tall Frenchman with a pencil moustache. The musicians were dressed in the assortment of suits, sweaters and leather jackets that had been looted from Marco Timoleon's forgotten closets. Ian Forster spotted the Dictator near the orchestra, dancing with a young woman.

'Stay away from that man, doctor,' he said. 'He's mad.'

Dr Patrikios nodded in agreement.

'Worse still, Mr Forster, he suffers from halitosis.'

The young man finished his champagne and took another glass. The doctor asked for lemonade and drank it standing next to the Englishman and watching him as if he were a long distance away. They chatted about the famous guests they each recognised in the crowd, commented on the canapés and both dismissed the choice of music but from opposite ends of the spectrum: Ian Forster would have preferred rock while the doctor, who had a weakness for classical music, would have compromised on contemporary jazz. The Englishman mentioned several bands that the doctor might like, but their names meant nothing to the older man. Ian Forster asked:

'Doctor, could I please have a word with you when you've got a spare moment?'

The other man raised his eyebrows.

'Aren't we having a word already, Mr Forster?'

'About the book.'

'Ah. That would be very difficult.'

The two men had first met shortly after the Englishman had approached Marco Timoleon to propose that he write his biography. Dr Patrikios was the only person Marco had asked for his opinion before making his decision. The doctor had not been in favour. He had said: 'It would be like playing with a loaded gun.' He had foreseen then that it would be very difficult for Marco Timoleon to hide from the ambitious biographer the secrets of his past that needed to remain secret. True, there had been several unauthorised biographies, but those had proved to be hopeless attempts that had not broken into Marco's privacy, revealing instead random and harmless details about his sex life and his business affairs. Dr Patrikios thought that the appointment of Ian Forster as his friend's official biographer meant the young man would have the key to the vaults and the opportunity to interview people close to the tycoon, picking up stray pieces of information not intended for the public domain, to say the least. For this reason Dr Patrikios always chose his words carefully whenever the young Englishman was within earshot.

As a matter of fact, it was the doctor who had suggested the confidentiality agreement to his friend. He himself had granted the Englishman just one interview, and this only after Marco Timoleon had intervened, but it revealed little that Ian Forster had not known already. They had met in Dr Patrikios's Brooklyn practice despite Ian Forster's willingness to meet him anywhere and at any time. They had talked for less than thirty minutes when Dr Patrikios stood up and offered his hand. The biographer had asked for a little more time, but the doctor had been resolute: 'I'm afraid this is the end of the talk show. I'm very busy.'

So when that evening at the birthday party Ian Forster talked to him about scheduling another interview, he was disappointed but not surprised that the doctor refused.

'Maybe you're here in a professional capacity, Mr Forster,' Dr Patrikios said. 'But I'm here as a friend. This is a birthday celebration, so I intend to celebrate.'

He gazed at the stars like an astronomer and began to study the clouds that had stood above the island all day but had so far brought no rain. Almost an hour had passed since the guests had gathered on the veranda and the mood was not improving. Boredom was beginning to overcome the crowd's curiosity about their host's whereabouts, and the danger of the food getting cold was now imminent. Suddenly, a loud cry brought the party to life:

'Intruder!'

On the stage a saxophonist dropped his instrument and tried to escape from the security guards. He first went towards the villa but changed his mind and turned in the direction of the gardens. The waiters quickly blocked his escape, and he ran towards the beach, taking off his shoes on the way, but was arrested as he was entering the water. They brought him back, wet and shaking from fear. The Dictator, who was the one who had recognised him, confirmed that he was a well-known investigative reporter. They searched him and found a miniature camera, which they immediately smashed on the floor, and a nautical chart of the area around the island.

'Look for the cyanide capsule,' the Dictator said.

He did not have one. When they interrogated him, he admitted that he had paid one of the musicians to take his place, and he had taken saxophone lessons for nine weeks. Who knows what they would have done to him if Dr Patrikios had not intervened to calm everyone down and suggest that they take him to their host to decide his fate. Dressed in his dinner jacket, Marco Timoleon had watched everything from the window of his study, smoking one last cigar before summoning the courage to face his guests. When they brought the man in, he looked at him, studied the broken pieces of the miniature camera and shook his head.

'What worries me most is not this nonsense, but that you're wearing my check suit,' he said.

The young reporter explained that Mrs Timoleon had dressed the orchestra in dry clothes while their cabaret suits dried on the line. Marco Timoleon listened in silence, his eyes betraying no emotion. Then he questioned the intruder to make sure he was the only uninvited visitor that night, threatening to set Soraya on him if he lied, and when he was satisfied that the reporter had acted alone, he ordered his guards to lock him in the basement with enough food and wine, and in the morning he would decide his punishment. The Dictator insisted that they should press charges, but Marco Timoleon disagreed.

'We will be playing his game if we do, Mr President. It'll be a great story for the papers, and it's certain your name will find its way into their pages too.'

In the end he convinced him. Then Marco Timoleon asked him and his other guests to return to the veranda where he would be joining them shortly for dinner, but he stopped his daughter from going too.

'Please,' he said. 'You stay.'

They sat in the armchairs facing the unlit fireplace, in a silence broken only by the first notes of music that flew in from the open windows: the orchestra had taken its place back on the platform. Marco Timoleon tapped his fingers and hummed the tune, waiting for his daughter to say something about the matter of the pregnancy. But she said nothing. He waited for a long time before her silence convinced him that his wife had not kept her word.

'I guess Olivia didn't have the chance to talk to you,' he said.

'Oh, she did.'

Marco Timoleon looked at his daughter.

'So?'

'She's worried about your health.'

'There's nothing wrong with my health. Was that all you talked about?'

Sofia nodded. Marco Timoleon had not expected that he would have to confront his daughter with the news himself. He had hoped that when they met the shock of the revelation would have passed, and they could have discussed the matter in a rational manner. So be it. He began by enquiring about her journey, asking whom the yacht she had arrived on belonged to, who was on board and whether she had had a pleasant time so far. While he listened, the phone on his desk rang, but he did not answer it. Sofia spoke about the trip a little, answering most of her father's questions with a shrug of her shoulders. This was the first time they had sat face to face after not being on speaking terms for some time. She had broken off diplomatic relations with her father because of his constant interference in her private life and his wish to marry her off to a man of his choice, an eternal plot of his made more frustrating ever since she had fallen in love with Ian Forster. While they talked, the smell of food began to fill the room. Marco Timoleon felt irritated. Despite the absence of both the host of the party and its guest of honour, someone had decided to serve dinner: Olivia, no doubt. He struck a match and lit a cigar. When he spoke again, he could have been speaking to himself.

'I know you don't like her,' he said. 'But I owe her my life.'

Olivia Andersen had been the saviour not only of his heart but also his liver: when he first met her, five years after the death of Sofia's mother, he was a certified alcoholic. She had pulled him back from the edge of the precipice with her common sense, devotion and patience when the world had written him off. Sofia Timoleon did not want to admit it but knew it was not far from the truth. She remembered her father's decline that had followed her mother's death, and it was what had ultimately convinced her that he had not killed her. It had been slow and imperceptible at first. Then he, who never fell ill, had started to complain of headaches and stomach pains. When his body could no longer take the daily punishment of his vices, he would collapse in bed where he lay naked for days on end, watching gangster films, smoking cigars and eating little. But he was still capable of staging remarkable resurrections that flew in the face of medical forecasts. When news of his condition had leaked to the press and his business partners threatened to dissolve their contracts, Marco Timoleon had called an extraordinary board meeting and two days later flew out to New York where he walked into the boardroom unaided, dressed in his black suit, white shirt and black tie, his hair combed back and shining with cream. He gave the board members a lingering look of contempt, took the cigar from his mouth and said: 'Treachery betrays itself in the end.' Then he got down to business. His appearance that day had calmed down his partners, terrorised his rivals and restored the confidence of the banks in him. For several hours Marco Timoleon had talked with great clarity and ease, and when the meeting ended, he saw off his associates at the door, shaking each one's hand and patting them on the back. After they were all gone, he shut the door and said: 'Bastards!' He then fell to the floor in a high fever.

Sofia Timoleon was too young at the time to have any influence over him. It was when Olivia Andersen had entered his life that he finally got out of bed, cut down on alcohol and tobacco and started enjoying life and work again. He did all this not because she talked him into it but because he had fallen in love. Now, almost six years since the couple had first met, he relied on no one but himself again. He took a puff on his cigar.

'But it's also true that my wife is the victim of her success,' he said.

Then he told his daughter the news that he knew would please her: he could no longer stay with Olivia simply out of gratitude. But before he could ask for a divorce, he had to safeguard his fortune from the storm of demands that her lawyers would certainly raise.

'You know that the only thing I hope for is that one day you'll take over the business,' he said. 'But only if you want to.'

He stood up and walked to the window. On the veranda his guests were already seated for dinner.

'I'd hate to lie in my coffin thinking I squandered my life for nothing,' he said, looking at the party.

Still facing the night, he pulled his handkerchief from his breast pocket and wiped his eyes. Then he took out of his pocket her birthday present, a sapphire and diamond bracelet bought over the phone from a Beverly Hills jeweller and which he had planned to give her at midnight. It was an illusionist's diversion: he wanted to soften the blow of what he was about to say. Not suspecting anything, Sofia gave him a kiss and stretched out her hand. He fastened the bracelet round her wrist with the solemnity of signing a peace accord, and for a second he forgot the reason for their meeting. When Sofia stood, saying that she had to return to the party, he realised he had run out of time and was forced to tell her without further delay:

'You can't bring a child into the world rashly.'

Sofia Timoleon did not have to turn and look at her father to know that he knew everything. His next words confirmed it: 'I know who he is.'

Only then did Sofia realise that the birthday celebration was part of a plan to bring her and Ian Forster to her father, so that he could persuade them to end the affair. Angry more at herself than her father for having let him deceive her, she unclipped the bracelet and let it drop to the floor, opened the door and walked out of the study, determined never to speak to him again. But she changed her mind and turned round.

'Go to hell,' she said.

She banged the door. Marco Timoleon picked up the diamond bracelet from the floor, put it back in its black velvet case, placed the case in the safe behind Eugenia Timoleon's portrait and relit his cigar. He considered his strategy not to allow the situation to get out of hand the way he would have considered a business plan: with the calmness that had saved him on many occasions in his life. He paced round the room deep in thought, oblivious to the music playing under his window. He lifted the phone and instructed his guards not to let his daughter leave the island, not tonight, not tomorrow, not any other day unless he gave them permission himself. He then turned off the lights in order not to be seen standing at the window and from the darkness of his study contemplated the dinner on the veranda. The trays of food on the tables stirred up a dislike in him as did the fakery of the whole occasion. But nothing could make him reconsider. He stayed at the window a long time, smoking, until the dinner ended and the guests stood again. The waiters cleared the veranda, carried the tables and chairs back to the villa, and the music grew louder, inviting the guests to the empty space in front of the bandstand where they began to dance under the stars and the paper lanterns.

HIS GREATEST MOMENT HAD COME IN THE 1950S, DURING the crisis that followed the nationalisation of the Suez Canal. Oil producers suddenly desperate for ships to transport oil over the much longer distance around the Cape of Good Hope came to him for help, and Marco Timoleon was able to profit by contracting his supertankers at extortionate prices, which he would never have achieved under different circumstances. When his clients protested, he shrugged: 'War is hell.' Within months he became one of the richest men in the world, but his refusal to negotiate also made him many enemies, who pursued him like the Furies for the rest of his life. Outwardly defiant, Marco Timoleon was in truth deeply worried about his rivals' attacks. Once he told his biographer: 'The whole world is after me, Mr Forster.' It was true, up to a point, that a big part of international business took a very dim view of him: a pirate with a peg-leg, an eye patch and a cutlass, a persona which he himself had encouraged in order to gain notoriety.

He did not have to admit it publicly for those close to him to know that over time this pressure affected him deeply. He became mistrustful not only of the people he did business with but also of his own employees, people who loved him and cared about the company because he was a generous employer whose door in those days was open to all of them. When he dared to accuse Sylvia Frank, saying that she, too, was undermining him, things came to a head.

'Stop trying to run this company,' he told her. 'It's not called Frank Enterprises for a reason.'

Mrs Frank was not the person to take insults lying down. In her lifelong involvement with Marco Timoleon, she never thought of herself as his subordinate but as his collaborator, friend and equal, not only because her ambition told her so but because he too thought of her in those terms. His attitude to her was in contrast to his generally low opinion of women. He liked to quote Aristotle: *The courage of a man is shown in commanding, of a woman in obeying.* He never said it in front of her not out of politeness but because her talent and accomplishments simply disproved it. Then one day he did say it to her face, and Mrs Frank answered back: 'Asshole!'

Marco Timoleon fired her on the spot. She said nothing but went to her office and started to put her things in a box: her tea service, her beloved Siamese cat, which she had had stuffed for posterity, the bust of Verdi, which reminded her of her life on the stage. Marco Timoleon waited until he heard the door of her office shut, and then he lit a cigar and paced round his desk, angry not only with her but with the whole world because they did not understand him. Besides, it was a matter of discipline and trust: she had to obey him even when he was wrong. After counting to ten, he called the doorman and told him not to let Mrs Frank leave the building. When she came back, he reinstated her. Neither of them offered an apology.

Sylvia Frank was close to him, and Ian Forster believed that the incident must have affected him more than he let on when he told his biographer the story nearly twenty years later. She was not just another of his employees; they had been together since 1939 when Timoleon Enterprises, Inc. was founded in New

York. The day he registered his company, one of the happiest of his life, he had walked into his offices in the Chanin Building with a bottle of champagne and a big cake. When Mrs Frank had asked him what they were celebrating, he told her: 'Mrs Frank, I've just made an honest woman of you.' Then he confessed that the company she had been working for for the past several months had not existed until that very morning, when he registered it. Sylvia Frank had been dismayed. Since then she made sure that she knew what went on in the company, down to the slightest detail, and this became the cause of their frequent clashes.

His confrontations with his employees led Marco Timoleon to reconsider his policy of keeping his office door open. He did more than to shut it. He moved to the top floor of the London building where the company headquarters were in the 1950s, and from then on saw only those members of his staff he asked to see himself. A private lift, operated by a liveried commission-aire, brought the visitor to a waiting room furnished with plush sofas. At a small desk, a secretary checked the visitor's name and offered him refreshments before notifying her employer. Marco Timoleon's office occupied most of the floor and had a view across the Thames. His large Louis XV writing desk took pride of place, of course, in a vast room laid with a yellow carpet woven with his initials in black. In the afternoons, Marco Timoleon liked to slip out of the office, usually down the emer-gency staircase at the back of the building, and walk along the bank of the river. He bought food from the street vendors, who had no idea that he was one of the richest men in the world, and he ate leaning against the balustrade of the Embankment and watching the slow barges that slid up and down the river.

It seems that loneliness did not overpower him in a single decisive attack but drew a little closer every time something happened to upset his calculations. It could be anything;

his universe seemed to stand in a strange balance. He was indomitable against attack by his business rivals, but a mere snub could instantly stir a deep sense of worthlessness within him. He was particularly vulnerable to aristocrats and old money, people like his father-in-law. Daniel Negri, who had quickly noticed his weakness, took advantage of it and tormented him in any way he could. One time Marco Timoleon was walking around an antiques shop in New York when he saw on display the Fabergé cigarette case he had bought his father-in-law the previous Christmas. The discovery hurt his feelings, so the next time he was in the Negri apartment he asked the old man why he had sold it. Daniel Negri had just shrugged: 'Because I've given up smoking.'

It was soon after Miranda and Marco moved to London that he began to suffer from the insomnia he would never really defeat but would learn, at least, how to use to his advantage. He could not remember exactly when it first happened, but he guessed it had to do with the demands of his business, which was growing rapidly. When the problem started, his peace of mind strayed into a labyrinth from which it never came out again. Anxiety would always be there even at moments when he was unaware of it, like the distant noise of traffic. Dr Patrikios, who examined him, found nothing wrong and simply recommended a glass of warm milk before bed and a better mattress. Neither helped. Finding it more and more difficult to have a nap, Marco Timoleon began to stay awake the entire night, reading the phone book in the hope that it would send him to sleep, but as soon as his eyes started to droop, and he lay down in bed, he woke up again. So he stopped trying to sleep and spent the night reading his father's books. It was his insomnia, therefore, that made him a lover of classical literature, which he studied in depth until he understood most of it and could repeat long passages from memory, to people's amazement because they thought of him as a philistine. His condition had an effect on his social life too. Since he could not sleep, he spent more nights in clubs and restaurants and invited friends to his house where he entertained, to his wife's despair, until four or five in the morning.

He always maintained that those were happy days. A year after moving to London, Miranda Timoleon gave birth to Anna Eugenia, later renamed Sofia, a healthy baby who kept the house awake at night with her crying. Because of his insomnia, Marco Timoleon did not mind, but after a while Miranda could not bear the torment and had the cot moved to a room two floors up in their six-storey house in Mayfair. To make amends, she decorated the room herself, painting clowns and animals in bright colours on the Georgian walls, hanging happy curtains and scattering soft toys everywhere. Despite Marco's objections, she breast-fed neither Sofia nor Daniel, a decision that had as much to do with the antiquated tradition that noblewomen do not breast-feed as with the popularity of infant formula in the 1950s. Shortly afterwards Miss Abigail Rees joined the family to oversee the children's education.

In London the family lived in a redbrick house on Green Street that had views towards Hyde Park. The pillared porch at the entrance led through a foyer into a panelled, high-ceiling hall decorated with a Persian carpet, a pair of Imari vases and a Chippendale longcase clock. Doors with architraves led to a reception room, an octagonal dining room with a vaulted ceiling, the main kitchen and a conservatory on two levels. A broad, curving staircase with wrought-iron balusters in the entrance hall led to the upper floors. On the first floor was the drawing room, which spanned the front of the house and had big windows that filled the room with natural light. Next to them was

Miranda's baby grand piano. This was where the Timoleons held their formal receptions. On that floor was also the library, with its vaulted ceiling and Orientalist paintings that Marco Timoleon had bought because they reminded him of his birthplace. On the bookshelves he displayed his father's large collection of classics. The house had seven bedrooms. The master bedroom was on the second floor, furnished and decorated in tones of blue and had windows above the street. There were four more bedrooms with *en suite* bathrooms on the third floor, and on the fourth a large games room, two more bedrooms and bathrooms and a small kitchen for preparing light meals. In the basement was a large swimming pool with a bar and the staff quarters.

Miranda Timoleon's waters had broken in a big gush one night in August 1950 while the couple slept, a normal event that had nevertheless worried Marco Timoleon. He knew nothing about childbirth, having rejected Miranda's attempts to educate him by insisting: 'All I need to know is the bottom line: babies are delivered by storks.' In the morning her contractions had been more frequent, and the midwife had come to be with her. The waiting had agitated Marco Timoleon even more, and suddenly the house seemed to become too small for him. He ran up and down the floors, taking the lift and then the stairs, smoking his cigar and giving orders to the servants about relevant and irrelevant matters, which he changed and later changed again. By early afternoon his behaviour had exhausted both the staff and Miranda, and she had to send him to work, promising that she would call if there was any change. He reluctantly agreed but decided not to take the car. Escorted by his bodyguard, he walked down Piccadilly, then Haymarket, and was on the Strand when he suddenly stopped and said: 'We have to go to the hospital *now*.' His bodyguard flagged down a taxi, which took them to the hospital. Miranda Timoleon had arrived five minutes earlier.

Many years later Ian Forster managed to track down his old bodyguard, who was by then living in a retirement home, and asked him about it. He did not remember the incident but gave the biographer the answer that he was given countless times during his research: 'If Mr Timoleon said it happened, then it did.'

Nothing shows better Marco Timoleon's exhilaration at the time than his decision to build a yacht in honour of his first-born. The project took twelve months to complete, by which time the matter of the baby's name had been settled, and the yacht was launched with a bottle of champagne broken against its bows before its name was unveiled: M/Y *Sofia*. At more than three hundred and twenty feet long, she was the largest and most luxurious yacht in the world until Queen Elizabeth's *Britannia* was built two years later, a fact that Marco Timoleon would grudgingly admit, always hastening to add that many more film stars, statesmen and aristocrats were invited to the *Sofia* in any given year than the royal yacht would ever see in its life. The white trim yacht sailed under the Liberian flag and had a crew of forty, who were instructed to fulfil any request of the passengers. These were accommodated in eighteen staterooms furnished in the same exquisite taste as the rest of the yacht, whose centrepiece was a luminous fireplace in the living room made from lapis lazuli.

The construction of the yacht confirmed Marco and Miranda Timoleon's place in the limelight. In summer the family flew to Monte Carlo where the *Sofia* spent the winter, and they sailed across the Mediterranean in the company of friends, stopping wherever took their fancy. Until Miranda Timoleon's death in 1964, their adventures dominated the pages of magazines and newspapers across the world. She was generally indifferent to the press, unlike her husband who had a voracious appetite for anything that was written about him: he received a stack of magazines and newspapers daily, which he scanned for his name while sipping his morning coffee. Not all the stories published were true, of course. Often they were written without the journalist having left his desk because it was impossible to catch up with the tycoon when he set off on his fabulous voyages. Saying now that Marco Timoleon sought publicity at the time would be an understatement. The captain of the *Sofia* had told Ian Forster the story of how one morning he was asked to go and see Marco, who was sitting at the stern, reading the news. Marco Timoleon showed him the newspaper.

'Your navigational skills aren't up to much, captain,' he said. 'We're in the wrong place. It says here we're holidaying in the Aegean.'

And then he had ordered him to set course for the Greek islands.

After Sofia's birth Marco Timoleon gave up philandering, a decision he was not aware that he had made until the presence of a beautiful young woman on board, a friend of a friend, confirmed it. Marco did not know her but treated her with the politeness and attention with which he treated all his guests without it ever crossing his mind that she was the type of woman who in the old days he would have pursued. One night they were alone at the bar of the yacht, and she touched his arm.

'This rocking makes me sick,' she said. 'I think I'll go to my cabin.'

'Take Dramamine,' Marco Timoleon suggested.

It was not until later that night, leaning against the rail to smoke his last cigar of the day, that he understood the historic significance of his words.

186

'Hell!' he exclaimed. 'I'm a saint.'

It was he who told Ian Forster the story, but the biographer had no reason not to believe him on this occasion: Marco was never a prude. He was sincerely proud of his newfound virtue. Knowing him – as well as one could know him – Ian Forster could well imagine what a great accomplishment he must have considered it. He began to tell his wife, with the intention less of boasting than of flattering her: she had saved him from sin. What was at first slightly amusing soon began to irritate her, but she said nothing; Miranda Timoleon was a woman unwilling by nature to voice her thoughts, her feelings and bodily functions (she suffered from chronic constipation). When one night in bed he confided to her that another woman had made a pass at him, Miranda finally replied with a stern joke that sent a chill down Marco Timoleon's spine: 'If I ever catch you cheating, I'll stuff your head and hang it on the wall.'

He never made the mistake of talking to her about such matters again but continued to defend himself against his own notoriety. All summer they travelled from one Mediterranean port to another, stopping to visit ancient ruins, religious festivals and other attractions, welcoming more guests on board and swimming in the green waters of coves inaccessible by land. They always returned to the *Sofia* to sleep because no hotel could match the opulence of the yacht and the service of its crew. In Sorrento they ate in a small restaurant and sang until the sun came out; in Piraeus they were met by an enormous crowd, a brass band and the starstruck mayor welcoming Marco Timoleon to town; in Istanbul they visited the Ottoman mosques where Marco impressed his guests, who did not know his ancestry, by speaking Turkish. They were in Cyprus for the Feast of the Dormition, they sailed on to Alexandria to see the Roman ruins and on their way back to Monaco stopped at Malta so that Marco could let his guests beat him at golf.

Sofia and Daniel were always taken along on those summer cruises, often a lonely time for them because they were mostly surrounded by adults. The situation seemed to affect Sofia more than her brother. Daniel was a late talker, a problem Marco Timoleon had not seemed to worry about when Miranda brought it to his attention. He had said: 'Einstein didn't talk until he was three.' But even when Daniel did talk, he preferred to sit silently in a corner of the room and play alone rather than join his sister and parents, and their summer cruises on the *Sofia* encouraged this personality trait. It was a tendency not towards loneliness but more probably solitude: a state of being alone without feeling lonely. It was then that Daniel began to turn into the person he would be at the time of his death: a happy castaway on a desert island who made no effort to return to the world. One night on board the yacht, where the children shared the same cabin, Sofia woke up and heard him sobbing in bed. When she asked him why, Daniel had said: 'Because one day I'll die.' It was perhaps not a premonition but rather a child's re-action when he understands once and for all the certainty of death. Sofia Timoleon's response was also typical of the elder sibling: she told him to shut up and go back to sleep. The incident quickly disappeared in the bottom of her memory, but she recalled it again after the accident when her brother's words, innocent and true, came alive in her mind all at once.

In September the yacht would sail back to Monte Carlo, and the family would fly back to London where the children resumed their education under Miss Rees's supervision. Marco and Miranda came and went, travelling together or separately all winter on business or for pleasure. At Christmas the family skied at St Moritz where they owned a chalet. Miranda Timoleon, an expert skier who had once trained with the American Olympic team but had failed to qualify for the Games, tried for a long time to persuade her husband to learn. One year he finally gave in. Putting on his skis, he predicted with a sigh: 'The first time will also be my last.' Later that day he hit a tree at a great speed and was hospitalised for several months, wrapped in bandages and writhing in agony, which medication could not alleviate. The accident was more serious than his failed attempt to fly with an umbrella some years earlier. Perhaps it was more tragic than comic: Dr Patrikios would always suspect that his friend's concussion altered his behaviour. He noticed that since the skiing accident not only was Marco more easily distracted and more irritable than before but that his anxiety and depression had increased, as did his violent temper: signs of brain damage.

In the first few years of their marriage, Marco and Miranda Timoleon were very much in love, which was obvious to whomever happened to be near them. They were affectionate towards each other in public, laughed a lot and seemed to enjoy similar things despite their age difference. Age was not one of Marco Timoleon's concerns then. He felt that he was only starting to live, having almost achieved what he had set out to achieve. It was a rare time of peace for him that would not last. Ambition, in addition perhaps to that ski injury, slowly ate away at his contentment until one day he sat up in bed and declared: 'Life sucks.'

He threw himself into work with more energy than ever before. During this time he was away from home for days on end, travelling to foreign capitals to meet customers, bankers and co-operators, visiting shipyards that built more ships for him or arriving unexpectedly in ports on the other side of the world to inspect his existing fleet that was operating at full capacity. Miranda Timoleon was not always able to get him on the phone. He often changed plans on the move without letting her know either because of a certain emergency that he had to attend to or simply to confuse his competitors, who, he was convinced, were watching his every move. It was not long before he looked back on his bachelor past with longing. Again he began to sleep with women he met at random places, safe in the thought that he was far from home and his wife would not find out. His rule was to flirt with no one at a distance of less than twenty miles in any direction from their Mayfair house. Inspired by the first hydrogen bomb test in the Pacific in 1952, he called this *The Damage Radius*. But he slipped up when one night he met someone at the Edmundo Ros' Dinner and Supper Club on Regent Street that was only a mile away. In the morning he returned home and dragged himself into the shower where he stood under the water but felt too tired to soap himself. It was a fatal mistake. When he later lay in bed next to his wife, Miranda had only to sniff him once to notice the unfamiliar perfume. She said nothing right then, but the following evening she confronted him at dinner.

'Tell me her name,' she said. 'If there's going to be three of us in this marriage I shouldn't be calling her L'Air du Temps.'

Marco Timoleon sliced his steak and chewed for a long time, holding his wife's stare.

'I can't help you,' he said. 'I don't know her name.'

Miranda Timoleon would not stuff her husband's head and hang it on the wall as she had once threatened to do but would soon do worse: pay him back in kind.

She had grown up in a Christian house with strict elderly parents and had tasted none of the freedom and privileges her husband had enjoyed as a child. She had been kept indoors like a museum piece unless she had had to go to school or sports or music lessons to which she was driven by the family chauffeur. It was a noble upbringing that had fascinated Marco Timoleon and led him to marry her in order to be accepted into the expatriate aristocracy. He had appeared out of nowhere, and she had welcomed his proposal because he was her only chance to escape the world of rules that she lived in, a decision she would not regret until much later. The discovery of his infidelity caused her a quiet storm that raged under her skin. Her Catholic education had instilled the shame of divorce in her, but her motive for not asking Marco to end their marriage was less religious than maternal. She had said once: 'I have to admit he's the less useless parent of the two of us. The children need him.'

She was reluctant to split the family, loving her children in her own way. Sofia was her favourite. Daniel she thought of as too docile, and she always worried that the world would swamp him as soon as he left home. The problem was that the only men she ever got to know were her father and Marco Timoleon, both men of great tenacity, almost ruthless, and compared to them everyone else seemed a coward. If she had lived longer, she would have seen how wrong she had been to worry, not so much because Daniel changed with age but because he did find a place that was perfectly safe for him: inside himself.

Her one eccentricity concerned books for children. It began when the children were little and Miranda Timoleon, following Dr Spock's advice, would read them to sleep. To her own surprise, Miranda found the books so absorbing that she began to read them for her pleasure too, first in bed at night and later at any time of the day, ignoring her husband, who was mystified by her pastime. Her interest in children's stories grew beyond books, and soon she was on the lookout for the next Disney film at the cinema, her excuse being that she was only escorting the children. Afterwards she made sure to buy the record and the score so that she could teach the children the songs on the piano.

It was an innocent pastime that offered her refuge from the reality of her life, which had not turned out the way she had expected it to. Not long after their dinnertime confrontation, Miranda Timoleon realised that her husband would never stop seeing other women. She did not confront him again because it would have made no difference, but she distanced herself from him, first at home and then also in public. They still lived together, entertained guests together, occasionally travelled together but slept in different rooms in the big house in Mayfair and spoke to each other little, even when they were both at home.

Marco Timoleon seemed happy with the arrangement. But the following summer, when they took a large crowd of guests on a cruise round the Caribbean, Miranda finally stumbled upon his weakness. While flirting without any intention with the younger men, she noticed Marco's livid expression across the deck. And so for the rest of the holiday, she meted out retribution for his sins: she let the men rub suntan oil on to her back, let them spoon-feed her ice-cream, took them on speedboat rides to explore the beaches and coves of the islands they came to and did not return to the yacht until late in the evening. Marco Timoleon did everything to show her that he did not care, but she was not fooled. Now she could see the jealousy behind his sunglasses, his wounded pride, his deep contempt, even when he joked about it, calling the whole thing *Penelope and her Suitors: A Farce*. When this did not work, he tried to retaliate, but his efforts were inept, half-hearted and desperate, having none of his usual charm. As a result, he only succeeded in embarrassing his guests, who all knew what was happening. In the end he conceded defeat and asked Miranda to his study to talk it over.

'Enough of this nonsense,' he said, standing behind his desk and biting his cigar. 'You're making a fool of yourself.'

Nothing changed. No: in fact, things took a turn for the worse because a few days later Stefano Tossi came on board. The same age as Marco Timoleon's wife, he was a tall and athletic Italian, the son of a powerful industrialist with whom Marco was negotiating a deal at the time. He joined the Caribbean holiday a week after the others, bringing on board an air of bad omen. Marco Timoleon had welcomed him warmly, but in secret he was not pleased. His feelings were confirmed when the young man rejected the cabin he was offered, demanding instead a luxury stateroom intended for some other guest, whom Marco Timoleon was forced not to invite.

From the moment that Stefano Tossi set foot on the *Sofia* he looked for company, which was the first thing he did wherever he went, putting his faith in his tracker's instinct that made sure he never slept alone for more than three nights in a row. It was not long before he took an interest in Miranda. The two of them spent the whole day together, sunbathing on the deck, swimming in the pool or playing draughts for hours, unconcerned about the damaging effects of the sun and the unfolding scandal. Stefano Tossi knew nothing about the competition between the couple, but he would have behaved no differently if he had – or, as he explained his actions himself in mechanistic terms to Ian Forster much later: 'I was not the *cause* of their split-up, but I made damn sure I was the *effect*.' Marco Timoleon tried to endure Miranda's retaliation for his own infidelities with patience, but what hurt him most was that it was all happening in public. He did not look away – even though he strove to give the impression that he did – but began to spy on them. He peeked through the blinds of the windows of his stateroom as Miranda and Stefano dived off the side of the yacht and swam away; he watched them in silence as they sat side by side a deck below. On the various islands where they dropped anchor, he followed them from a distance under the Caribbean sun, from one fishing village to the next, up and down volcanic rocks, across dry stream beds, in and out of abandoned gold mines, sweating and hiding behind the candlestick cactuses and the divi divi trees bent by the winds. He reacted on impulse, which was the exact opposite to his level-headed response to the attacks that he faced in business, the market collapses that threatened to wipe out his fortune, the indictments in international courts that could have sent him to prison for a long time. His behaviour only encouraged Miranda Timoleon to prolong his punishment. One night, towards the end of the holiday, Stefano Tossi and she were playing draughts in the Italian's stateroom when she stretched out her hand to take the dice, and he kissed it.

'It'll do no harm to your reputation if you stay the night,' he joked – perhaps. 'They all think we're sleeping together anyway.'

Miranda Timoleon slowly pulled back her hand.

'I went to a Catholic school,' she said.

'It's all right. My father knows the Pope.'

It was almost twenty years later when Ian Forster interviewed Stefano Tossi for his book, but the playboy had lost none of his charm or good memory. He was forty-five but attractive, fit, with hair turning a perfect grey at the temples and his voice had the persuasion of an elderly statesman. He insisted that back then Miranda had wanted to marry him, but Marco had refused to give her a divorce.

The affair did not end when the yacht returned to the Mediterranean as Marco Timoleon hoped but continued for the next two years among instances of confusion, mutual accusations and hatred. Whether Miranda fell in love with Stefano Tossi and wanted to marry him or not, he did become to all intents and purposes her companion. They met at least once a month either in London or in continental Europe, usually in Rome where he lived and ruled the city after dark. On that occasion Marco Timoleon did not have to hire a private investigator to know the details of the affair: he had only to open a magazine to read about it, which he did almost daily. At the same time, he tried to keep up appearances in public, telling the journalists: 'We don't live in the Middle Ages. Mr Tossi is a good friend of our family.' He fooled no one but made a fool of himself. When he could no longer take it, he had another long conversation with Miranda to try and repair the damage.

'You proved your point,' he said.

It was too late. Miranda Timoleon was no longer the schoolgirl he had courted in New York. She now saw her husband as the ageing man that he was, full of conservative ideas and vices. He was someone with whom she had very little in common. By now she had overcome her earlier doubts.

'I want a divorce,' she replied.

He refused to give it her, threatening that he would fight for the custody of their children using the best lawyers in the world, and then, maddened by humiliation, he locked the outside doors and chased her through the house with a poker. If they had lived in a smaller house, perhaps he would have killed her, but in that six-storey house Miranda Timoleon managed to elude him, hiding in storerooms her husband had no idea existed, taking the stairs when she heard the lift coming, erecting barricades of furniture. She did this for three hours, until he calmed down and went to bed, leaving behind him a trail of destruction: the shards of the Imari vases, the keys of the piano scattered across the drawing room, the torn Orientalist paintings, the upturned longcase clock – everything was destroyed. When she had later told Stefano Tossi about the incident, saying that she was lucky to be alive, he asked her why she had not called for help. 'Impossible,' she had explained. 'I would've died of shame.'

Miranda Timoleon always maintained that this violence was incidental, and the true punishment that Marco had in mind for her was to ruin her father, whose fabulous wealth he had always envied. It is true that Marco Timoleon considered Daniel Negri responsible for Miranda's behaviour because he indulged his daughter all her life and took her side in her disputes with her husband. According to Stefano Tossi, Miranda believed that Marco set his plan in motion during a Christmas family visit to the Negri estate in the Hudson Valley, outside New York, a week-long annual ordeal during which Marco was forced to listen to his father-in-law reading from the Bible for hours on end. The right opportunity came the day before the Timoleons were due to fly back to London. In the afternoon Marco went to look for Daniel Negri in the garden to say goodbye. Following the trail of footprints in the snow, he found him reading in a rocking chair on the gazebo, next to a petrol heater. Under his coat, scarf and gloves, Daniel Negri was always a giant who towered above Marco Timoleon even when seated. He had the hands and shoulders of an oarsman, big feet and a sweet, calm expression on his face that turned reproachful the moment he saw his son-in-law. Marco Timoleon asked him what he was reading, and his father-in-law held up the newspaper: big squares were missing from the page. Marco passed his finger through the holes.

'For my health,' explained Daniel Negri.

For a long time he had been suffering from a heart condition, and so his wife had taken to censoring the news she judged unsuitable for him. Every day after lunch, Anna Negri would sit in the living room, scissors in hand, and scan through the newspapers, paying particular attention to the obituaries. Only after she had removed all the upsetting stories would she hand over the papers to their maid to take to her husband, saying, 'What he doesn't know won't hurt him.' She had saved his life. Over the years she had concealed from him the deaths of many good friends and contemporaries, news that would have broken his heart, she had concealed from him stock market crashes that would have given him nightmares and liberal editorials that would have made his blood boil, but above all she was concealing from him everything written about Marco and Miranda, their failing marriage and the scandal of their affairs.

According to Stefano Tossi, Miranda was convinced that from the day Marco Timoleon found out about her father's heart condition he became obsessed with the idea of killing him. In the end he came up with his plan. At that time Daniel Negri was seventy-eight years old and had officially retired from business to devote himself to philanthropy. He contributed to several good causes, including the New York Philharmonic and the Metropolitan Museum of Art, of which he was a patron, but his main occupation was running the Anna and Daniel Negri Charitable Foundation, which offered grants and fellowships to underprivileged students and artists from his homeland. He had thrown himself into this activity with the same enthusiasm that he had shown for business, deriving great satisfaction from the good he did and taking himself a step closer to heaven. He liked to see his Foundation, always in need of funds, surviving him and continuing to help young people for as long as possible. This meant that he had to secure its future with good investments. Marco Timoleon knew all this when some time after that Christmas he proposed to him that they invest together in a fleet of luxury cruise liners, a deal that could secure the future of his charity for generations to come.

His father-in-law promised to think it over. Despite having dissolved his team of advisers when he retired and despite being out of touch with the business realities of the day, he still wanted to do it. His wife, always worried about his health, advised him against it, but he silenced her with a short-tempered comment: 'If I worried about my health, I'd be dead by now.' Marco Timoleon knew it was difficult for his father-in-law to resist the thrill of a good business deal. He fabricated statistics to show him, he paid experts to lie about the future of luxury cruising, he underplayed the cost of building the ships, but above all he relied on Daniel Negri's passion.

The secret was that Miranda's father belonged to the last generation to grow up with sea travel, the only means of crossing the oceans for the largest part of the twentieth century up until the 1950s and still the most comfortable. A committed sea traveller, he had, in fact, only been on a plane twice, but it had been enough to seal his opinion: 'It's inhuman.' Every spring he and his wife sailed to England to visit their daughter and grandchildren. In the summer they crossed the Atlantic again, this time on SS *Constitution* to cruise the Mediterranean. He had no interest in sailing boats but loved cruises for the uninterrupted views, the fresh wind and the luxury, and yet he did not want to own a yacht because of the extravagant running costs and because he suspected that if he indulged himself he would sooner or later lose his passion for the sea. Once, in his son-in-law's presence, the shipping magnate had said:

'The sea is my mistress.'

'Since you make so much money out of her, one may say you're more like her pimp,' Marco Timoleon had said.

Indeed, it was this passion that had made him a fortune in shipping, but it also brought about his downfall: he failed to predict the advent of the jet engine. Marco Timoleon knew all this, of course, when he proposed that they go into business together. Before the end of the decade, transatlantic flight would have all but put an end to sea travel and Daniel Negri would be dead of a heart attack, having lost most of his vast fortune in the luxury cruise business, his ships rusting away at the docks. On the other hand, Marco Timoleon, who had secretly sold most of his shares in the company long before, had made a profit.

While all these conspiracies, love affairs and fights were taking place, no one thought of the children. Daniel was too young to understand, but Sofia, an intelligent five-year-old, kept notes of everything that was happening in her diary. Her refuge at that time was not her room in their Mayfair house, which was defenceless against the visits of her parents, but her governess's terraced cottage in Ilford, on the eastern outskirts of London. During the week, Miss Abigail Rees lived with the family, but on weekends she went home where she fed her cat, looked after her garden and attended church. Most of her time she devoted to reading historical romances, seated in her armchair in her narrow front room from where she could keep an eye on the street. It was there that Sofia liked to go when she was little, and her parents had no objection. At Miss Rees's house, she was free to drink what she wanted, to eat what she wanted, to go where she wanted, anything, but was not allowed to speak. While Miss Rees read, Sofia listened to the radio in the kitchen, played with the cat or searched the small rooms for Victorian secrets. The house existed in another world that was not disturbed by bad news, the changes of weather or the arrival of visitors; all the years that Sofia knew Miss Rees she never heard of her having any friends or relatives. Considering the chaos of her own family, Sofia Timoleon envied the sombre balance of that small solitary house with the jumble of clothes on the sofa, which Miss Rees never felt like sorting out, the simple furniture, which she never felt like dusting, the old appliances, which she never felt like replacing, the clock on the mantelpiece that did not always tick.

More than a year after Miranda and Stefano Tossi's affair had begun, an incident would give both her and Marco Timoleon time to reconsider the madness of the situation. One Sunday in winter, he was sitting in the conservatory with Herodotus' *Histories* on his lap, catching the last drops of the evening sun, when he took off his glasses and rubbed his eyes. Then a strange thing happened. He looked at the yellowed pages for a long time as if he were seeing them for the first time, and a single tear rolled down his cheek and fell on to the paper that was parched by time. He surrendered himself to a grief that was almost forty years old and relived the damage and humiliation that his father's disappearance had caused him, then caught sight of his reflection in the windows of the conservatory. Instead of being himself, the man dressed in his clothes and holding the book was Victor Timoleon: Marco was then not much older than his father had been when he had walked out on his family.

The incident stayed in his mind for days. Time had dissolved his contempt and anger, and there only remained nostalgia for his youth. The boy would never have forgiven his father, but Marco the husband and father felt sorry for him. The only person he talked to about all this was Sylvia Frank.

'You should hire someone to find him,' she said.

Marco Timoleon was not convinced it was possible.

'It happened thirty-eight years ago.'

It was Sylvia Frank who suggested that he hired a psychic, and Marco Timoleon, whose faith in the paranormal remained unwavering, agreed at once. These days the idea may sound ridiculous, but at the time there had been many stories in the news about clairvoyants who had earned the respect of important people in governments and helped the police solve impossible crimes, convincing even the worst sceptics. No one was more successful than Harold van Ness. A suave Dutchman specialising in psychometry, which is the ability to receive and interpret information by touching inanimate objects or visiting places, he had acquired his mental gifts after falling from a ladder and suffering a brain injury. He had lapsed into a coma for several days before regaining consciousness to discover that he could walk through the barriers between past, present and future as easily as between rooms, and he could see into the unknown with great accuracy. He had been decorated by police forces around the world, blessed by Pope Pius XII and acted as a consultant to the President of the United States, so Marco Timoleon was certain that he was the best person to help him.

He arrived in London a week later and visited the house in Mayfair early that same evening. His appearance matched his reputation. He had shiny black hair, an intense gaze and was dressed in an immaculate black suit, white shirt and bow-tie. As soon as he stood in the hall, he closed his eyes.

'You're a very lonely man,' he said.

Marco Timoleon showed him in himself and asked if there was anything else that he could tell him. His guest replied: 'Not yet.' They were served high tea in the drawing room; for hours they discussed the details of the case while the world went by outside, distant and irrelevant. The clairvoyant was an intelligent man who paid attention to everything his host was saying, nodding occasionally and scribbling in a small notebook. But he truly demonstrated his talents when he stood up from his chair and, out of the blue, asked Marco Timoleon to show him his book collection. When he entered the library, he walked up to the shelves and without any hesitation took out a book, seemingly at random. Marco Timoleon, who had not mentioned the incident in the conservatory to him, was stunned: it was

Herodotus' *Histories*. Next, Harold van Ness did even better than that: he opened the book to the very page where the mark of Marco's tear was, again without knowing about it, and placed his palm on the page. He closed his eyes.

'Mesopotamia,' he said.

Then he began to speak without stop, describing the images that passed in front of his eyes as if he were watching the view from inside a moving train. He said he could see a short man walking alone in a vast expanse of barren land; he said the man had broad shoulders, a thick neck, grey hair and hollow eyes; he said the man was dressed in a black suit and top hat, that when he passed through towns he stayed in guesthouses but in the country he slept under trees, that he liked to be alone, but above all it seemed that he wanted to get as far away from home as possible.

'He is following the railway line,' said the clairvoyant.

He collapsed on the sofa, his mind exhausted from its journey through time, and asked for water. Marco Timoleon was speechless. He wiped the sweat from his forehead and sat with his head in his hands, deep in thought. It was a wet and windy evening with the rain tapping against the windows and the honking of cars interrupting the peace. Later Marco Timoleon offered his guest dinner, during which his host talked little. Before returning to his hotel, the clairvoyant said that his gift was at his client's service if he wanted to continue his search. For this, he informed him, they would have to travel to the Middle East. Marco Timoleon handed him the envelope with his fee and nodded in agreement: 'I won't rest until I find the truth.'

This is how he fell victim to the famous charlatan who deceived him for several months, demanding exorbitant fees, first-class travel and luxury accommodation, all of which Marco Timoleon paid without objection, driven by his desire to trace his father's whereabouts. At first, Harold van Ness insisted that Victor Timoleon was alive and well. He could see him living quietly in a modest house built around a paved yard with a well in the middle, in Amman or Baghdad or perhaps a smaller town, with a wife and children to whom he spoke in Arabic. He told Marco Timoleon all this and much more, the information getting more precise the closer they came to their supposed destination. In the Middle East, they began to visit one place after another, starting with the big cities, then the towns, then the villages, knocking on doors, interviewing alleged neighbours, looking through hotel registers, asking retired mayors and local historians, but no one seemed to have seen or heard anything about Victor Timoleon. Then the clairvoyant changed his story.

'He suffers from amnesia,' he said. 'He forgot his name shortly after leaving Izmir.'

And so they continued to roam Mesopotamia, crossing and re-crossing the Tigris and the Euphrates, leaving behind them an endless trail of money. When the news spread that Marco Timoleon, the Richest Man in the World, was searching for his father, a crowd of impostors approached them wherever they went, claiming to know his father or to be him, the most implausible of whom was an elderly man with white curls and very dark skin, who was reduced to tears when he saw Marco Timoleon and fell into his arms, thanking God in Sumerian.

Finally, Harold van Ness had to break the bad news to him that his father had been alive when they started their journey but was now dead. He had passed on peacefully in his sleep, a few days earlier, yes he could see it now, but the clairvoyant could not help Marco any longer because he had to respect the wishes of the dead: Victor Timoleon did not want to be found. Years later, following the seaplane accident, Harold van Ness would again offer his services to help the tycoon find out who killed his son, but on this occasion Dr Patrikios would manage to bring his grieving friend to his senses: Marco Timoleon declined the offer reluctantly.

The only good news that Marco received was when he returned to London from Mesopotamia, and Miranda announced to him that she had ended her affair with Stefano Tossi: their marriage had been granted a reprieve.

THE REASON WHY IAN FORSTER WANTED TO SPEAK TO the doctor at the birthday party was to give him the opportunity to comment, according to the ethics of journalism, before his findings were made public. He still had doubts about the validity of many of his claims, admitting that he had relied more on his intuition than on solid evidence. During his research he had come to realise that he could prove many lies beyond a shadow of a doubt, but this had not always been the same as proving the truth. It was a compromise he was willing to make because it was his belief that there was never smoke without fire. What he did not expect to find was that there would be so many fires: inconsistencies, deliberate and not, cover-ups and confusions that made him waste a lot of time on illusory paths that led nowhere. He did not lose hope. He peeled off the layers of deception slowly, one by one, until he reached, exhausted but satisfied, what he thought was the closest one would ever get to the truth about Marco Timoleon. The problem was that, seduced by his success as a biographer, he stopped questioning what it all meant as long as the pieces fitted together.

He knew that the Ian Forster who was now putting the finishing touches to the book was not the same as the man who had begun to research it two years and seven months earlier. As far as biographies go, it had been done in no time. He had expected to take five or six years, but his enthusiasm as well as Marco Timoleon's money and influence had quickly cleared most of the obstacles from his way. If his subject's direct involvement had compromised the project, Ian Forster did not want to admit it. What he had no doubt about was his determination to see behind the smokescreen.

Dr Patrikios's constant presence in Marco Timoleon's life had first caught his attention: he was there in Buenos Aires, he was there in New York and even though he never lived in London or Paris, he was there often too. When Ian Forster mentioned this to him, the doctor shrugged his shoulders and replied that it was natural because he was Marco Timoleon's private physician. He was, but the tycoon's strong constitution meant that there was little need to see his doctor more than once a year when he flew to New York to have his comprehensive check-up that simply confirmed his clean bill of health. No. Their relationship was based on more than that: a deep, mutual and discreet affection that endured the passage of time. There was only one place where the two men's paths had not crossed, and that was Izmir. Intrigued by this, Ian Forster prepared to make the journey to Marco Timoleon's birthplace, telling his sponsor that he wanted to go in order to be able to describe it better in his book. Marco Timoleon had no objection.

'Fine,' he had said. 'But don't go searching for the Holy Grail, Mr Forster. It doesn't exist.'

The Englishman travelled to Turkey by ship from Greece. As soon as he set eyes on the city from the sea, he knew that his mission would be a difficult one. So little resemblance did it bear to the old photographs Marco Timoleon had kept that he had to ask a deckhand whether this was indeed their destination; he confirmed it. Destroyed by fire in Marco Timoleon's youth, large parts of Izmir had been rebuilt with more eagerness than taste, the harbour had been expanded and new neighbourhoods had sprung up along the bay to accommodate the rise in population. It was difficult to make out any of the neoclassical buildings that used to adorn the seafront. Most of them had long been demolished, and the last remaining ones were squeezed between modern concrete buildings that could have been found anywhere in the world. The ship slid into port with two long blasts of its whistle, waking the stevedores on the quay sleeping inside their carts. Ian Forster wasted no time. He found a taxi and gave the driver the address, having very little hope that the house would still be standing after so many years.

It was there. The house where Marco Timoleon had grown up stood on top of a hill where an asphalt road ended and a dirt track continued towards the outskirts of town where modern construction had not yet reached. It was exactly the way Marco Timoleon had described it in their interviews: the big iron gate, the wild garden with the two palms that rose above the tiled roof, the windows with wooden shutters, which now seemed permanently closed, a house existing in a state of peaceful neglect. It was dying, but it was a happy death after a long, contented life. Ian Forster had to wait a long time for someone to answer the bell, but when he saw the old woman, he was in no doubt that she was Pandora.

'No visitors,' she said.

She said it in Turkish, the only language she claimed to remember, having not spoken Greek in thirty-two years, since the day Eugenia Timoleon had died. Ian Forster did not understand. He had to come back the following morning with a tourist guide whom he hired to be his interpreter and who persuaded Pandora to let the Englishman interview her. Almost deaf, she had to use a brass hearing trumpet from Ottoman times, which she held close to her ear and turned in the interpreter's direction every time he asked her a question. She was surrounded by clucking chickens that walked in and out of the house as they pleased, pecking at the rugs, resting on the rickety chairs, having turned the once magnificent house into an enormous coop that smelt of droppings. Ian Forster asked her many questions whose answers he knew already, in order to determine the state of her memory as well as her sanity, before shifting his attention to Marco Timoleon's adolescent years. He wanted to know who were his friends, why he left Izmir, how Eugenia Timoleon reacted to his departure. Pandora did not reply. The interpreter repeated the questions louder.

'Don't shout, damn it,' she said. 'I'm not that deaf.'

She folded her arms and remained silent, making it clear that she wished to speak no more, and no amount of pleading made her change her mind. Ian Forster left but did not give up. He spent several days in the city, searching for answers: he visited the offices of the local press to examine their archives, poring over papers still smoking from the Great Fire of 1922, the year Marco Timoleon had left for South America; he visited the public library; he visited the hospital where Eugenia Timoleon had been diagnosed with dementia; he talked to people who knew her and people who knew Marco Timoleon in those days, taking detailed notes. He did not stop there. When he returned to Athens, he postponed his flight back to London in order to visit the medical school where Aristide Patrikios had taken his degree, a visit that proved very useful to his research and that had prompted other journeys.

A waiter carrying a tray tapped Ian Forster on the shoulder and told him that his host wished to see him at once. The birthday dinner had ended, and the party was in full swing, with the orchestra playing and the guests dancing on the veranda. Ian

Forster's eyes searched among the crowd for Sofia, but he could not find her. He felt uneasy. Marco Timoleon's absence from the celebration had not seemed significant at first because Ian Forster knew that since the accident his host disliked people and social gatherings. He now thought it could not be a coincidence that both Sofia and her father were not at the party. He helped himself to three glasses of champagne, but they did not help. When he knocked at the door of the study and entered, he saw Marco Timoleon waiting for him behind his desk.

'Come in, Mr Forster. Christmas is coming early this year for you.'

The room was lit only by the lamp on the writing desk. The draught blew the curtains out of the french windows, and they flapped briefly in the dark before Ian Forster shut the door behind him. Despite the open windows, the room was covered in a haze of smoke. On the veranda the music and dancing continued. Ian Forster sat where he was told to sit while his host began to pace in the shadows with his hands clasped behind his back and a cigar in his mouth. The biographer, who had seen him faced with difficult situations many times before, from emergencies to the recent oil crisis, had never seen him looking as stern as that night.

'Are you enjoying the party, Mr Forster?'

He emerged from the shadows, tapped his cigar in the ashtray and leaned back against his desk with his arms folded across his chest. Ian Forster suddenly felt as if he were meeting the tycoon for the very first time. All the hours he had spent listening to his stories, all the pages he had filled with their conversations in shorthand (Marco Timoleon never allowed him to record them on his Dictaphone), all the journeys across the world, nothing of this had really mattered. He realised with a pang of disappointment that he had wasted his time searching for Marco

Timoleon in the wrong places: Izmir, Buenos Aires, New York, London and Paris. He was in front of him all along, as close as he was standing now, furious and supreme. Ian Forster felt the sweat on his palms, the throbbing in his temples, the squeeze of his clip-on bow-tie. He managed to smile.

'You're missed by all,' he said.

'Naturally.'

Marco Timoleon turned his back and watched the party on the veranda. The paper lanterns were flickering in the breeze. Some had burned out, and a waiter with a long stick came to take them down and put new candles inside.

'You must be wondering why I have taken you away from that great party,' continued Marco Timoleon.

'Is it about—'

'I wanted to congratulate you, Mr Forster, that's why.'

'I don't understand.'

'I have good news. You have won.'

'Won?'

Marco Timoleon nodded.

'I'm at your mercy.'

The Englishman was puzzled. Marco Timoleon puffed at his cigar and studied him for a moment. Then he walked behind his desk, lifted Eugenia Timoleon's portrait and dialled the combination on the safe. He opened it, took out a typed document several pages long and threw it on Ian Forster's lap.

'I had my lawyers send it to me,' he said. 'It's the original. Check the signatures. If you remember, no other copy exists.'

It was their confidentiality agreement. Ian Forster stared at it.

'It could be yours,' Marco Timoleon said, sucking his cigar. 'To do as you please.' He leaned over his biographer and whispered in his ear: 'I recommend that when you get it you burn it right away. I might change my mind and ask for it back.'

'You . . . decided against our book?'

'What? Oh no, no. Quite the contrary.'

Ian Forster looked at his host lit by the desk lamp. Marco Timoleon seemed to be mocking him, but at the same time he was admitting defeat. He could not believe that what he had been hoping for, namely to publish his book without censorship, was going to happen.

'I'm prepared to sign the necessary documents that would safeguard you against libel actions, et cetera,' said Marco Timoleon. 'In other words you could write whatever you want. Tell them I'm from Mars. Or that I was born a woman. Or any other truth you want, Mr Forster.'

'I can publish the book? Unedited?'

Marco Timoleon nodded.

'You'd be limited only by your imagination.'

His biographer sat deep in his armchair, sweating under his dinner jacket, still unable to celebrate the fulfilment of his dream. Then it slowly dawned on him. He began to think about the wealth and the fame that were in store for him, and then he began to answer in his mind the questions that imaginary interviewers were asking him about his book. A triumph, a triumph! He thought about all this until Marco Timoleon's voice brought him back to reality.

'I only ask for one thing in return – no, two.'

Ian Forster looked up.

'Don't have a child,' Marco Timoleon said. 'Not with my daughter.'

Ian Forster would never admit the sense of relief he felt then, he would never forget – not without guilt – how that night he came to the crossroads in a life that so far had not asked him to choose. Things had happened easily to him; having persuaded

Macro Timoleon to let him be his biographer, he had lived a comfortable life in the shadow of his famous subject. He had uncovered conspiracies, proved theories, clarified facts, committed to history long-forgotten incidents from Marco Timoleon's life, telling himself that he was a servant of the truth and not of his master. From the biographer's point of view, he could not imagine a better stroke of luck than having Sofia fall in love with him, which gave him an advantage over all other biographers, past and future. And then came the baby that risked everything. Sacrifice was a portentous word.

'And stop seeing her,' Marco Timoleon said.

Out on the veranda, the orchestra was now playing slow love songs. The ageing tycoon stood at the window and contemplated the party. Couples were dancing under the paper lanterns, and other guests stood in small groups and watched the sea where the stars of a cloudless sky were reflected like diamonds. In the bay, the white hull of the *Sofia*, illuminated by electric lights, stood out against the Mediterranean night. He noticed his wife in front of the bandstand. She had changed into a long white dress and was dancing with the Dictator. Before turning round, he also caught sight of an awkward couple standing quietly at the edge of the dance floor and recognised the anaesthetist and the nurse he had hired for the procedure.

'With or without your help, I'll somehow still get my way, Mr Forster. But you, hell, my boy, you'll never publish your book. I promise you that.'

The Englishman thought in silence. His affair with Sofia Timoleon was not a plan as her father assumed or pretended to assume for the sake of argument; it was the result of an intimacy that had grown from their interviews. His persistent questions had unearthed her loneliness, her insecurities, the memories of failed relationships and other bits and pieces whose existence she had forgotten. It was all recorded on the tapes that Ian Forster played back day after day, making notes, transcribing quotes, studying them for clues, listening to Sofia's voice until he arrived at the conclusion: the rich are all screwed up.

'What you're asking me is impossible,' he told his host. 'Even if I agreed, I don't think I can impose—'

'I don't want you to stop seeing her right away. Losing the baby would upset her enough. Keep her company. Then go quietly at a later date . . . Two months from now perhaps? Unless *she* throws you out before that, of course. I wouldn't be surprised. Think about it.'

He walked up to his guest, who was still trapped in the leather armchair, took the legal document from his hands and locked it back in the safe. When he was alone again, Marco Timoleon checked himself in the mirror, had a few sips from the bottle of Scotch he kept in his desk and went downstairs to join his guests on the veranda where his late arrival was greeted with spontaneous applause. After hours of waiting, many of those queuing up to greet him had forgotten the reason for the celebration and made the same mistake the Dictator made when he gave him a military salute and shook his hand: 'Happy birthday, Mr Timoleon.'

Fuelled by alcohol, the misunderstanding spread quickly, and soon a large part of the crowd seemed to assume that it was Marco Timoleon's birthday instead of that of Sofia, who was nowhere to be seen. Rather than trying to correct their mistake, the tycoon took part in the situation with a zest that just about hid his contempt for his guests, some of whom had never met Sofia before but were there because the Richest Man in the World had invited them. Olivia Timoleon, embarrassed by the misunderstanding, walked through the crowd putting the world to rights with a smile until she persuaded the guests that they were making a mistake. When everyone was dancing again, she stood next to her husband, passed her arm round his and kissed him on the cheek. Then she asked him how his meeting with his daughter went, and he was telling the truth when he replied: 'It couldn't have gone any better.' He also thanked her for having saved the party even though he had not asked her to and wondered why she had bothered. She replied not with anger but fatalism: 'Because I am still your wife.'

Their relationship was doomed to fail from the start because of their irreconcilable differences of opinion on everything and everyone, but it was the unkindness that had sped up its decline. One evening the couple were playing bridge against Dr Patrikios and Daniel, a formidable pair that seemed to communicate by telepathy, and they were losing. They were in the living room of the Timoleons' Parisian apartment where all the windows were open because the doctor could not stand the smoke of Marco's cigar. It was winter. A cold wind blew in snowflakes and threatened to scatter the cards on the green table, but Marco Timoleon refused to put out his cigar. Olivia had to play wearing her fur coat.

'One of you will have to give in,' she said, shivering. 'We have to close the windows. Pass.'

Dr Patrikios smiled at her but did not change his mind. He was wearing his hat and gloves.

'Science is on my side,' he said. 'Passive smoking is known to cause cancer. Two hearts.'

Marco Timoleon drew on his cigar and looked at his cards. He had unbuttoned his shirt and rolled up his sleeves as a sign of defiance.

'Constant nagging is known to cause irritation,' he said. 'Three clubs.'

And so they continued for a long time while the temperature

in the room dropped and dropped. Eventually Olivia Timoleon stood up.

'Don't do it,' Marco warned her.

But she did. She closed the windows, pulled the heavy curtains and turned up the heat to melt the snow that had piled up against the walls, and then she put out her husband's cigar in the ashtray and took off her fur coat. No sooner had she sat down again to continue their game, pleased she had resolved a diplomatic deadlock, than Marco Timoleon slapped her across the face. Dr Patrikios immediately intervened, but the glass had cracked: it was their first fight.

So started their estrangement. It did not help that Marco Timoleon had always detested Olivia's circle of friends. He did not understand their humour, he disagreed with their politics, he ridiculed their taste in art and fashion. Bored with them, he would leave their parties without telling his wife, who would look for him in vain, and he would ask his driver to take him to a nightclub where he enjoyed the attention of strangers, who recognised him as soon as he walked in. He was almost seventy at the time but with enough reserves of strength still, the last rays of light before the total eclipse. His son's death a year later would shake his health, and old age would quickly catch up with him.

Marco Timoleon knew how to hurt Olivia. Only days after their separation, he had emptied their Paris apartment of her things and shipped them to New York in big crates that contained not only her clothes and books but also her nail clippers, her hairbrush and her squeezed toothpaste: he was erasing her from his life. When she took delivery of the boxes, Olivia Timoleon had stored them unopened in the basement of the tower on Fifth Avenue to wait for what she privately called *The Second Coming*: the day he would ask her to come back to Paris.

In the meantime she was convinced that he was seeing other women despite the rumours about his impotence, which she refused to believe. She was prepared to forgive him and try again because she did not blame their separation entirely on him: she blamed Sofia at least as much. She would admit it to no one, but the first thought that crossed her mind when she heard the news of Daniel's seaplane crashing in the sea was why could it not have been Sofia instead of him? She had said: 'Death is unreasonable.' She was fond of Daniel. She liked his polite manners, she liked his sensitivity, she liked the distance he kept from the carnival of fame, which she herself could not resist, but above all she liked it that he had sided with her against Sofia in the undeclared war for Marco Timoleon's affections.

The relationship between the two women had been bad from the start. Following Marco Timoleon's suggestion, Sofia had agreed to be Olivia's maid of honour at her wedding, but the attempt to reconcile the two women had backfired: Sofia failed to show up. The ceremony took place at Saint Mark of the Cypresses in the summer of 1970, a grand affair with many guests. Sofia's absence embarrassed Marco Timoleon, but the ceremony went ahead with only Dr Patrikios, who was Marco's best man, attending to the rites, dressed in his cream linen suit and a borrowed bow-tie. The problems did not end there. Sofia Timoleon, who was twenty at the time, had long moved out of the family apartment in Paris, but when the couple returned from their honeymoon, they found that she had moved back. Marco Timoleon was not pleased.

'It's only a temporary measure,' Sofia reassured him.

A year later she was still living on avenue Montaigne, doing everything she could to disturb the life of the newlyweds. She had frequent confrontations with her stepmother, embarrassed her in front of their guests and gave interviews to popular magazines in which she declared that Olivia Andersen was taking advantage of a senile old man. Marco Timoleon apologised on her behalf to his wife, explaining her behaviour as stemming from her grief for the death of her mother seven years earlier and suggesting that they had better ignore her. The truth was that Sofia was trying his patience too, and he confided to Dr Patrikios that he was this close to disinheriting her. In the end it was Daniel who had brought his sister to her senses, persuading her to move out of the apartment and live her own life rather than ruin the life of others, but perhaps the damage in the marriage had already been done.

Across the dance floor, Dr Patrikios raised his glass of lemonade to Olivia and Marco, who returned his greeting. Olivia Timoleon smiled at him and the other guests who had become hers during the course of the evening. She had advised the orchestra what music to play and when to play it, had directed the traffic from the kitchen to the tables, had made sure there was enough drink for everyone so that they would not notice the absence of their host and Sofia. Someone asked Marco Timoleon to make a speech, but he resisted until the cheers drowned out the music and forced him to give in. He invited Olivia to join him, and together they climbed the bandstand hand in hand where, speaking in a solemn voice without a microphone, he thanked his guests for their presence in this distant corner of the world, apologised for his absence that evening and regretted the breach of security for which he intended to punish the intruder mercilessly. He then expressed his gratitude for everything his wife had done on his behalf that day and added: 'I don't know what I'd do without her.'

He ended his speech with a toast to his daughter, who was no longer there. The applause reached Ian Forster's ears in the garden, where he had sought refuge after Marco Timoleon's ultimatum. He had strayed from the paved path, lost his way in the dark and ended up among the rose bushes whose heavy odour always reminded him of state funerals. On a stone bench, he sat and smoked a cigarette with nervous hands. Disturbed by the music and the lights, the birds were still singing in the middle of the night. His bow-tie and collar were undone, the carnation pinned to his lapel was long gone, and he was shivering despite it being warm. The meeting had been so unexpected and brief that it had shattered his confidence, leaving him trapped in a situation that was forcing him to do exactly what Marco Timoleon wanted him to. He looked at the floodlit villa in the distance where dancing had resumed after the host's short speech. He had not tried to deny that he was the baby's father, he had not tried to negotiate a settlement, he had not protested but had silently accepted a solution that was a defeat for his morality and a victory for his book. He had to speak to Sofia.

He walked back to the villa, following a path that steered clear of the crowded veranda and led to the back entrance where he could go in unnoticed. That part of the house facing away from the sea was unlit. The long search for the door in the moonlight increased his frustration. When he finally found it, he entered and walked along the dark corridor on the ground floor, hearing his heels on the tiles over the sound of dance music coming from the veranda and the clamour of the waiters at the other end of the house. He found the staircase in the dark where he thought it would be, and he climbed to the first floor where a sudden growl stopped him. Lying in the shadows, Soraya raised her head, but she recognised him and went back to sleep. The door was locked. Ian Forster knocked softly and waited a long time before Sofia Timoleon opened and greeted him with a warning.

'I have bad news,' she said.

She seemed calm and dignified, in a way she had never appeared to him before, as if her predicament had tamed her eternally bad mood. She told him she had decided to defy her father but was worried about the consequences that this would have for her lover and his work. Ian Forster saw the small plastic bottle on the night table and immediately understood that she owed her courage to the tranquillisers. He stopped her before she told him more: 'I know.' Then he held her in his arms, which he guessed was what she wanted him to do, but the smell of her perfume added to his apprehension.

They had become lovers a year and four months earlier but since then had spent no more than sixty days together and never two in succession. In order to keep their relationship secret, they followed a set of simple rules borrowed from spy films: they did not use their real names, they did not wear the same clothes twice, they did not arrive or leave together, they did not meet at each other's houses. It was Ian Forster who had come up with those rules, and although Sofia Timoleon made fun of him, she did obey them because she knew that her lover's fears of what her father would do should he find out were not unreasonable. They always met in London, in one of the big hotels where Sofia booked a room under a false name and Ian Forster could come and go unnoticed. He took the lift up to the room, waited until the corridor was empty and then knocked on the door, his heart pounding with fear. They never broke any of their rules, they talked to no one about their affair, not even their most trusted friends, and all that time never had reasons to suspect that their cover was blown. In fact, one time Ian Forster had woken up in the middle of the night and thought he saw someone spying on them from behind the curtain, but then he had gone back to sleep, thinking he had dreamed it. It was not until his meeting with Marco Timoleon on the night of the party that he remem-bered the incident again, and then he shuddered: someone had been spying on them all along.

They had learned to live with the situation without consid-ering its consequences because they did not really expect it to last. The truth was that their affair was put on hold the moment they parted in the morning and began again when the letter arrived – typed, no sender – that let the Englishman know of the place, date and hour of their next meeting. There was no way of replying to it even if he wanted to alter the arrangement: he had to go. Once he failed to keep one of their appointments and received a letter containing several pages of abuse and the warning not to do it again. He had not. At that time their affair was still a revolutionary act against Marco Timoleon, and sooner or later it, too, would have suffered the fate of Sofia's previous relationships if it were not for silence.

It was not one of their rules. It began out of tiredness, or lazi-ness, or from having nothing to say, but gradually they said less and less to each other until it became awkward to speak at all. When he arrived in the hotel, Ian Forster would simply walk into the room and greet Sofia Timoleon with a kiss before they undressed and made love without a word being spoken: no declarations of love, no truths, no lies, no gossip, no jokes, nothing. Then they slept and in the morning showered and left separately without saying goodbye, melting into the lonely crowd that flooded the streets outside. After a while Sofia Timoleon had asked him what he thought of all that silence, and he had shrugged and answered: 'I like it. We sort of fuck like Trappists.'

They agreed that it was a good thing. Rather than driving them apart, silence was bringing them closer. It was strange. Slowly their hotel room became a sanctuary where they escaped the noise of their lives for a few hours, the silence turned the air-conditioned air into something like cotton and their ears became attuned to the slightest movement: their breathing, the crumpling of sheets, the treading of naked feet on the carpet. And so their affair went on, shrouded in mystery, silent, tender and honest, their bodies saying all that needed to be said, not through the mouth but through the other orifices.

It seemed as if it could last for ever in that state, which was not true love or even counterfeit, no, it was something different altogether. Then, one morning, after having spent the night in a suite at the Savoy, Ian Forster had opened his eyes, looked at the view over the Thames, then looked at Sofia sleeping next to him and without realising it broke their vow of silence with two words that set off a chain reaction: 'Good morning.'

It became love. And now that Marco Timoleon knew, there was no need to hide any more. They undressed without the urgency of the past and got into bed. They listened to the music coming from the veranda.

'There's no reason why everything should not continue according to plan,' Sofia said.

She knew very well to what lengths her father was prepared to go in order to impose his will, but not even she could have guessed that he had converted one of the guest rooms into an operating room where Dr Patrikios, an anaesthetist and a nurse were standing by to fulfil Marco Timoleon's wishes.

'He's just an old fool,' she said.

Ian Forster had been thinking about it from the moment he left Marco Timoleon's study – not thinking what to do, because he had accepted the logic of Marco Timoleon's argument before walking out of the door, but how to persuade Sofia to do the only thing that made sense under the circumstances: not to have the baby.

'Let's try to be sensible,' he said.

'We *are* sensible.'

'Listen. This is perhaps not the right time to have a child. Irrespective of the book.'

Sofia Timoleon stared at him.

'You owe me,' she said.

They both knew it was true. She had opened doors to him that would have stayed locked despite Marco Timoleon's repeated reassurances that his biographer had his total support, told him any secrets of her father that she knew, intervened to persuade friends and associates to grant him interviews, allowed him access to the family apartments and houses, dug out photographs and documents.

'It's not a matter of who owes whom what,' Ian Forster said.

'No. It's a sacrifice.'

He had expected it.

'No need to be melodramatic.'

Sofia's reply was to cover herself with the bed sheet.

'There's no risk,' he said. 'It's a straightforward procedure.'

The moon slanted through the windows, lighting the furniture, the walls, the clothes scattered across the floor. The music coming from the veranda was no longer as loud; the party was losing its verve.

'It should be a joint decision,' Ian Forster continued. 'You can't make it on your own.'

He was tired. The evening before, dinner with Marco Timoleon and the doctor had gone on late into the night, and this morning he had woken up early to work on his book. He added with a sense of helplessness:

'I don't give my consent for you to have that child.'

When she did not reply, he stood up, put on his clothes and left the room. As soon as the door closed, Sofia Timoleon began to think about her life, day by day, incident by incident, place by place, with gloomy fascination. Everything came to light then, clear and vivid. While she was thinking what to do next, she became aware that the music had stopped outside, and she wanted to know why. She left her room naked and walked across the corridor into a room overlooking the veranda. From the window she saw an enormous birthday cake decorated with sparklers being carried outside on the waiters' shoulders. Everyone broke into *Happy Birthday*. When the singing ended, the crowd applauded and the waiters began to cut the cake. Mellow instrumental pieces accompanied the end of the party as the veranda was emptying of people. When Sofia Timoleon returned to her room, she had decided. Her hands shaking, she groped in the dark for the bedside table until she found the bottle with the tranquillisers: there were not enough. In the drawer she found two more unopened bottles, and she swallowed those pills too, helped down with cola, before lying in bed to wait for eternity or the doctor.

NOTHING WOULD EVER CONVINCE MIRANDA TIMOLEON that her husband was not responsible for her father's sudden death only months after he was declared bankrupt. The truth is that Daniel Negri was too astute an investor to be fooled by anyone and even more so by his son-in-law whom he did not trust. But he was a stubborn man too, and it was as difficult to talk him into doing something as it was to talk him out of it. Once he agreed to invest in luxury sea travel, he refused to change course despite the warning signs. He would say: 'Success demands a leap of faith.' He had lived by this rule all his life, but then the day came when he was too old to jump any more: times were changing too fast for men of his generation. It was also bad luck. In July 1956, not long after Daniel Negri had signed the contracts for the building of his large fleet and construction was about to start, the Italian luxury liner SS *Andrea Doria* sank off the north-east coast of the United States after a collision with another ship in thick fog. The tragedy caused the death of more than fifty people and marked the end of ocean-liner travel.

Marco Timoleon did little to correct Miranda's perception that he was Daniel Negri's ruin. He knew how much it cost her to witness her father's financial collapse, how much it hurt her that she was unable to defend his fortune from the whirlwind of claims, lawsuits and court orders that arrived, wiping out everything in its path: the bank accounts, the houses, the art collection. That was not all. The auditors discovered that Daniel Negri had been siphoning off money from the Anna and Daniel Negri Charitable Foundation to fund his luxury liners venture, and the bailiffs seized the assets of the charity, which was forced to shut down. Daniel Negri remained calm throughout the ordeal, not expressing his true feelings in public so as not to please his enemies – his son-in-law among them – or sadden his daughter. When bad news was given to him, which happened frequently, and he sensed that emotion was about to overwhelm him, he would excuse himself and leave the room to hide in a distant part of the house where he could cry in private. He fooled no one, but they all pretended not to know what he was doing. In fact, it was he who did not know that his wife and daughter had taken up his habit too: in order not to upset him they went into another room to cry. One day Daniel Negri touched his daughter's cheek and said: 'You'll soon be the only proof that I ever existed.' Overcome with emotion, Miranda Timoleon stood up to leave the room but broke down before she reached the door and began to cry in front of him, which made her mother cry too. Then little Daniel, who was sitting on his grandmother's lap, burst into tears because his mother was crying and Sofia joined in, a torrent of grief that finally tore off Daniel Negri's mask and all five cried together until their tears flooded the room to one inch above the floor.

Marco Timoleon did offer to pay some of his father-in-law's colossal debts, but Daniel Negri, who would be damned if he were going to let an upstart humiliate him, turned down his offer with a brief reply: 'Thank you, but fuck off.' The next day he asked his chauffeur to drive him to his estate in the

Hudson Valley, knowing in his heart that he would never return. From the back seat of his Lincoln, he looked at the city for the last time, at its streets, its pavements, its skyscrapers, not with the eyes of a magnate but like an immigrant seeing New York for the first time: a foreign land. A few months later, in November 1959, the bailiffs came to take possession of the country estate too, and it was they who found him dead in the gazebo, seated in his rocking chair, next to the petrol heater, with his bible on his lap. He was eighty-two years old.

After his death, Miranda Timoleon took to wearing black at all times, at home and in public. She mourned her father with all her heart even more than her mother did, whose age had long forced her to come to terms with death. In fact, Anna Negri lived for several more years in an old people's home, which Marco Timoleon paid for, having survived against her will not only her husband but also her daughter and grandson.

It was after her father's death that Miranda Timoleon discovered the consolation of pills, which helped her bear her mourning but also her disappointment with her failing marriage. She took pills in the morning to get out of bed, dropped them in her coffee instead of sugar, took one after lunch to go to sleep, took another to wake up, a great quantity of chemicals, which she hid among the diamonds and pearls in her jewellery box, which she carried everywhere. Marco Timoleon, who had many vices himself but illegal drugs were not one of them, knew about her addiction from the start. He warned her, but Miranda ignored him and soon she was not even trying to hide her habit from family and friends. Her supplier was one of the servants, who made a fortune thanks to his underworld connections who could provide him with medicines without prescription. When Marco Timoleon found out, he immediately fired him and stopped giving his wife cash in an attempt to put an end to the situation. Fourteen years later Ian Forster managed to trace the man to a Mediterranean island where he agreed to speak to him on condition of anonymity. It transpired that far from disappearing from the scene, Miranda Timoleon's ex-servant remained close to her until her death, supplying her with any chemical she asked for. The biographer was not convinced. He asked him how she could afford to pay him since Marco Timoleon had stopped her allowance, and the man explained to him that Miranda would sell any valuables she could get hold of, from her jewellery to her antiques collection and the house furniture. To prove it, he took Ian Forster around his house and pointed out some of the items he had received from her in lieu of payment, among them the Chippendale long-case clock, the Orientalist paintings and the baby grand piano from the house in Mayfair, items which once had been the target of Marco Timoleon's domestic rage but which Miranda had afterwards repaired and given, among many other things, to her ex-servant.

Marco Timoleon would have tried harder to stop her if he had known that Miranda's habit would also contaminate his daughter. Sofia Timoleon, who was at the time entering adolescence, discovered peace for herself when she stole a pill from her mother's jewellery box, went into her room, locked the door and swallowed it with a glass of cola. It was enough to lull her to sleep where she floated in a sea of contentment for several hours, indifferent to the bleakness of her surroundings, which seemed to have been invaded by a storm of butterflies. She would always be grateful to her mother for having introduced her, without intention, to a way of escaping reality a few hours a day.

Marco Timoleon himself found refuge elsewhere. When the

novelty of sailing the seas on the *Sofia* wore off, he began to contemplate owning a house where he could spend the summers in greater luxury than even his yacht could offer – and in greater privacy too because the scandal of his failing marriage was attracting more photographers and journalists than ever before. He did not want to buy one but to build it exactly to his specifications, and the opportunity presented itself when a small island in the eastern Mediterranean came up for sale. He immediately entered into negotiations that went on for months even though he secretly considered the asking price good, but he did it out of the sheer pleasure of bargaining, which he could never resist. Once the island was his, he set about finding the best location for his villa, a tireless search that lasted several days. Finally he stood on a slope above the cove of his island, took off his dark glasses and studied the view for a long time. The wind carried over the sound of the waves breaking at the bottom of the cove, the shrieks of the seagulls diving for fish, the rustling of the pines. He lit a cigar and smoked it against the wind, looking at the mainland in the distance with the stern eyes of a wooden Neptune at the bow of a ship. When he finished smoking, he said: 'Here.'

His island became his obsession. He neglected his businesses – which he said could run themselves, knowing very well that it was Sylvia Frank who ran them for him – and spent days and nights bent over long rolls of paper, drawing the plans of his villa in between sips of coffee and puffs on his cigar. The plans, with their errors in dimensions, geometric impossibilities and construction challenges, drove his architects to despair. Many nights, having finally gone to sleep, he would suddenly jump out of bed and rush to his study to add something to the drawings that he had just dreamed, something that would make his villa the most beautiful house in the world. Miranda, who until that moment was sleeping peacefully next to him thanks to the pills, would also wake up, her heart beating fast with fright, and not sleep for the rest of the night, which she passed reading children's books. The design of the villa was not enough to satisfy Marco Timoleon's appetite. As soon as he finished with it, he began work on the plans of the church of Saint Mark of the Cypresses that would stand on top of the tallest hill on the island, which he wanted to be his mother's final resting place. Next he busied himself with the landscaping of the gardens, the planting of trees and the construction of the jetty, which he originally conceived as a large marina that proved impossible to build because the waters round the island were not deep enough for big yachts.

He divided his time between his London home and the island where he stayed in a big tent pitched in the middle of the camp, among the engineers and workers. Living conditions were basic, but he did not mind. He was at his happiest there not only because he had escaped the evenings of long silences with his wife in Mayfair but also because he found it easier to relate to construction workers than to people of his own social circle. It was not high regard or affinity that drew him to them. Ian Forster's research revealed that his claim about hailing from working-class stock owed more to his inborn romanticism than to fact. He was self-made, indeed, since Victor Timoleon's disappearance and the war had ruined the family financially, but this does not mean he was not bourgeois: the good school, the big house, the Christian values were all there while he was growing up. But his powers of autosuggestion were so great that he could convince himself he was an interloper in the upper classes, a belief that helped him sustain his ambition and antagonism.

Inside a concrete pillbox built on the side that faced the mainland, he found a mechanical air-raid siren from the days of World War II, and he used it every morning to wake up his workmen. He ate the food they ate, with good appetite, and then he began his daily inspection, walking around the island with a stick tucked under his arm like a general, stopping to ask questions here and there, ordering eleventh-hour adjustments after having changed his mind in his sleep. Thanks to his photographic memory and his aptitude for numbers, he could remember the details of the architectural drawings by heart, he could recite the lists of building materials and the exact quantities needed, and he could do rapid calculations in his mind. He did not eat lunch but smoked another cigar, contemplating his Pharaonic army of labourers from the shade of an olive tree, taking pleasure in the noise of the excavators, the pneumatic drills and the dumper trucks as if they were music.

His satisfaction in the project was the only good thing that happened to him at a time when everything else seemed to be going against his expectations: his marriage, the raising of his children, even his business was stagnant. His love affairs did not please him the way they used to either. What he liked most about the island was that there he believed he could start with nothing and create, piece by piece, something that obeyed his own laws and not the laws of physics: something that would not be damaged by time. By the time he finished creating his earthly paradise, his desire to distance himself from the rest of the world had grown so strong that he would observe the coast of the mainland with a hermit's eyes and wish that he could cut the anchors and let the island float out to sea because eleven nautical miles from civilisation was not far enough for his mood. In thirteen years of marriage, he had run the gamut of emotions from happiness and expectation to sadness and fury, then to acceptance, then to infidelity before settling on a state of boredom.

To celebrate the end of construction work on his island, he decided to treat the workmen to a ride in his seaplanes. This was the early 1960s and air travel was the privilege of the rich, so his announcement was received with a big cheer, which turned into quiet terror when the crowd realised the recklessness of the undertaking. No one dared refuse, either from curiosity or the shame of being branded a coward, and they lined up in alphabetical order to board the Piaggios, ten on each plane at a time, whispering prayers and crossing themselves. Marco Timoleon went up on the last flight, taking his seat next to the pilot to provide a running commentary. He explained the purpose of every switch and dial in the cockpit; he asked his pilot to demonstrate the principles of flight and told him to fly the plane at a lower altitude over the mainland so that his workers could have the chance to see their houses. Then he talked about the space age, which had commenced with the launching of the first Sputnik satellite in 1957, saying that it would not last unless private enterprise was allowed to compete too because the race was weighed down by politics, espionage and scientists with bad haircuts. He would have said more, but the Piaggio was suddenly hit by turbulence and began to shake, terrifying the workers to the limits of their nerve. While they recited the Lord's Prayer over the noise of the engines, Marco Timoleon, as terrified as they were, tried to calm them down with humour. 'Don't panic,' he said. 'My contract with the Devil hasn't expired yet.' Some years later that same seaplane, old and in need of repair, would crash into the sea, killing his son.

Once Saint Mark of the Cypresses was completed, Marco Timoleon travelled to Anatolia to oversee the exhumation of his mother's remains and carry them to his private island. He was there when the gravediggers lifted the heavy tombstone, removed the earth and used a crowbar to break open the lid of the coffin, half expecting to find his mother still beautiful inside, the way he had known her as a child, ready to be canonised by the Church. But he only found Eugenia Timoleon's bones stripped of flesh, yellowed and brittle, arranged at the bottom of the rotting box as if for an anatomy lesson.

Back on the island, Marco Timoleon invited the archbishop of Athens to officiate at the memorial service before the burial of the bones in the ossuary. The archbishop accepted but turned down Marco's offer to send his seaplane to the capital to pick him up, choosing to come instead by car and boat. He explained to Marco Timoleon his decision over the phone: 'Air travellers are today's builders of Babel.' The memorial service was an unassuming affair, attended only by the Timoleon family, Dr Patrikios and the staff who looked after the island: maids, servants, cooks, gardeners and guards, all dressed in clean uniforms and white velvet gloves in honour of the matriarch. Only Pandora was not there, having refused to come even though Marco had already paid for her trip. She had said: 'It is enough to die once.' Dressed in a black suit, with a black tie and black armband, Marco Timoleon remained silent throughout the service, hidden behind his dark glasses, which he did not even remove inside the church. It was not grief, he had already felt that twenty years earlier when his mother had passed away, but fear because he was now almost at the age when Eugenia Timoleon had died, and for the first time he, too, felt the certainty, however distant, of the end: from that day on, the prospect of death would never leave him.

And so his days changed. He began to think of time as a liquid that slowly but surely filled every aspect of his life, every thought, every sensation, every undertaking. Until then he had relied on his indomitable confidence to achieve everything that he wanted, but now confidence, too, was starting to fail him. He began to fear an impending danger whose source he could not define but was convinced that when it arrived he would not be able to beat it, an elusive but constant fear that caused his muscles to stiffen, his palms to sweat, his stomach to ache, his heart to pound. He had suffered these symptoms before and had learned how to live with them, but then, some months later, something stranger happened: one night he was woken by the ticking of a clock. He immediately jumped out of bed to locate the source of the noise, puzzled because he never used an alarm clock: he could wake up any time he wished to, even in the middle of a dream, a habit he had picked up after years of his mother having forced him out of bed because it was time for Sunday school. He searched his bedroom for a long time but found nothing, and then he began to search the rest of the house with growing irritation, going from room to room and smashing every clock that he came across, even the electric wall clock in the kitchen that made no noise. The ticking continued. The next time he was in New York, he asked Dr Patrikios to examine his ears, but the doctor had found nothing and diagnosed him as suffering from anxiety. Marco Timoleon was not convinced.

'Nonsense,' he said.

Dr Patrikios suggested that he take medication or at least start psychotherapy.

'These things are for nuts,' his patient said.

'You said it.'

Later the ticking inside his head stopped as suddenly as it had started – but not for ever. It would return to torment him in his sleep now and then, until the end of his days, and he would come to accept it, the way he accepted so many other strange and sad things that life threw at him, naming his condition *The Night of the Clocks*.

Among these strange goings-on, Miranda Timoleon remained silent and indifferent. Perhaps it was the pills. By that time she was taking them by the handful after her continual and indiscriminate use had lessened their potency and caused side-effects, which she could only control by taking yet more pills. It was a vicious circle that she could not escape without help, but she shrugged off the warnings by telling anyone who dared bring up her problem: 'I'm only addicted to happiness.'

She was secretive about her alcohol habit, as she never was about the pills. There were reasons for it. Her grandfather on her mother's side had been a pharmacist who had become an alcoholic and distilled ardent spirits in the basement of his house. He spent endless hours making brandy from wine, rum from molasses, whisky from grain mash, any kind of substance that could be turned into alcohol. He lived in an Athens suburb where Anna Negri and her daughter visited every summer from New York, in a house shrouded in the mist of alcoholic vapours escaping from the still in the basement. Miranda remembered his nose, enormous and purple, his dragon's breath that burned and smelt of fermented grapes, his constant hiccup. He had been a source of embarrassment to Anna Negri, who had once taken her young daughter to one side and told her: 'Promise me never to touch it.' Miranda had kept her promise for many years until the misfortunes of her own life forced her to reach for whichever lifebelt she could grab. She hid bottles at the back of wardrobes, inside drawers, behind the shelves of children's books. If she ran out, she took the risk of drinking her husband's alcohol, which she then topped up with pure spirit from the medicine cabinet.

At that time certain rumours began to spread about her, which people believed without hesitation. They told of orgies that Miranda Timoleon organised and took part in, parties where famous people went wild with sex, alcohol and illegal drugs handed out free, bacchanals that started in the evening and lasted all night in country houses under tight security. They told of masked lovers involved in abominable acts, swimming pools filled with champagne, exotic fruits laced with opium and bonfires burning cannabis and rare South American roots whose psychedelic fumes, blown by the wind, doped unsuspecting grandmothers and little children miles away. The rumours soon found their way into the pages of popular magazines, and the police were forced to act, but none of their many raids found any criminal wrongdoing.

The truth is that behind those lies was none other than Marco Timoleon. He had set off the whispering campaign in order to pave the way for keeping Sofia and Daniel after the divorce, which was now inevitable. When his wife had started her affair with Stefano Tossi, Marco Timoleon had tried everything to win her back, and later he had celebrated her surrender without ever pausing to think whether he really wanted her back or not. He was now losing interest: the hunter had killed his lion. One morning, sitting with his wife in the conservatory of their London house where they always had coffee, a ritual they maintained even in the darkest moments of their marriage, he suddenly spoke up.

'Let's call it quits.'

Miranda Timoleon did not raise her eyes from the newspaper.

'Good,' she said. 'I want the children.'

'I'd sooner see them grow up in an asylum.'

'Then forget about the whole thing,' she said.

The couple sat in silence again. Marco Timoleon sipped his coffee and watched the eternal drizzle that fell against the large windowpanes of the conservatory and his wife turning the ironed pages of the newspapers. This was what their married life was like in 1963, one year before Miranda Timoleon's death. They communicated more with noises than words: the sipping of coffee, the rustle of pages, the chink of the cutlery. If one said something, sometimes the other replied but more often did not. For a long time Marco Timoleon had been waiting for her to admit defeat and walk away so that he could accuse her of abandoning their children, for a long time he had been smearing her reputation, for a long time he had been taking his lawyers' advice until he exhausted both his patience and malice. That morning he offered her a large sum and a generous monthly allowance in return for sacrificing any custody claims to their children. After saying that he was prepared to award her reasonable visiting rights, he warned her that if she fought him in the courts, he would seek an order to ban her from ever seeing the children again on account of her well-documented depravity.

He did not manage to intimidate her. The legal battle for the custody of the children was long, bitter and public, feeding the pages of magazines and newspapers with scandal and intrigue that increased their circulation. Miranda Timoleon refused to move out of the house in Mayfair, wanting to be near both her children and her enemy while the hearing lasted. She moved to another room on the top floor of the house, and there she spent most of the day, making it her headquarters where she invited her lawyers to discuss tactics against her husband. Marco Timoleon had it bugged and would listen to the tapes of her private conversations late at night in his office, taking notes of her secrets, learning what moves she planned, discovering weaknesses of her legal defence that would help him determine his own strategy. After a while his habit changed purpose and gradually turned into an addiction. He could not go to bed without having listened to all the tapes of the previous day or start work the following morning without having played them back again. It was then that he developed the insatiable appetite for information that later would lead him to keep his daughter under constant surveillance too. Every morning he took delivery of more tapes and sat down to uncover the hidden meanings in Miranda Timoleon's trivial remarks, sudden coughs and innocent laughs, stopping and rewinding the tape to listen to them again, then again and again until he thought he had deciphered what they meant. Soon his office was full of tapes. They were in every drawer, on every shelf and stacked against the walls, but they still kept coming until one could not cross the room without stepping on them.

The family battle was still raging in the early summer of 1964 when Dr Patrikios received a long-distance phone call in New York as he was about to leave his practice. It was Marco Timoleon.

'Come at once,' he said. 'A plane is waiting. JFK.'

'Do you need my expertise or my friendship?' Dr Patrikios had only time to ask.

'Both,' was the answer.

The doctor filled his medical bag with needles, bandages and bottles and took a taxi to the airport where a scheduled flight to Athens was being delayed so that he could catch it. He arrived on the island the following evening. He stepped off the seaplane and felt the wind through his coat and saw the seagulls sheltering on the beach from the summer storm. Marco Timoleon was waiting for him on the jetty, alone, in the rain, without a raincoat or umbrella. After so many years of answering urgent calls, the doctor could tell when he had arrived too late.

'Someone has died,' Dr Patrikios said.

Marco Timoleon did not answer but took his bag, and together they climbed the steps that led to the house. Inside the villa it was dark. The doctor wondered whether there was a power failure, but then he saw a lit table lamp. Something else intrigued him more: he noticed that there was not one servant around in a house where there was always more staff than furniture. Marco Timoleon took his coat and led him upstairs, to a guest room at the far end of the corridor. The choice of room misled the doctor.

'A guest?' he asked.

Then he approached the bed, lifted the blankets and saw Miranda Timoleon, her eyes and mouth shut, her skin pale, and he could not help but feel the grief of an outcome that could not have been prevented.

'I found her in the living room,' Marco Timoleon said.

Dr Patrikios felt resentful: his friend's superstition had led him not to place the dead woman in the master bedroom. He lifted her eyelids and looked at her pupils then pulled back the covers to examine the rest of her body. Even though she wore a dressing gown, she was also wearing her jewellery and her nails were varnished. The gold slipper missing from her foot was a poignant detail: it must have fallen off when Marco Timoleon had carried her. As soon as he took her arm, he noticed the onset of rigor mortis, but even so he tried to take her pulse. Behind his back Marco looked on.

'I'm going to say this, doctor, only because it will help your job: I'm innocent.'

The doctor opened his bag and found his stethoscope.

'Save your breath,' he said. 'I'm not the judge.'

He went through the procedure of certifying Miranda's death without stopping to think whether what he was doing was really necessary, but he kept busy in order not to let emotion take over. He was concentrating so much on his work that he began to undress Miranda to examine her body for signs of violence. Then he stopped: that was the job of the medical examiner. The doctor's refusal to look at him was angering Marco Timoleon.

'My pilot will fly you back whenever you wish to go,' he said.

Dr Patrikios looked out of the window where the rain had grown heavier since he had arrived.

'Nah. Not in this weather.'

He covered the body again with the blankets, put his equipment back in his leather case and only then did he ask what had happened. Marco Timoleon replied: 'Not here.' They sat in his study where the only light came from the lit fireplace. Ten years later Dr Patrikios repeated to Ian Forster their conversation that night. Marco Timoleon told him that he had found his wife in the living room lying on the floor, pale and breathless. He had wrapped her in blankets and tried to bring her round with water and cups of coffee, but her condition had not improved. She had finally died almost three hours before the Piaggio carrying the doctor had landed.

'Why didn't you call some local doctor?' Dr Patrikios asked.

'The scandal,' Marco Timoleon said. 'I was thinking about the children. This must be contained. There're people who'd love this to get out . . . this . . . tragedy . . . to hurt me.'

'You should call the police.'

Marco Timoleon nodded. He picked up the phone. Before dialling the number, he looked briefly at the doctor.

'I hope that you'll tell them the truth.'

'Which is?'

'That she died of natural causes.'

Dr Patrikios felt the blood rushing to his head.

'She was only thirty-five,' he said.

Dr Patrikios never fully convinced himself about the circumstances of Miranda Timoleon's death, but chose to accept his friend's explanations, presuming him innocent because he could not prove him guilty: given the extent of Miranda's addiction, her sudden death was a likely outcome. The next morning two policemen arrived from the mainland with a local doctor who was asked to conduct the autopsy, but from the moment they stepped ashore it was obvious that the case was already closed. They saluted Marco Timoleon, asking his pardon for the inconvenience, reassuring him that the whole matter was a formality and that it would be over very quickly. Then the doctor came forward, an elderly man dressed not for a medical emergency but for the occasion of meeting the Richest Man in the World: an evening suit, tie, gold cufflinks and hat. He bowed and shook Marco Timoleon's hand.

'A great pleasure, Mr Timoleon, a great pleasure.' Then he realised the inappropriateness of his comment and rushed to add: 'I mean to say, my deepest condolences.'

The forensic examination lasted indeed only a few minutes, enough time to satisfy the local doctor that Miranda Timoleon's death had been caused by pulmonary oedema; he omitted to mention in the death certificate, which Ian Forster had later seen, that it was the result of a drugs overdose. The policemen signed the necessary papers, and the body was released to the care of her husband. Miranda Timoleon was buried in the yard of Saint Mark of the Cypresses the following day, no archbishop, no pallbearers, no guests: just Marco Timoleon, his children and the staff.

In the only interview that Dr Patrikios granted to Ian Forster, in 1974, he explained at length that the appearance of an acute overdose of tranquillisers is similar to that of a narcotic overdose. The patient may be comatose or convulsing and their ability to breathe decreases, which can lead to apnoea, that is, a temporary halt in breathing. Blood pressure falls and cardiac performance deteriorates, which is what ultimately causes pulmonary oedema unless the respiratory depression is corrected and ventilation is restored quickly. The effects can be more severe and death may occur if large amounts of aspirin have also been ingested: it was well known that Miranda Timoleon took aspirin for her everlasting headaches.

This theory did not convince the media, and the circumstances of Miranda Timoleon's death would give rise to a predictable rumour that would never quieten down: Marco Timoleon had killed his wife. Perhaps it was his attempt to protect his children from the bad publicity by taking them on the long cruise on the *Sofia* soon afterwards that fuelled suspicions. As soon as they returned, he sold the house in London, accepted Miss Rees's resignation and moved the family to Paris where he tried to put the past behind him, reverting to his old lifestyle.

He became a regular presence in Parisian nightspots where he arrived late at night and always with company. His favourite was Maxim's, the restaurant on rue Royale that still preserved the *fin de siècle* atmosphere of its early days, a place popular with holders of titles, celebrities of the entertainment world and big businessmen like him. He did not go for the elaborate haute cuisine. He ordered sole Albert, lobster Newburg or *chartreuse de perdreau* but rarely tasted them, preferring instead to listen to the orchestra playing tunes from Franz Lehár's *The Merry Widow* and pop music of the time for anyone who wished to dance on the rudimentary dance floor. Marco Timoleon was often seen there at three or four o'clock in the morning, several evenings in a row, always in a good mood and showing no signs of tiredness, a fact that made people wonder whether there were more than one of him.

When they suggested this to him, he laughed and took it as a compliment. But then one evening at the Opéra, where he went because it was a charity event, he left his box in the middle of the performance and went outside to breathe some fresh air, and on the steps he saw a man who was as tall as him and had his silver-grey hair and suntanned face. Not only that. He was wearing the same suit as him, the same glasses as him and was smoking the same brand of cigar: his identical twin. The man disappeared as soon as he saw him. Marco Timoleon did not meet him or hear of him again until years later when he read in the papers that Marco Timoleon had been found dead in a cheap hotel on the Côte d'Azur. In the following days, he learned that his double was an unemployed Belgian, who had lived on small loans given him by people gullible enough to believe that the real Marco Timoleon would ever ask for credit. Intrigued, the tycoon paid the hospital to keep the dead man in the mortuary and dispatched his private investigator to find out everything that he could and learned that the Belgian had been following him across Europe for more than a decade, eating at exclusive restaurants, sleeping with *Playboy* centrefolds and being dressed by bespoke tailors. A mild-mannered man and a tee-totaller, the Belgian had trained himself to throw tantrums that resembled Marco Timoleon's and drink Scotch in order to fulfil the requirements of his role, but his body did not have the strength of Marco Timoleon's: he had died of cirrhosis. In retrospect, there were many photographs of him in magazines, and Marco Timoleon, the only man in the world who could tell the difference, made it his pastime to collect them, arrange them in chronological order and study them in the hope of learning more about the Belgian. But, in fact, he soon forgot that he was looking at a stranger, and he began to see himself in those photographs, the way God saw him from heaven: a man growing older, heavier and uglier year after year. Moved by the futility of it all, he decided to pay for the impostor's funeral, which he also attended not in order to amuse himself or the media but out of sincere sadness. He even gave a speech in which he paid tribute to the man whose great misfortune, he said, was that he looked like him, and he ended with a poetic comment: 'We, mortals, are made of the discarded spares of the gods: heads that lose their hair, teeth that fall out, hearts that do not love.' Then he left in his limousine, not waiting for the service to end because he could not bear to see himself being lowered into the grave.

Despite the great social upheavals of the 1960s, Marco Timoleon managed to maintain the success of his businesses and increase his wealth. Ideologies did not interest him; he took an interest in politics only when politics took an interest in him. Reckless by nature, he disliked rules, laws and regulations even when they protected him from his own temperament. When a military coup overthrew the Greek government in 1967, Marco Timoleon saw it as a golden opportunity to invest in the country without the obstacles of democracy and arrived in Athens while the city was still under martial law. The streets were deserted apart from occasional groups of soldiers squatting in the shade of the trees, armoured vehicles standing at crossroads and the old public buses that crawled towards their depots with no one on board. Headed by police motorcycles with their sirens on, Marco Timoleon's motorcade drove from the airport to the city centre without stopping at traffic lights. The Dictator, who only two months before was an unimportant army colonel, received him with reverence. Marco Timoleon shook his hand, noticing that under his pressed suit he still wore his uniform.

'Welcome to the birthplace of democracy,' the Dictator said. 'I am a great admirer of yours.'

They had lunch under the trees in the garden, surrounded by security guards and flowering shrubs that released a sweet fragrance, a hidden paradise in the middle of the sprawling capital that was bracing itself for a scorching summer. Marco Timoleon asked his host how long it would be before martial law was lifted, pointing out that it would be good for the image of the country abroad.

'Not martial law,' the Dictator corrected him. 'Just measures to ease traffic congestion.'

It was the beginning of a great friendship that was based on mutual admiration and endured the fall of the dictatorship seven years later. When the Dictator was tried and sentenced to life imprisonment, Marco Timoleon, now close to the democratic government, managed to lighten his sentence by negotiating a secret release for his friend to spend his summers on his private island, and it was there that Ian Forster came across him in August 1975 when they were both guests at Sofia Timoleon's twenty-fifth birthday party.

After Miranda's death, Marco Timoleon vowed never to remarry. When he met Olivia Andersen, five years without a wife had taught him that, although he would never learn to resist having affairs, he was too old to live without a steady companion. What attracted him to her was what had attracted him to Miranda Negri more than twenty years earlier: despite his wealth and fame, which surpassed almost everyone else's, he was still fascinated by the aristocracy. Their wedding took place on his private island a year after they met. No expense was spared. The preparations that had begun months before soon turned into a military operation. The Dictator put the army at Marco Timoleon's service, sending a detachment of soldiers to help in any way the bridegroom saw fit. They cleaned the beach of flotsam, opened paths, planted flowers and used DDT, which was used in the Vietnam War at the time, to spray the island from end to end in order to kill the bugs and bees because Olivia Andersen suggested they would be a nuisance to the guests. Afterwards the Dictator decorated every soldier with a commemorative medal for his efforts, and Marco Timoleon gave them envelopes filled with banknotes, thanking them for their help and promising them jobs after their release from the army. More than a thousand guests were invited to the wedding to wish Marco, sixty-seven, and Olivia, thirty-three, every happiness. Despite his age Marco Timoleon had insisted on lifting his bride and carrying her over the threshold of the villa according to the custom. But when he attempted to climb the stairs to their bedroom with her in his arms, his years defeated him, and he was forced to put her down. He caught his breath and addressed his wedding guests, who had been watching from the hallway.

'Ladies and gentlemen,' he said. 'I promise you I can do it. But I need every drop of my strength for later.'

They applauded. Marco then took Olivia by the hand, and they went upstairs to their bedroom where he locked the door. He had instructed his servants to decorate the room in a manner worthy of the occasion, but they had gone too far in fulfilling his wishes. There were vases filled with flowers everywhere, on the tables, the mantelpiece and the windowsills, baskets hanging down from the chandeliers and garlands of carnations on the walls, making the room look like a greenhouse. It did not end there. The bed was covered with rose petals, which Olivia was about to discover she had an allergy to. As soon as the newly-weds lay in bed, she broke out in a rash and had difficultly breathing. Dr Patrikios was called at once, and he gave her cortisone to check the allergic reaction, but the damage to her mood was already done. Unable to stay in a room that was contaminated by pollen, the couple was forced to spend the night in another room.

'This is a bad omen,' Marco Timoleon said.

Throughout their engagement Olivia had resisted his attempts to sleep with her, honouring her promise to Father O'Malley, who constantly reminded her of her vulnerability to sin after her first divorce. The couple finally made love three days after their wedding. Olivia was feeling better even though she had not fully recovered from her allergic reaction. She announced her decision at dinner: 'I'm ready.' Marco Timoleon nodded with satisfaction. When they finished their meal, he followed her to their bedroom where, without applause, without fanfare, without pomp and circumstance, they undressed in silence and lay in the bed that had been carefully disinfected.

Olivia Timoleon would always remember that night as the moment she fell in love with him. Holding him in her arms and stroking his grey hair and ageing seal's body, she decided that she would do everything she could to make their relationship work not because she was short of marriage proposals or money, as people thought – quite the opposite, in fact – but because she fell for his humour, his enthusiasm and his generosity. Soon she would also discover his fits of rage, but even these she would think for a long time childlike: unexpected, uncontrollable and dissolving as suddenly as they appeared. She would say, 'He's a good man,' and in the first years of their marriage nothing could make her change her mind: not other people's opinion, which she dismissed as malicious, not the magazine articles that revealed his scandals; not even her own eyes.

She suggested that their honeymoon should be a journey to all the places where Marco Timoleon had lived from the day he was born until then, so that she could see the world the way he had seen it, in chronological order, smell it the way he had smelt it, listen to its sounds the way he had first listened to them in the long trajectory of his life. He indulged her, refusing, however, to visit Asia Minor, the most important place of all, because of his superstitious fear that the moment he set foot in Izmir his life would come full circle and there would be nothing left for him to do but die. Instead, they began their honeymoon in Buenos Aires, where Marco Timoleon had come ashore after a long sea voyage to lay claim to the world almost fifty years earlier. He had not prepared himself for the inevitable disappointment. In 1970 he was no longer the poor young man from a small Mediterranean town but one of the richest and most famous men in the world. The noble city seemed to him much smaller than he remembered it even though it had clearly expanded a lot since he was there. Its old buildings were not all that tall, its avenues not as wide, its parks not as green.

'Damn, Olivia,' he said good-naturedly. 'You stole away my memories.'

The following days he took her on long tours of the city with only his indelible memory as a guide, showing her everything, including his various haunts, which no woman would have dared to visit back in the 1920s but were now tourist attractions for the whole family. More often than not, they found that the old buildings he remembered had been demolished and in their place stood modern apartment and office blocks. They also went to the Strangers' Club where Marco gave a speech, at the end of which he amused everyone by admitting that he had cheated in order to become a member. He was forgiven with loud applause, and the club president immediately granted him lifelong membership.

In the storms of his life, Marco Timoleon never forgot the name of his benefactor, the man who had offered him his first job: Colonel Stanley Nicholls. He knew that the Colonel had been more than sixty when he had walked into his office, so there was no way he could have been alive now, but hoped that he was buried somewhere in the city. He was disappointed to hear that after his retirement the Colonel had, in fact, returned to England where he had died only months later.

There was one more visit Marco Timoleon could have made. From the moment the local newspapers first wrote about the trip of the Richest Man in the World to South America, Flor Alcorta, aged eighty-four, convinced that he would like to see her, prepared to receive him in the big apartment where she had lived with a maid and Borges, her blind parrot, ever since the death of her husband. A venerable great-grandmother with a face pitted with the marks of age, she sometimes forgot the names of her many great-grandchildren but not the adventures of her youth. She had followed Marco's rise to fame not with jealousy or regret but with a loving interest, happy for his success because she knew how much it meant to him. Yet, the more that she read about him, the more convinced she became that she had made the right decision to leave him before he left her, which was inevitable considering his compulsive philandering: she had at least saved herself from heartbreak and loneliness down the road. So in 1970 she had her apartment cleaned, dug her best dresses out of mothballs and sent them to the cleaner's, filled the refrigerator with cocoa cakes and refreshments, stocked up on cigars and whisky, which she had read was Marco's favourite drink, and then sent her maid to his hotel with a handwritten invitation to him and his wife for any evening they wished to come. Every day Flor Alcorta bathed with the help of her maid, dressed up in one of her ancient dresses and sat in her living room with Borges on her lap to wait, but her guests never called.

From Buenos Aires Marco and Olivia Timoleon flew to New York, then to Los Angeles, and the couple returned home to Paris via London a month after their departure. Their trip brought to the surface many of the lies that Marco Timoleon had told about his life over the years and the lies that others had told about him. But it was no longer possible to tell the truth because whoever had told them had not been an honest liar but a storyteller whose stories had not come out of a hat but been inspired by real events: he had moved them across time and place, swapped them with others and turned them upside-down so that ultimately Marco Timoleon's life had turned out to be a mix of history and theatre. Olivia Timoleon realised this, and also that it would be futile to try and discover what her husband was really like. When he asked her opinion about the Englishman who wanted to write his biography, she said: 'Let him. I'll be the first to buy a copy.' She was not joking. She looked forward to reading the book, and every time she met Ian Foster she enquired about it with sincere interest.

The 1970s saw a change in Marco Timoleon's fortunes. He refused to invest in new technologies, which he did not understand because he did not have the patience, and kept the bulk of his activities in shipping, which had made him a billionaire. But things were different now. His fleet was ageing, there was competition from newer fleets and oil prices kept rising until they went out of control. In 1973, during the first oil crisis, demand for his ships dropped to an all-time low. Old and tired, Marco Timoleon could no longer outrun his shadow. He was always an aggressive capitalist, a stubborn negotiator and a cunning diplomat whose dealings had been risky and dubious, but the truth was that he could no longer do as he pleased. Democratic governments, congressional committees and fraud squads were after him, trying to stop him with laws, embargoes and treaties. He should have freed his parrot, thrown away his cutlass and lowered the black flag, but Marco Timoleon refused to admit it: the Age of the Pirates had come to an end.

ELEVEN YEARS AFTER MIRANDA TIMOLEON'S DEATH SOFIA, LET DOWN by her father and her lover, would try to imitate her mother and overdose on tranquillisers. But unlike her, she had not thought over her decision to end her life. The truth was that Miranda Timoleon had done it after a long deliberation that had begun when things between her and Marco Timoleon were at their lowest point. Once, while the War of Timoleons was raging, she had told a friend: 'My husband is doing every-thing he can to convince me that life isn't worth living.' Soon he convinced her, and Miranda Timoleon set about planning her suicide. She did it meticulously, educating herself with relish even though all she needed to know she knew already: an overdose would kill her. She read about sleeping pills in medical encyclopaedias, how they worked, which were the best for her purpose, how to enhance their effect by taking aspirin and alcohol, and then she scanned the papers, looking for suicide stories, how people succeeded and others failed, knowing that she would probably only have one chance because Marco Timoleon would then lock her up in a private hospital or she herself might change her mind. She set a date after a pilgrimage to Los Angeles to visit Marilyn Monroe's crypt in Westwood Memorial Park, and early in the summer of 1964 she told her husband:

'All this is killing me. Let's just discuss the custody of the children, the two of us. No lawyers. Perhaps it could be resolved amicably.'

Marco Timoleon was elated.

'I'm listening.'

'Not here. On the island. It might be the last time I visit.'

She did not want simply to erase herself from Marco Timoleon's life; it had to be a ritual, an immolation. She wanted to shock him, shame him, perhaps even incriminate him; he was, after all, responsible too.

Over the years her innate despair had trickled down to her daughter and continued to flow slowly after her death, a thin line of blood that ran from her grave at Saint Mark of the Cypresses to wherever in the world Sofia Timoleon happened to be. So, Sofia's decision to take the pills that might or might not kill her – she never liked to plan far ahead – was not exactly an impulsive reaction. Rather, it was the combination of a biological legacy, of years of frustration and of hundreds of incidents, important and trivial, that on the night of her birthday caused an avalanche of feelings that swamped her and made her do it. Knowing the grief that her father had felt for Daniel's death, she began to swallow the pills one by one, deriving little satisfaction from their taste but great pleasure from the guilt and regret she hoped to cause both her father and Ian Forster, not the first man she had fallen in love with but the one above suspicion: the honest one.

Now she was glad about the lie and also convinced that it had been the right thing to do. It had started with a visit to her gynaecologist after missing a period. The examination quickly showed that she was not pregnant, but she had to miss two more periods before her doctor ordered full tests and concluded that her condition was the result of rapid weight loss from her determined diets. Sofia Timoleon, who had never considered the possibility of a child before, was relieved. She listened to her gynaecologist's warnings, took his advice regarding her eating habits, promised to attempt nothing as drastic again, thanked him for the good news and left his practice, meaning to tell Ian Forster the results of her examination at once. She knew that he was worried from the moment that she had told him 'I'm late.'

They were having coffee in the living room of her Monte Carlo apartment and were going through the manuscript of the biography. Sofia was answering Ian Forster's never-ending questions, the curtains drawn as usual to protect them from the photographers and Marco Timoleon's spies. Ian Forster checked his watch.

'Give me just a few minutes,' he said.

Then he understood, and he was surprised and worried but also intrigued.

'I know what you're thinking,' Sofia Timoleon said.

'You do?'

'About the baby. Not wanting it.'

'I wouldn't like you to write my biography,' he replied with an ambiguous smile. 'You don't know me well enough.'

As soon as she had walked out of her gynaecologist's, Sofia Timoleon had looked for a public phone to call Ian Forster with the news but could not find one. She walked for a while, observing the people, the traffic, the shop fronts, and it was then that the idea crossed her mind that she could use her illusory pregnancy to discover who Ian Forster really was: to interview her interviewer. There were many things she would have liked to know, namely what he thought about her, what motivated him in their relationship, what future he saw in it; the imaginary situation with all its implications for his book and his precious relationship with her father would give her a sufficient answer. She passed by several phone boxes, which she either missed in her pensive walk or simply ignored, but finally stopped at one and dialled the number that she knew by heart. When she heard the voice on the other end, she took a deep breath and said: 'Ian, I'm so happy.'

And the litmus test had worked: now she knew. It was only the fact that her father had her under surveillance that meant she ended up fooling him too, which was not part of her plan. When she found out that he knew, Sofia Timoleon could not resist punishing him by not telling him the truth right away. She would have done it later, of course, but then Ian Forster had come to her room, and his reaction had stunned her. She now lay in bed, waiting. Love: she repeated the word many times until it lost its meaning. At last, out of breath, she felt the savage pleasure of having killed an animal that caused no harm, and she shut her eyes.

On the veranda the musicians were packing their instruments and leaving the bandstand. A few guests continued to dance among the confetti and streamers until they left for their rooms too, discouraged by the silence. Drunk and loud, the Dictator refused to accept that the celebration had finished, and he stayed alone on the empty veranda. Marco Timoleon came and persuaded him that the party was over. His guest clicked his heels, gave him a military salute and walked away. When he was finally alone, Marco Timoleon lit a cigar and sat on the edge of the veranda to smoke, watching the waiters collecting the empty glasses, carrying away the tables and sweeping the floor while the lights inside the villa went off one after another. Earlier on, when the party was still in full swing, he had interpreted the darkness in Sofia's window as a good omen: she had probably gone to sleep.

After the rough weather that had almost drowned the orchestra on its way to the island, a steady breeze was clearing the clouds away, revealing a sky full of stars and a bright waning moon. Marco Timoleon felt relieved: the party had ended. He had persuaded the Englishman to do what he wanted him to do and had squared up to his daughter successfully, considering the seriousness of the matter. When the waiters blew out the lanterns and turned off the last electric lights, the moon cast the shadow of the villa over the veranda, over the steps that led to the jetty, over the small beach. A moment later the festoons of light bulbs on the *Sofia* went off too. Marco Timoleon was finishing his cigar when a voice behind him interrupted his thoughts:

'It was a nice party.'

Olivia stood almost invisible at the edge of the veranda. She said that she had come to say good-night, but one look was enough for Marco Timoleon to know that she was prepared to forgive him and try again, without misgiving, without rancour, without lawyers. She leaned over to kiss him on the lips, but he turned his head, offered her his cheek and doused her hopes.

'Let's take things one step at a time,' he said.

When she had heard in the news about Daniel's death, Olivia Timoleon had tried to contact her husband, but it had proved impossible. She tried calling him on the phone, sent him telegrams, wrote him a hand-delivered letter but received no reply. Marco Timoleon had cut off all ways of communication, telling his secretaries not to connect her if she called, throwing away her messages without reading them, instructing his guards to turn her away if she came to the house. Impervious, Olivia Timoleon had taken the plane to be with him, arriving on the island the day of the funeral without prior notice. 'This is a family matter,' he said when he saw her. He had let her stay, but she had to suffer the humiliation of having to follow the coffin not next to her husband and stepdaughter or even with Dr Patrikios and the few close friends who followed behind, but with the servants at the back. As if this were not enough, she had had to listen to the memorial service from the churchyard because there had not been enough room inside. She had not complained but maintained her poise throughout it all, just as she would weather all the storms of her marriage to Marco Timoleon. In the evening she took the launch to start her return journey, having offered her husband her condolences and thanking him for having let her stay.

Now on the veranda she thanked him again for having invited her to the party, telling him that she would be leaving in the afternoon. He did not ask her to stay. 'Good-night,' Marco Timoleon replied and watched her walk away. It was four o'clock in the morning. The veranda was clean and empty, without any sign that a big party had taken place a short while earlier. Only his ears, still ringing from the music, reminded him of the charade. He stubbed out his cigar and went inside with a mind to work, but as soon as he entered his study he felt tired, the way he had never felt since he had begun to suffer from insomnia. He dropped in an armchair with just enough strength to stretch out his hand and touch a forgotten tumbler on the table. That moment summer seemed to end and autumn to begin with a wind entering through the open windows, dissolving the heavy smell of smoke, scattering the papers on his desk and making him tremble with cold.

His bedroom was no more welcoming. He undressed and got into a bed whose fresh sheets only made his flesh crawl more, and he had to get up as he was warming up. Normally, no drop in temperature would affect him, but something told him not to repeat the dare of the previous night: he shut the windows.

He moved around without turning on the lights, knowing where everything was like a blind man, after having spent so many sleepless nights pacing round his bedroom in the dark in failed attempts to cure his insomnia. But tonight he fell asleep as soon as his head touched the pillow.

He had the same dream that he had had the night before. He dreamed he was a boy again living in Izmir and was standing on the promenade dressed in his pyjamas. But the current that yesterday had swept the dead sailor out to sea tonight brought him back into the harbour, and there he came back to life. He climbed the jetty and stood on the promenade to wring out his cap, calm and a little amused as if he were not dead but simply caught in a sudden thunderstorm that had drenched him to the skin. Marco Timoleon looked at his white steward's uniform, defiled by a big bloody mark on the chest, he looked at his hands that were pale from the frostiness of death and then looked at his face: it was Daniel.

He woke up as suddenly as he had fallen asleep. It was afternoon. He sat up in bed, filled a glass from the jug of water on his bedside table and drank it, thinking about his dream. The sun shone through the windows, but it was not warm. He lit the first cigar of the day but after a few puffs forgot it in the ashtray from where its smoke slowly spread across the room. By the time it stopped burning, Marco Timoleon had made his decision. His tiredness having all but disappeared, he jumped out of bed and dressed. For the first time in his life, he had changed his mind about something, big or small, admitting to himself not that he was wrong but that perhaps he could forgive one more of his daughter's mistakes: he would consent to her having the baby.

He went to his study, locked the door and spoke to his lawyers on the phone for a long time before sitting down to draft an agreement in his own hand that would safeguard Sofia's legacy against claims by Ian Forster. When he finally knocked on her door with the draft document in his hand more than an hour later, he received no answer but did not worry even when he tried the door and found it locked: his daughter was probably out. The long sleep had put him in a good mood, and now he felt hungry – that also happened rarely. He had lunch on the balcony of his bedroom, savouring the food, the view and the silence, promising himself never to spoil the beauty of the island with another party – real or fake. After lunch he made a cursory search for Sofia in the villa before whistling at Soraya to follow him out to look for his daughter, still not suspecting that something might be wrong. He knew that Sofia liked to go for a swim as soon as she woke up.

She was not on the small beach below the villa. The water was calm and seemed pleasantly warm, and he decided to come back later on for the last swim of the season. On his way back, he stopped to say goodbye to the last guests leaving on the Piaggio and was pleased to see Olivia among them. No, none had met Sofia that day. He kissed his wife on both cheeks, wished her a safe journey and gave her a promise he knew he would not keep but did it for the sake of their guests who heard it: 'I'll call soon.' When the seaplane took off, he resumed his search, feeling a little intrigued now because it was strange for someone to go unnoticed for so long on the small island. He snapped his fingers. 'The church!' he said. The dog followed him up the path that led to Saint Mark of the Cypresses where Marco Timoleon was convinced he would find Sofia at her mother's grave. The closer he came to the top of the hill, the more his optimism grew; he was certain his daughter would be surprised to hear his decision.

There was no one in the churchyard. He looked inside the

church, but Sofia was not there either, and then his cheerful-
ness turned into worry. He came out of the church and stood
at the edge of the hill, shielding his eyes from the sun with
his hand. Below him spread the familiar landscape of his island,
the trees and bushes, the cove, the beach, the cliffs, the paths
that branched out in every direction. He knew his daughter
did not like to walk, but still he wasted a long time looking
for her where it was certain she would not be. When he
returned to the villa, he could not help making an even bigger
mistake.

It was his dream of the previous two nights that led him to
think that Sofia had been swept away by the currents. In his
panic he did not stop to think that his daughter was as good a
swimmer as him, perhaps even better, but raised the alarm, calling
everyone to the jetty. They used every dinghy, every lifeboat from
his yacht, plus the launch from the mainland to search round
the island for a long time, but still no trace of Sofia was found.
The sun was beginning to set when it occurred to Marco
Timoleon that they had not actually looked in her room.

Her door was still locked. He ordered his servants to unlock
it, but the key would not fit in, and someone who looked through
the keyhole said that the key must still be in on the other side.

'Then break it down, damn it!' said Marco Timoleon.

They brought a sledgehammer and hit the solid oak door
three times before they managed to split it down the middle.
They squeezed through one after another and found Sofia
Timoleon lying peacefully in bed, her hands clasped on her chest.

'Thank God,' Marco Timoleon said. 'She's only hung-over.'

Dr Patrikios was not convinced by his reassurances. He pushed
him aside and held the young woman's wrist. Her arm felt limp,
but he was relieved that her skin was not cold. While he took
her pulse, he noticed the empty pill bottles on the floor and

thought that eleven years before, in a room only a few doors away, he had held her mother's arm too.

'To the operating room,' he said. 'Hurry up.'

Apart from his host, only two other people knew what he meant: the anaesthetist and the nurse the tycoon had hired for the abortion. Marco Timoleon ran to unlock the door of the guest room where the procedure had been meant to take place. The servants laid Sofia on the operating table and stood round doing nothing until Dr Patrikios ordered everyone out except for his colleagues. At that moment the seaplane was heard returning from the capital, and Marco Timoleon immediately asked whether they should fly Sofia to hospital. Dr Patrikios shot him a withering look.

'It won't be necessary. We have everything we need right here. Stand aside, please.'

Marco Timoleon went to sit on the ledge of the window from where he watched the pumping of his daughter's stomach in silence. First the doctor inserted a tube through Sofia Timoleon's nose and passed it through her windpipe to make sure she could breathe during the procedure. Then he asked his two assistants to place her on her side with her head lowered, and he inserted another small tube through her mouth and into her stomach. He rummaged through his leather case for his pump, which he attached to the end of the stomach tube. When he finished draining the fluids of her stomach, he gave her a spoonful of activated charcoal and a dose of cathartic. The emergency procedure completed, Dr Patrikios examined Sofia Timoleon again. He listened to her heart with the stethoscope, shone a small torch into her pupils and held down her tongue with a spatula to examine her throat. Satisfied with her condition, he swabbed her forearm with a piece of cotton and gave her an injection. He waited until Sofia drifted into sleep before taking off his glasses.

260

'She'll be fine.'

'Thank God,' Marco Timoleon said.

'Thank me,' the doctor said.

He asked his host to bring him a chair, so that he could stay a little while Sofia slept, and then told him to go because his patient needed sleep. Marco Timoleon obeyed. He found refuge in his study, among his ancient books that smelt of soot, the leather furniture, the cold fireplace. Out on the balcony, the evening breeze carried the smell of the rose bushes, which on some other day he would have found agreeable. Leaning against the balustrade, he considered the possibility of his daughter having succeeded in her attempt and felt his heart beating with a belated horror. Some time later Dr Patrikios walked out on to the balcony.

'I knocked, but you didn't answer,' he said.

He was tired. He stood next to his friend and gazed at the sea. It was sunset.

'Well?' Marco Timoleon asked.

'She's comfortable. She'll be asleep for a while.'

'Can I see her?'

'Later.'

After the sun had set, the doctor went back inside. Marco Timoleon followed him.

'And the baby?'

Dr Patrikios poured himself a glass of water and drank it slowly.

'What about it?'

'Will it be all right?'

'Oh, forget about the baby.'

Marco Timoleon's face showed no emotion.

'A miscarriage?'

The doctor smiled bitterly and refilled his glass.

'Don't fret. You're innocent.'

'Was it the pills?'

Dr Patrikios shook his head.

'You don't understand.'

The door had been left ajar; Soraya slipped in and went and sat quietly under the desk.

'I wanted her to have that baby,' Marco Timoleon said.

The doctor frowned.

'You did? Well, you fooled me. The operating room, the anaesthetist, the nurse – good props. What an elaborate hoax.'

'I mean, after what happened.'

'Ah, I see.'

Marco Timoleon took from his pocket the draft of the agreement that was meant to protect his daughter's fortune and tore it up. The doctor watched him throw the pieces in the wastepaper basket, unable to interpret the gesture.

'I thank you for your help, doctor.'

'It was an emergency. I did my duty. As far as the baby is concerned . . .' He looked at his friend: 'Zilch.'

'Will you tell me what you mean?'

'Sofia was never pregnant.'

Marco Timoleon looked at the doctor with disbelief. He thought back to the day he was told his daughter was pregnant. It was not a mistake: he had listened to her conversations with Ian Forster. A deception? For a moment he wondered whether this was bad or good news.

'Impossible.'

'Possible,' the doctor said. 'It's called amenorrhoea. There're all sorts of things that can go wrong in one's body.'

Marco Timoleon sat at his desk to solve the riddle. He tried to smoke but his mouth was dry. Deep in thought, he did not notice when the doctor left but continued to ask him questions, unaware for a long time that he received no answers. Then he raised his head and shuddered at the sight of the empty study. Unable to bear the solitude, he left too. At Sofia's room he opened the door softly. Sitting on a chair next to his daughter's bed, Ian Forster was reading. Marco Timoleon waved at him not to stand up.

'Any news?' he asked.

The Englishman shook his head. Marco Timoleon stood at the door for another minute, looking at his daughter, then left as quietly as he had come. Down the corridor, he found the door to Ian Forster's room open, and he strolled in. He paced around with his hands in his pockets, examining the unmade bed, the suitcase in the corner, the wardrobe, not touching anything. On top of the small desk, he saw a thick bundle of pages next to the Englishman's typewriter. He read the first few lines: *The Société des Chemins de Fer Ottomans d'Anatolie had been founded with the main purpose of building a railway line that would link the Bosporus* . . . A day earlier he would have been very curious to read more, but now the manuscript seemed to him as irrelevant as a piece of fiction. He decided to let his biographer publish anything he wanted, as long as the book came out after his own death.

Night was falling fast; there was no time to go for a walk. He went downstairs to the kitchen where he talked to the cook and his staff about the birthday party. He wanted to know what they had cooked for the party and if his guests had enjoyed it, and then he thanked them for their efforts and asked them to have whatever was left, including the wine. He walked around the villa, inspecting the work of the servants, which had begun in the morning and was still going on, the vacuuming of floors, the changing of bed sheets, the closing of guest rooms in preparation for winter: the holiday season had ended. Suddenly he remembered: 'Hell! The reporter.' He went to the basement, unlocked the door and found the intruder from the previous night sleeping on the floor. He woke him up and asked him to follow him upstairs where he told the servants to put him in a guest room for the night.

He followed his servants around until they finished work for the day, and then he was alone. There was nothing left for him to do. He expected the Afghan to be under the desk in his study, but she was not there. He walked out on to the balcony where at least he could breathe. A phone rang somewhere in the house: a business call, his wife from the airport, maybe a guest thanking him for his hospitality. Whoever it was, the staff did not dare to disturb him. He leaned against the balustrade with the light from the french windows on his back and stayed on the balcony for a long time despite the cold. The wind blew in from the sea, and he began to shiver, not only with cold but with an ill-omened tremor that would not wane for the next two years, three months and nine days when he would finally die. But for now he was still alive in his villa on the slope of the hill, among the biblical trees, the futile flowers, the paved paths, not far from the church where three generations of his family were buried – he, as much as they, stranded on a faraway island, in the middle of the night.